Choices

By dhtreichler

Dedication:

To Don Sloan

CEO of Publishers Daily Reviews and Brilliant Trailers.com

Vice President, Reelization Global Media

The first to see the merit in my stories and help me become a better author. Also, a great friend.

Ghosts

I've run this course every morning for years. Fog, rain and sleet. Hot and cold. Shadows that scare the bejeesus out of me. Then I find they are now familiar features of the fantasy my mind plays when it has not yet fully engaged after a five am alarm. I guess it would be fair to say I run on autopilot. No need to think of the turns I need to make. My body knows where to go. I seldom think about lengthening my stride or relaxing into the pace. All of that just happens. My mind seems to finally engage after I've nearly completed my shower. Shampoo in my eyes is the reminder that I'll be off to work shortly.

Seldom do I see anyone this time of day. Shadows are from overflowing dumpsters. Movements are cats seeking out rodents feasting on the contents of garbage bags. Generally, I ignore the shadows, the movements, the sighing winds. Even on nights when the moon is full, like it has been tonight, the co-inhabitants of my running space generally pass by without registering on my consciousness. But this morning is different. I don't know what it is, but my senses seem more alert. Why am I more awake than normal? No idea; but I am. Hearing, seeing things I've simply run right past hundreds of times. And then I see her. She's running towards me, apparently running a course similar to mine, but going in the opposite direction. Even with the full moon I have difficulty making out a face; but she has blonde hair in a long pony tail, just like mine. As she gets closer, I notice even her running clothes are the same as another pair I often wear. I can't tell about her shoes.

"Morning," I call as I do to anyone I see along the way.

"Morning," returns to me. The voice is familiar. Do I know this person? But she doesn't slow to talk, keeps her pace and doesn't even turn to look at me as she moves away into the shadows. Knowing she is likely to loop around, I may see her again where the street crosses. I'm more awake now. Decide to lengthen my stride and pick up the pace just a bit so I will get to the corner before she does. All the way to that corner I wonder if I know this runner. Have I seen her at one or another race in Dallas? I haven't run that many, but once in a while I'll join a charity event to help raise money.

And then I see her. She comes out of the side street, turns left and then left again down the Katy Trail. I thought I'd catch up to her, but she must have picked up the pace even more than I did. I don't sprint to the corner, but want to catch up to this other runner. Who is she? Why do I care? I shouldn't. But my competitive juices are flowing. In only a moment I'm at the corner and turn left, scanning for the mystery runner. I look in all directions. She should be right about there, a point I judge her rate of speed would have delivered her to. But nothing. No movement. No blonde ponytail swaying in rhythm to her stride. No shadows. Where did she go?

I follow the street as I do every morning, continually watching, expecting her to come out of hiding at any moment. At the next residential loop I run every morning, I take a quick unsatisfying glance around and turn into it. No sign of the other runner here either.

No need to keep up the pace now since there's no chance I'm going to catch the runner. I lengthen my stride and slow a bit so I can just cruise along on autopilot once more. This particular loop is about a mile, so it doesn't take long to come back to where I entered it. And there she is, already in the intersection, passing by from the opposite direction. She's going back towards where I first saw her. I sprint this time to the corner, turn to my right. I should be right behind her. But I'm not. I'm not behind anyone. There is no one there. She has to be. So, I speed up to overtake anyone who might be somewhere along this stretch. My long stride covers the distance from this corner to the next where I would normally turn right again. I'm surveying every inch along the way. No runner. No cats chasing mice. Several overflowing dumpsters as they were when I passed this way a few minutes ago.

I slow and come to a stop at the corner, looking again for any sign of the runner. Nothing. I'm still a mile or so from my apartment. As I lope along passing back into my morning trance, not seeing much of anything about me, I wonder: who is she? But more important, who am I? What do I really want out of life? Most would think I have a great life, but if I do, why am I so unsettled? So empty?

The stairs await me, as I only take the elevator when I'm dressed up. I certainly don't qualify for the elevator in my running clothes. I've seen women wearing this outfit around town, but I'm not ready to do that just yet. Comfortable for running, not for impressing anyone.

A flash of my keycard and I'm in my apartment. The first thing I do is go to the window and look out. I see shadows of movement, as though people are walking in a fog. But it wasn't foggy when I was out running. In fact, it was a full moon. Clear night. So, where did the fog come from? I look out again. Maybe it's not fog. Maybe it's just the way the shadows are affected by the first rays of dawn that are hinted at in the distant horizon. I look for rosy fingers. Who was it, Odysseus, who was always looking for the rosy fingered dawn that portended trouble or at least bad weather coming in? Is this ghost a portent of changes in my life? If it is, will I welcome those changes or will they turn my hard-earned comfortable life upside down? I don't know, but if the troubles of Odysseus are any indication of what is to come then I should be very worried.

A Prototype

Mia Mastrangelo is a pixie princess. That's the only way I can describe her. Barely five feet tall and maybe ninety pounds soaking wet, she has a Mediterranean complexion. Long jet black hair. It falls only to her shoulders. This is a recent development. She kept it short the whole time I've known her. What's it been? Less than ten years because I met her here at the law firm. She graduated from Texas Tech Law School in Lubbock. I graduated from Southern Methodist Law in Dallas the year before. We have helped each other make our way up the ladder here. Mia is a better researcher than I am. But I'm better in front of a jury. Maybe it was all that amateur theater I did in high school and undergraduate. No time for that now. Another thing I used to enjoy that has dropped by the way. Why is it things we enjoy disappear from our lives in order for us to become something that we don't enjoy in the same manner but is dressed in the trappings of success? Maybe it's just choices we make, like Mia with her shoulder length hair and me with my long hair. Am I more successful than Mia? I wouldn't say so. She is very well regarded in her specialty; just as I am. But what does 'well-regarded' mean anyway? I think it means you're good. Are you the best? No. People talk about the best differently. The best never lose a case. The best can influence legislators to change laws. The best become the senior partners of their firms because they bring in clients and billable hours for the firm. The best become judges or governor or something that spreads their influence even further.

I'm getting there. I'm regarded the best trial lawyer in the firm and 'one of the best' in Dallas. I need a case to elevate myself up to that next tier. I'm close, but I haven't eliminated the competition as yet. My current case may do it. An Intellectual Property infringement case of significant complexity. My client is well established in its industry. Has had a leadership position for a decade. All the best talent was drawn there. Enabled them to establish the state of the art. That is, until recently. A start-up firm hired one of their key design folks early on. But non-compete clauses required that he couldn't work in the same area where he did for my client. So, the start-up hired several other people from my client, none of whom worked directly in the competing areas. However, a year later the start-up came out with a new product that was easily a generation ahead of my client's current offerings. So, now I'm trying to prove the pattern of hiring from my client established an intent to circumvent the non-compete prohibited transfer of intellectual property. It's a complicated case. The law leaves room for interpretation. Our Managing Partner, Stevenson Wainwright III would say room for interpretation is another term for opportunity for substantial legal fees. And for Stevenson Wainwright III, that is the name of the game.

Mia stops outside my door and looks in. "J'ne?" she calls, timidly, probably wondering if I have a client in here.

"Come on in." I return her call.

She does so tentatively, sees I'm alone and then relaxes. "I've found a few more cases you can reference, but none would be precedential."

Not what I was hoping for. If I can find one case where a similar fact pattern had been established and the court found for the claimant, I'd be resting a lot easier. Giving a judge discretion is never a good thing. Reduces the odds to no more than fifty-fifty. "All have direct IP application?" I surmise.

"Yup." Mia is pithy at times. We noted that what is different in this case is the new product does not use my client's direct IP in their new solution.

"So, how do we establish this linkage?" I ask Mia who has been working this issue for weeks.

"What if we could establish that someone had built a prototype at your client's firm before the defendants left? That we could establish at least one of those who departed to the start-up had seen the prototype and discussed at least the architecture of it before leaving?"

"Do you think you have something?" I like where she's going, but…

"I don't know." Mia seems unsettled. "I was talking with this one engineer. He seems to remember a prototype that was built. He's been looking around trying to find it. The problem is it was built by an intern."

"So, not an employee." I muse. "But I think the case law is clear that intellectual property designed, developed or deployed while working for hire at the firm belongs to the firm and would be considered their property."

"Yes, I know. But the issue is no one knows if the intern kept the prototype when he left."

"Why would he do that?" I have to ask, not sure where she's going.

"He needed it for a class grade. And they think he intended on entering it in the Science Fair."

I know I have a puzzled look now. "Isn't Science Fair like high school?"

"It is. And this intern was a high school kid. Sort of."

"What are you saying? Sort of?" I'm lost now.

"He was a freshman. But he was already taking college level physics and math."

"You're telling me a kid designed the most advanced system of its kind in the world at that time?" I'm not believing this as it could just blow up my whole case about an IP lineage.

"The engineering manager said he was the smartest kid he'd ever met. Was always talking about way-advanced kinds-of-things. Systems that don't exist. But he was theorizing about how such systems could be built. The engineering manager said he didn't know all that much about some of the things the kid was talking about."

"Fine. Happy he's a child prodigy. But can we get our hands on that prototype?"

Mia looks at me unhappily, "You're assuming I haven't tried?"

"What's the story then?"

"The kid is in the middle of a custody fight." This seems way too hard.

"Parents splitting up?" I jump to the usual custody fight scenario, although I find it odd that the kid is probably what? Sixteen? "Why should that be a problem? Either he built a prototype, or he didn't."

"I haven't been able to talk directly with the prodigy. The government is holding him."

"This custody fight a result of a homicide?" I'm still missing links and Mia is doing it to me on purpose. She wants me to understand this is no ordinary situation.

"Parents are together, no divorce. The government simply wants to ensure the kid can work on some top-secret project."

"Top secret? The government. You're saying the government is taking this kid away from his parents because he's too smart? What's the deal? They want to make sure he does his thing for them and not what, for the Russians or Chinese?"

"No one wants to talk but I've pieced together the kid has a theory. Something about multiple different dimensions that periodically bump into each other. When they do, you see ghosts, shadows of people on the other side of the dimensional wall."

Not relevant to my case. "See if you can talk to the kid's parents. Maybe they can give you some insight. If he built such a device for a science fair, they should remember it."

"You would think. But the scary part is if the kid's that smart, he just may have built such a device and entered it in high school science fair."

Prototype

Stevenson Wainwright III is not an impressive looking man. You could be standing in line behind him at a grocery store and think he's just another wage slave working for one of the thousands of firms occupying offices in the many towers of downtown Dallas. That is, until he speaks. "J'ne." He pronounces it like my father. It sounds like Jay-nee. My mother always pronounced it with a soft J to make it sound more like 'zuh-nay'. Said it sounded more European, which is what she intended when she gave me the name.

"I take it your case is air-tight." That's what Stevenson says to each and every one of us before we go into trial.

"Getting there," is the best I can offer at the moment. The only thing worse than losing a case is not informing Stevenson there is risk.

Stevenson looks around my office, "I see Mia is helping you. What other help do you need?"

"Finding a prototype." I respond so he understands we are working a specific resolution.

"I won't ask. I'm sure that would take too much of the time you need to find it. You believe the device exists?"

Mia responds for me, "An engineering manager at the firm remembers seeing it."

"So, it does exist."

Mia shrugs, "The manager doesn't remember if it worked or even if it was designed on the relevant architecture."

Stevenson darkens. "What's your fall back – if this device either doesn't exist or didn't work?"

"At the moment, a blizzard of partial precedents." I respond. "But we're continuing to look for something more definitive."

"You understand this particular client is responsible for more than a million dollars of fees every year." Stephenson's voice lowers to be more threatening. "This case alone will be worth half that amount in addition to the annual billings. If we don't prove we provide the closest thing possible to guaranteed verdicts we will lose the client. That reduces the fees needed to add new partners."

"What are you saying?" I don't have to ask, but I want him to verbalize his threat.

"If we have a million dollars less to support our firm next year, we will clearly need to reduce our staff. And reductions won't come just from junior staff members. Senior members will be asked to leave as well. If we must reach into the ranks of partners, it will be difficult at best to make up for what you will have lost for the firm."

I have to push back, "I do more than my share of litigation billable hours. And that's because I have the best decision record in the firm."

"But when we are trying to make up for lost revenue, you have the lowest billings from new clients in the firm. You carry the water for existing clients, but you're not bringing in anyone new."

"We've had this discussion before." I point out. "Someone has to earn those billable hours."

Stephenson closes his eyes. Never a good sign. "If you win your case, you keep on satisfying our existing clients. We take a hit? Well, all bets are off."

I think if Mia could have crawled under the table she would have. But this was not the first time she has been subjected to Stevenson's hardball tactics with the staff. Put the fear of God into us. Make sure we win every case. Create the expectation that if we let a client or the firm down, even once, we will be relegated to the small firms that never see the kind of litigation or fees we do every day. And then where would I be?

"I better let you get back to it." Stevenson says in parting with a dark look at each of us.

The next day I'm in court pleading my case. "Your honor, I believe the facts of this matter speak for themselves. The defendant never would have been able to make the leap to its solution if employees, restricted by non-compete agreements, had not seen a prototype of the architecture while in the employ of my client before joining the defendant's firm. We have provided summaries of dozens of relevant cases where employees knowledgeable of Intellectual Property from a prior employer but not working directly in that technology area for the new firm were found to be in violation of the restrictions under non-compete agreements. The courts found for the complainant each time. I urge you to follow those precedents and find for the complainant in this instance as well."

I take my seat and wait for the judge.

"Would you please present your opening arguments Mister Mills?"

Ted Mills is tall and rail thin. He's been compared to Abraham Lincoln in looks, but not in demeanor. He has bounced from one to another of the larger firms in town. Always a hired gun, but never on a partner track. He finally got tired of working long hours and never having a chance to argue the important cases, so he went solo. It says a lot that the defending firm would go to him in this instance. Says to me they were unable to get a major firm to take the case since we would be prosecuting for our complainant. Sometimes reputation is a good thing.

"Your honor. Generally, the firm of Victor, Vargas and Utley is known for meticulous investigation of all relevant facts of a case. I expected nothing less having been employed at the firm for two years and having helped Miss Wilcox prepare cases personally. The firm of Victor, Vargas and Utley leaves nothing to the court to interpret. You are supplied with all the relevant facts, you get to hear from all relevant witnesses and experts. And that is what is so startling about this case. You have the facts. You have testimony from the experts. And yet not one person or fact draws a straight line towards a violation of a non-compete agreement or a systematic encouragement of such a violation by my client. You have supposition by experts that my client would not have been able to make the technological leap they did without detailed understanding of the requisite architecture. Miss Wilcox postulates that was formalized in a prototype device. She further asserts employees who chose to move to my client's firm from her client's firm would have had knowledge of that architecture. She has not produced the claimed prototype. In fact, all she has done is produce the testimony of a single engineering manager from her client's firm where he recalls seeing such a prototype. He freely admits Miss Wilcox's client did not build a production unit from the alleged prototype. We do not know if in fact it may have solved basic problems of the design. So, even if a prototype exists her client's firm did not perfect their interests in such intellectual property. My client's firm solved those design problems and filed a patent for their solution. I am disappointed, your honor. When I took this case, I expected to go up against the best that Victor, Vargas and Utley could bring. To be amazed at how they once again discovered case turning evidence. What we have been fed and asked to believe is an allegation of a conspiracy to circumvent non-compete agreements to steal intellectual property. And what we have been shown is that not only did my client not conspire with former employees of her client, they were able to develop a next generation product that was not infringing in anyway upon the intellectual property of her client. I ask the court to find for my client and award all court costs."

"Very well." The judge begins her summary as Ted Mills returns to his table. "Having heard the opening arguments, we will reconvene

Monday at 11:00 am."

I don't know. I generally try not to infer things from body language and voice, but it seems to me the judge is agreeing with Ted Mills about my lackluster handling of the case. Premonition maybe? I don't know, but I'm not confident leaving the court room. Maybe because Ted drew the straight line I was trying to draw. Only his straight line was the lack of hard evidence. I pack up my papers.

Bill Rodgers, the representative of my client firm stops me. "What can you tell me about that prototype you discovered?"

Dreaming

Mia is in my office before I even set my briefcase down. "Don't look so happy," she remarks.

"I wonder if Cambridge Partners is looking for trial lawyers," is my unfiltered thought.

"You obviously need some serious mood adjustment and I know just the place." Mia puts her arm around my shoulder and isn't about to let me not leave with her.

Of course, we end up where we always end up on Friday nights. I'm just arriving a little earlier than normal since I'm generally not out of the office much before 7:30 even on a Friday. Mia goes to the bar and returns with a red wine for me and a vodka tonic for her. She has a much better tolerance for alcohol than I do. That's why she starts out with vodka.

"Okay sunshine," Mia begins. "What could we have done differently?"

"Not taken the case?" I suggest and I'm serious. "We probably should have taken a look at it earlier and told them they didn't have a complaint. Unfortunately, as Stevenson mentioned, a half million in unplanned legal fees doesn't just walk into your door on a daily basis."

"Now you're whining." Mia isn't feeling sorry for me. "You're saying it was out of our control from the first, but that's not true. There has to be a way to win the case."

"I'm listening." I am feeling sorry for myself. I wait for her to volunteer an insight but hearing none, "I think we did everything we could. We just don't have enough to work with." I pronounce as the preppy sandy-blonde haired Noah Williams enters the bar.

Noah is a pediatric oncologist of some note. He's been a part of our little Friday get togethers for as long as I can remember. At first there was a whole group of young docs who would come in and hang with us. Docs and Lawyers – what a combination. Great discussions, but over the years the docs thinned out and now just Noah represents them most weeks. While the other docs got married and started families, Noah has never married and not professed a girlfriend, at least not to any of us. So, he's the last doc standing.

"Doesn't sound particularly promising." Noah notes as he fetches his standard red wine. After all this time I don't know what kind of red he drinks, but then again, I long ago challenged the bartender to surprise me with something unusual.

I nod and look away. "Some people at my practice will most likely lose their jobs, not because they're not good employees, but because one of our clients will go across town and hire a different firm. People at my client's company will most likely lose their jobs because the defendant company has built a better product and customers are already preferring their solution to my client's solution. Some people will say I'm not a good lawyer because I didn't win this case. And ultimately that will probably cause me to have to go someplace else to practice law."

"Hey!" Noah gets up and right in my face. "Stop feeling sorry for yourself. I lost one today. Does that mean I ever gave up or gave in? Never! I did everything I could for him right up until he took his last breath. Is it any easier for me to lose a patient than it is for you to lose a case? It should be much harder because in most instances if you lose no one dies. Am I responsible for his death? Yes, I think I am. If someone else, who is maybe a little more skilled, or has other experiences, or learned of newer techniques than I've studied had been working with him, maybe he's still alive. I was given a patient and a chance to save his life. I failed. As a result, that patient will not grow up. He won't enjoy high school sports even though he loved football and baseball. He will never marry or have children of his own or raise a family and have grandchildren. He won't experience the wonder of the holidays or learn something new each and every day. I am responsible for that. I think I have you beat." Noah says as he sits back down, glances into his wine before a long sip.

I feel ashamed I was whining about my situation.

"Way too heavy for a Friday night." Mia exclaims. "This is supposed to be a time to laugh. We tell ridiculous stories about each other. We let everyone know that despite what you've heard tonight, we are all good people, doing the best we can to help others. We take what we do probably way too seriously, with the exception of the doc there. He doesn't get a pass. He's got to be way too serious. Just what he signed up for. Sorry. So, who's got a story to tell?"

I feel ashamed at my self-absorption, decide to ask a general question. "Has anyone seen a ghost recently?"

I see the expressions change as people are trying to figure out if I'm being serious or this is some kind of joke. "I think I saw my own ghost this morning when I went out to run." I put it out there, probably a little exaggerated, but not too far from the truth.

"Bullshit," Colton Reynolds, Jr., one of the lawyers from my firm at the bar responds. "You can't see your own ghost by definition. If you're dead you're not seeing anything, and if you're not you're not a ghost. So, what's the deal?"

"I saw someone this morning." I respond. "She had long blonde hair in a ponytail like I run with. She was about my size. When she spoke I recognized the voice. But I just figured out it was my voice. That's why I was having so much trouble placing where I'd heard it before," I realize as I remember the morning run.

"You were probably dreaming." Noah suggests still upset with me.

"You know I thought that." I try to be soft with him. "But I've come to the conclusion I was awake, and it really did happen."

"How do you know it was a ghost?" Mia asks trying to figure out where I'm going.

"She disappeared on me. Twice."

"Could you put your hand through the apparition or anything?" Colton Reynolds still is trying to burst my bubble.

"No, she was running ahead of me, turned a corner and by the time I got there she was gone."

"You never saw this person before?" Noah asks apparently willing to re-engage me.

"Nope. I've been running this course for years. Know it like the back of my hand. I know where the cats are, where the wind blows, where I can expect the moon to peak through on a cloudy night. Nope. I've seldom run into anyone on this trail at five am. That's why this one is so strange."

"I suggest we all drink up, go home and go to sleep early. Then we can all get up and run with J'ne at five o'clock. See if the ghost comes back." Noah suggests.

"Tomorrow is Saturday. I've never seen a Saturday morning." Mia announces to everyone. "You go on without me. But take pictures."

Fees

The wind blows in my face stronger than usual. That means I'll have to bear down harder to finish this run than most. I let my mind wander as I usually do. Today is Saturday, and since the judge is reviewing the filings and testimony, I really don't have anything I have to do. Normally, given my concern about the outcome I'd start immediately on the appeals strategy, writing up a draft and running it past a few of my colleagues so I can file it immediately upon an adverse outcome. It's been a while since I had to do this as I've been confident of the outcome in every case I've tried for a quite a while now. Why is this one different? Is Stevenson trying to bring me down a peg? Ruin my winning run so he can justify not offering me a partnership? And at the same time ensure none of the other firms in town come looking for me. Would he do that? I hate to think I believe he would do anything to advance his agenda. If only I knew what it is.

I find myself on the same street where I saw my ghost. That realization brings me out of my reverie about Stevenson. I look around, opening up my senses to hear, see and smell anything that might be different than all the other mornings I've run this street. Will I see myself running away from me? Offering a fleeting greeting, but not evidencing any curiosity about me or what I might be doing out this early. Nothing comes to my attention. So, I go back into my thoughts of how to approach an appeal.

I turn onto another street. Movement instantly pulls me out of my thoughts. I see shadows up ahead. They seem to inhabit a foggy area which seems… small. Didn't know a fog could cover such a small area. I always thought fog rolled in covering everything as far as you can see and then dissipates when the sun comes out and burns the fog off. I generally wouldn't run that far, but I decide to check it out. So, I lengthen my stride to cover the distance a little faster.

It seems strange the fog doesn't get closer. I'm approaching where it was originally or where I thought it was. Has it moved away from me? It certainly seems no closer than when I first noticed it. The shadows come and go convincing me there are runners or pedestrians. People up there in any event. But strangely no one between me and the fog. My still mostly asleep mind tries to deal with this anomaly. I realize no people out this early is the norm. What's different is the people in the fog ahead. And with this realization I become more determined to reach the fog and figure out why it's different. So, I pick up the pace and concentrate on the shadows and fog ahead.

As I watch, a figure comes out of the fog running straight towards me. She's not running as fast as I am now, but we still close the distance quickly. And as she gets closer, I see the long blonde ponytail bouncing behind her in rhythm to her stride. It's my phantom me. Her face remains obscured by the shadows but I'm intent on answering the question of whether this runner is another me.

She's getting close now, I should be able to see her face when she passes under the street light that's about midway between us now. A crash right next to me causes me to look to my right, finding a garbage can rolling towards me and a cat scampering away. I change my stride to leap over the rolling can. When I'm past it I turn back to look at the face of my approaching phantom. But when I look around, she's gone. Again, I stop to look about. Could she have passed me when I was distracted? Possible. I look back, but there is no retreating blonde ponytail. Where is the cat? Why did it dump the garbage can now? Just when I'm about to answer a question I've been wondering about since I first saw the ghost's ponytail?

No cat. Was there really a cat or am I dreaming this all again? I look up to find the fog and shadows, but they have also disappeared. Was it really ever there? Here I am near where I turn off into my mile loop. This is where I saw her before. She disappeared in the same way. Did she come out of a fog then too? A fog I just didn't see that morning? I'm tired and still half asleep. All I want to do is finish this run, shower and get on with my day. I don't care if she was there or not. But if anyone from last night had come along with me that might have settled this.

The mile loop is uneventful. I'm back thinking about what else I may need to incorporate into the appeal when I come back out to the Katy Trail where I'd seen my ghost. As I come out I'm about to turn right when a flash of a blonde ponytail moves past me going back towards where the fog and shadows had been. I'm so surprised I stop still and just stare after her. I think about looking for the fog and realize there is something about four hundred yards away. The ponytail is heading right towards it. A quarter mile. Could I catch her in such a short distance? I decide to try, even though thinking it through has delayed my start. I realize it's not likely. But I'm sprinting and the blonde ponytail is not.

The distance starts to close. The more I look at the blonde ponytail the more I realize she really is built very much like I am. Same height, about the same weight and a similar loping stride. Today she's wearing the same running outfit I was wearing when I saw her earlier. Of course, I'm not since that outfit's in the hamper to be laundered.

The other runner seems to be oblivious of my rapid approach. If I really push it, I just might be able to reach her before she disappears into the shadows she seems to be running toward. I put my head down and strain to get even a bit more speed. I never run this far this fast. I'm a distance runner not a sprinter.

I look up to judge how much further I have to keep this up and she is gone. I instantly slow my headlong rush. Let my legs continue to cycle at a slower and slower rate so I don't pull a muscle or something. Then I finally begin to walk. I keep approaching the shadows until I feel something I can only describe as an electric pulse in front of me. I pull back away from it. Then the shadows begin to break up and disappear.

There is something happening here. I'm convinced it's real, but I don't know what 'it' is. In the distance I see the first rays of the morning sun sending colors out to paint the clouds quickly passing overhead in pinks and grays. That wind I first encountered when I came out is still in my face. Apparently, it's blowing at not just the surface but also moving the clouds about in the sky.

Is there some connection to the sky, or the day break, or the time of day? I only have two data points so far, but it seems the ghost only comes out at 5:00 am or a little after that. The ghost only looks like me, so is there only one? But I see movement in the fog or whatever it is. There are others in there. So, why is the one ghost able to come out and run the streets with me, but no one else? Is this a sign? I don't believe in signs, so no it's not a sign. But why someone who looks like me? If someone else were out here running, would the ghost look like them instead of me? I don't know, but it's certainly possible.

I turn around and walk a short distance before starting to jog. Having sprinted I need to make sure I'm loose before I try to start running again. It doesn't take long and I'm able to settle into a comfortable pace. I'm thinking about what I've witnessed. Why me? I've never experienced anything like this. I can't think of anything that would have changed. So, that makes it even more curious as to why me and why now?

I come to the garbage can that rolled in front of me and come out of my thoughts long enough to stand it up and look around. I know the runner went back where she came from. With the fog gone I'm not going to see anything now that would give me any more insights about what is happening to me.

When I reach my turn, I know I have about a mile yet to go, but that will only take a few minutes and I'll be home. I certainly will need a shower after my extra effort trying to catch the blonde ponytailed ghost. I never did see her face. Is it possible that I wasn't supposed to see it? That it really isn't me, but someone else altogether?

I have so many questions. It seems that whatever it is must to be aware of me. It has made sure I can't get into a position of actually seeing what it is. But isn't that what ghosts supposedly do? The closer you get the less distinct they become until they disappear when you get real close? I've never heard of anyone actually touching a ghost. They aren't really there. But does that mean my ghost is simply a figment of my imagination? A hallucination? Am I creating this runner in my mind for some reason? Is she supposed to be symbolic? Is my mind trying to tell me that I'm running away from something? That I'll never reach my goal, whatever that is? That I'm simply not up to whatever task it is I'm setting out for myself?

If I believed any of these scenarios is behind what I'm seeing, I'd have to come to the conclusion that I've lost confidence in myself. That I think I'm incapable of something. But what could that be? I most likely will lose this case but could still win it on appeal. So, no. I'm not feeling a lack of confidence. But I am angry about Stevenson setting me up. The more I think about the whole situation the more convinced I am that Stevenson sold the client on the suit even though he knew we probably couldn't win it just because it was a lot of fees for the firm either way.

The Courier

"Your honor," I continue my objection. "The defense has not affirmed any positive action his client has taken to ensure that intellectual property obtained from prior employment cannot be introduced into engineering discussions or product design considerations."

"Your honor," Ted Mills, the defense counsel seeks to rebut my statement. "I have already introduced organization charts that show the former employees of the complaining party at my client's firm do not have a role in the design, development or deployment of technology solutions they worked on in their prior work assignments."

"Your honor, Mister Mills has not shown that they were not in a position to discuss prototype devices which they would have seen and possibly even discussed with the design teams, but for which they were not given direct day-to-day active involvement. And that is exactly what we allege happened in this instance. A prototype of the device Mister Mill's client has brought to market was built by my client more than two years ago. Prior to any of the employees retained by Mister Mill's client had left my client's employ. If you carefully examine the affidavits filed by the former employees, their words are carefully selected. They affirm they did not work directly or indirectly on my client's primary technology. Or if they did, in several instances, they have affirmed they did not work directly or indirectly on the design, development or deployment of the new firm's new technology. No where do they affirm they did not have access to product roadmaps or prototypes. No where do they affirm they never spoke to any of the engineering staff about the roadmap or prototypes under development. Your honor, with all due respect, Mister Mills has not provided an air-tight defense for his client. He has not built a credible scenario where it would have been impossible for those employees who chose to take employment opportunities with Mister Mill's client to have impacted the architecture, design, development and deployment of their new solution."

"And your honor," Ted jumps right back in. "Miss Wilcox alludes to a prototype of a device that does substantially everything my client's product does that conveniently heralds back before my client's new employees decided to pursue new opportunities. I for one would like to see this prototype with supporting documentation that will prove beyond a reasonable doubt that this prototype could have been seen and discussed with my clients. Any substantiation of my client's employees discussing the prototype would go a long way to bridging the river where it is the widest in your arguments."

Ted's calling my bluff. I can't take the bait because at the moment we only have the testimony of the one engineering manager. I have to let him off the hook and sink it further into my own mouth in the process.

"Your honor, the average product development lifecycle for a device of the kind that Mister Mill's client released in the market this year is five years. That is how long it took for my client's firm to produce the first operational versions of their world recognized device. So too we must expect at least a five year product development period from Mister Mill's company. Five years. And Mister Mills' client was able to design, develop and begin deployment of their product in less than two. That is not reasonable unless they had access to prior art as defined by the patents that have been filed by my client's firm along with the trade secrets that enabled the Intellectual Property to properly function."

"Your honor," Ted rebuts. "We have been over this ground on Friday. Miss Wilcox was not able to provide any hard evidence for her assertion. In fact, she obtained her data from only one company in the industry and we have no clear tangible evidence that their design period was typical or substantially delayed in their intellectual property development."

"Your honor," I can't let that stand. "It is a well-established fact that the more intellectual horsepower a firm has, the more rapidly it can adjust to new products, new markets and innovate across industries. A small firm, such as the one Mister Mills represents, generally does not have the depth of resources to innovate. They may make a breakthrough in one area of design, but rarely are they able to innovate across the full range of sub-elements to evolve an entirely new architecture."

"Speculative, your honor." Ted objects.

"Your honor," I continue. I have to push every thought I have that Ted will permit me to put forth. Preponderance of the evidence might carry the day. "But that is exactly what we have in this case. It is a next generation product and everything within it is next generation. How could such an under-resourced firm conduct all of that original research across a broad spectrum of industrial components and come up with novel designs for each and every one? And do it in two years? They had to have access to the design concepts of multiple vendors. They would have had to have the engineering expertise across the board to design all these new components. They would have needed depth of engineering expertise to design the integration packaging to ensure each and every one of the new elements would plug and play together. It's just not reasonable, your honor."

"Your honor." Ted rebuts. "My client's firm is well known in the industry for rapid prototyping. They have an industry recognized capacity to deliver first article items for testing faster than the industry averages."

I hear someone enter the court room. I turn and see a courier with a long blonde ponytail carrying a briefcase. The woman appears to be about my height and weight. Am I hallucinating? She approaches Bill Rodgers and transfers the briefcase to him. I look at her and realize she doesn't look all that much like me. Prettier in some ways but much more casual about her appearance. She is clearly athletic. If not a runner, maybe a gymnast.

Bill opens the briefcase, removes a CD and hands it to me. "Smoking gun."

"Your honor. Mister Mills has requested that we introduce into evidence the prototype device and clear evidence of its lineage. If you would permit me to play this disk?"

The bailiff rolls in a player and monitor and set it up so the judge and litigants can see the image. I hand him the disk which he inserts into the player, turns on the monitor and gets out of the way.

The image that comes up reads: 'Dallas Independent School District, School of Science and Engineering at Yvonne A. Ewell, Townview Center - Science Fair.'

"There's the date." I point out as it comes up on the screen, "And the thankyou note indicating that this prototype device was built with the cooperation of and under the auspices of my client."

A young man, probably not more than fourteen comes on screen and starts describing the device. With him in the lab are three of the employees who later moved to Ted Mills' client's company. I point them out, "Jackson Potter, Abdullah Mustafa, So Chin Su. Three of the seven employees who moved to Mr. Mills' client company six months after this video was made for a high school science fair showing them discussing the approach."

I then raise the device from the brief case. "Your honor, one copy of the prototype, which is the subject of the video and the discussion regarding intellectual property transfer in this case. There were five and this is the only one surviving at my client's firm."

I carry the prototype to the judge and set it before her.

"Please provide this to the bailiff who will label it appropriately and enter it into evidence along with the video disk." The judge nods to Ted Mills. "Mister Mills. Beware what you ask for. It appears that Miss Wilcox has now provided the prototype and clear lineage and linkage of at least three of the individuals your firm has denied having any knowledge of a prototype device. What say you?"

It's over, but I'm looking for the blonde ponytailed courier.

An Overnight Bag

The bar is crowded, not just with the people from my office, unusual for a Monday. We're here to celebrate the impossible win. At best it would have been a long drawn out appeals process without the smoking gun provided by Bill Rodgers. He was able to locate the team that worked the prototype project with the high school prodigy I saw on the video. They found not only the first of five prototypes they built but also the video explaining the device that Elijah Mohammed Mason showed at the high school science fair that year.

"You know I was down there with them, tearing the place apart." Bill confides in me over my glass of red wine. "In fact, I found the video. They'd all forgotten about it. I didn't recognize the board. The lab manager had to identify it as we didn't think much about it. A school project. Left in a desk drawer. Who would have thought our carelessness almost let a competitor eat us for lunch?"

Noah comes in. I'm surprised to see him since it's not Friday. "Heard you won the impossible case." He kisses me on my cheek. I instinctively pull back and instantly regret doing so. "Oh, shock. Are you full of static?" I try to cover my reaction with an explainable response having nothing at all to do with the real reason.

"Don't think so." Noah checks his clothes.

"Must be me." I respond, knowing the truth to that response.

"You feeling good about the verdict? You were completely down in the dumps on Friday. I take it you worked all weekend?" Noah frowns and then continues.

"A lot of people worked all weekend including Bill Rodgers," I nod to Bill. "…from my client's firm. So, what's going on with you today?"

"It was a good day. Nobody died." Noah responds with a shrug.

"Is that how you evaluate a day?" I'm surprised. "You don't look at whether some kids are getting better?"

"I do." Noah responds simply. "That's a great day. But it's not an everyday occurrence so I have to start somewhere."

"How do you do it? Stay positive when kids are struggling?" I have to ask.

"I don't understand how you stay positive when you have to be under just enormous pressure to win every case, even when you probably shouldn't."

"What are you saying?" I don't like the implications.

"Should you have won the case today or did you just find a loophole that allowed you to win even though the other guy was right?"

I don't know if I'm up to having this conversation with Noah right now. I'm actually feeling very tired. I didn't realize how tense I was about probably losing the case. I take a sip of my wine before responding. "Your world is pretty black and white. Someone lives, someone dies. Some hang on in the middle, but they are just dying at a slower rate. Does that pretty much sum it up?"

Noah frowns. "I don't know as I'd go quite that far, but I know where you're going."

"In my world everyone is right. And that's the problem. In a contested case someone has to change their position and, in some cases, both parties have to change their positions. That's what happened today. My client won the case, although there wasn't a verdict handed down. The judge telegraphed her intentions. She suggested a settlement on my client's terms. Since it was a settlement, neither side 'won'. Both had to compromise. Both gave up something to get something. So, was either side right? Not exactly. Was either side wrong? Most definitely. Both were wrong about parts of the case. I like to think the outcome resolves the infringement case and settles the non-compete violations. Everyone can get on with life. That's what's most important, isn't it? Certainty?"

"You know I couldn't do what you do." Noah confides.

"Why is that?" He's never been this dismissive of my work.

"Too much moral ambiguity." Noah places an order for a glass of red wine with a waitress and returns his attention to me. "I like things simple. I like to know what I'm doing is the best thing for my patient. I like to think I'm respectful of the wishes of the family. But when I'm dealing with a three-year-old with a tumor the size of a quarter, there's not a lot of moral ambiguity. If medicines won't shrink it, then it's radiation and chemo. If that won't shrink it then it's surgery. Pretty much clear decisions depending on how the patient responds to the approved protocols. But in your world, at the end of the day you can't go home and say the good guy won. From what you're saying, in all too many instances that will never be known."

"How did we ever get into this discussion?" I'm too tired to keep this going. "Kind of heavy for a Monday night. Particularly a Monday when I should be celebrating and so should you. No one died."

The wine comes and Noah clinks glasses, "To celebrating. Something we should both do more often. Speaking of which are you ever going to accept my standing invitation for dinner?"

That's almost become a joke because he asked me out the first time we met, when was that? Five years or more ago. And we still haven't gone out. But I don't go out with anyone except the crowd from work on Fridays. I'm not ready to go down the whole romance route again. Been there, done that. Have the scars and t-shirt. "Maybe someday. If you're going to try to make me happy, you're going to have to come up with a better line than it's been a good day because no one died."

"Touché." Noah clinks his glass on mine. "No seriously. I used to come here on Fridays with all the young docs and we'd just about swamp the place. Now I come here and I'm the only one. At some point I'm going to stop waiting for someone to accept my invitation. I'm going to make a commitment to someone who wants the patter of little feet to keep us both up all night."

"You certainly know how to romance a girl," just comes out. "That's not fair. No, I'm sure you do, but I've been living alone for a long time. It's hard to admit things could be better with someone else jockeying for the bathroom. Having to pick up after someone else, washing two loads of clothes at the same time, or actually cooking a meal for two. I don't know as I'm in a comfort zone or a habit zone. I actually think habits are harder to break than discomforts are to overcome. Is that where you're at? Thinking you need to start breaking some of those self-defeating habits you've gotten into because they're easy? Necessary? The only real choice?"

"I think you need to finally accept that dinner invitation, listen to my quips, and laugh uproariously while I do the same for you. I think it would do you good to have someone laugh with you in celebration. As a doctor I can tell you laughter is absolutely the best medicine. You'll live at least twice as long if you laugh once a day than you will if you don't. Now doesn't that get your attention?"

"Oh, my god. You mean I might have to live twice as long just because I'm laughing? That would be awful. I'd probably have twice as many gray hairs, twice as many hemorrhoids. Instead of only running half way to the moon, if you add up all my morning runs, I might actually get there. And then what would I do? I'd be too old to make it back."

"See. You and I are made for each other. I'm a doctor. You're a lawyer. You'd get to the moon and argue with St. Peter that he needs to wait until you get home to take you because you can't go to heaven with just an overnight bag. Now me being a doctor, I'd give you a prescription for a pain killer so you could walk home."

How Do You Decide?

Mia finds Noah and me over in the corner and joins us with her vodka tonic. "Oh, oh. A lawyer and a doctor walk into a bar…"

At least she's in the proper frame of mind to join this discussion.

"Didn't know it's Friday." Mia aims at Noah since he never comes out except on Friday.

"Heard there was something to celebrate, so decided to come by and check it out."

"Pulled a miracle from the jaws of certain defeat." Mia raises her glass. We do as well.

"If it was a miracle, was it the right decision?" Noah asks still playing devil's advocate.

"For our client it certainly was." Mia responds without having to even think about the question.

"Then by definition it wasn't the right decision for the other party." Noah considers the implication.

"Who cares?" Mia shrugs. "If they want the right decision, next time they'll retain us rather than Ted Mills. They should have known better. A lone practitioner just doesn't have the resources or expertise to be on equal footing with a large firm like ours."

"Am I hearing you right?" Noah seems displeased. "You're saying the law has nothing to do with right or wrong? It's all a matter of who you have argue the case?"

"I wouldn't go quite that far." Mia retreats in tone, but not in attitude. "You have to know the law thoroughly, you have to know precedent, you have to know the judge and what she or he focuses on, you have to have researchers who will find witnesses, evidence and documents that can be used in court to support your arguments. All I'm saying is a plaintiff or defendant gets what they pay for. You put up the money to have people working together to find every shred of evidence that can support your argument you have a better chance of winning the case."

"Do you ever suppress evidence that's contrary to your argument?" Noah pushes looking for something he's not voiced as yet.

"Define suppress." Mia goes right back at him.

"Failure to bring forward to the court." Noah tries.

Mia considers his question for a moment, takes a sip and then responds. "We gather much more evidence than we present. Our job is not to present every shred of evidence. Our job is to present what will support our argument and the cause of our client. Does that mean we sometimes find evidence that is contrary to our argument? Yes, that is often the case. Do we present it in court? It depends on how it will affect the case. Many times, we do not present it because it would make a clear verdict harder to achieve. Is that suppression? No. The other side has the opportunity to find the same evidence. If they present it in support of their case, then we have to deal with it. If they don't, well, as I said, the clients get what they pay for."

Noah contemplates her description of how evidence is handled by the legal teams, appearing as if he is about to ask another question, but Mia heads him off.

"Isn't it the same in the medical profession? I mean if you have to have a procedure and you go to the cheapest doc, aren't you likely to get an adequate result? But if you pay for the top doc in that specialty, you're more likely to get a better outcome. How is that different?"

"Doctors use all of the evidence and information presented to them about a particular patient's case. For us it's more often trying to de-conflict different symptoms. Trying to understand contradictory indications of what may actually be going on. We have to be good enough detectives to be able to follow the path to the true culprit."

"Good enough detectives?" Mia picks up on his comment.

"Being a detective is not my primary job, but I have to be good enough at it to find the right cause. It all comes from experience, because it's not something that is easily taught in med school. It's one of those things that the more you do it, the better you become. Having seen a set of symptoms more than once gives you clues of where to go look. But every patient is different. Every time you embark on that process the more you learn. You could say that an experienced doc is going to get to your root cause quicker because of the number of patients she or he has seen. But a younger doc may know of cutting-edge treatments that better address the causes of the symptoms being experienced."

"Lawyers are different." Mia suggests. "We play a team sport. So, we get to bring in the collective wisdom and experience of younger and older attorneys as we look at a case. From what you've said and I've read, it appears docs tend to work from generalists to specialists and hand patients off to one another depending on their ability to address the symptoms."

"Patients often seek second opinions, when it comes to major procedures. In those instances, multiple docs look at the same lab results, images and patient history and recommend a procedure or treatment. Then it's up to the patient to decide which approach they would prefer to pursue."

"Again, that's different since the patient decides what they are going to do." Mia confirms.

"Correct." Noah seems to be reflecting on something he's not talking about.

"So, there's more differences between docs and lawyers than how we bill for our services." Mia offers apparently expecting to conclude this discussion.

Noah has other ideas. "We deal with absolutes. A patient either gets better or not. In the law it seems to me to be all about moral ambiguity. The party that brings the most money to the table is much more likely to get the result they want regardless of whether that decision is right or wrong."

Mia takes a sip of her vodka tonic, gestures that she has more to say, then gets to it. "That's where I thought you were going earlier. You seem to have some notion about right or wrong. As I said before a decision that is right for one client is often not for the other party in the case. The fact that someone has to make a decision is a reflection of reality. Who decides? Who can look into the hearts of men and be able to know what is right or wrong? We have laws to guide us. We have legislators who sometimes change their minds and what's wrong today is right tomorrow. So, how do you decide when the standards of justice are constantly changing?"

Choices

Stevenson Wainwright III sees the three of us in the corner, pulls up a chair and joins us. Stevenson Wainwright III never deems it worthy of his time to talk with members of his firm at social occasions. In fact, he seldom joins the Friday events here. So, it is highly unusual he would be here at all. Even more unusual he would come to talk with us. I have to assume his focus will be on Noah since he is a client of the firm.

"Ladies, Dr. Williams." And as I expect he goes right to Noah. "I understand congratulations are in order. Are you all aware that Dr. Williams has been asked to assume the role of Chief of Staff in Pediatrics for the Baylor system of hospitals? That's quite an honor for someone as young as Dr. Williams. He's replacing my older brother who has been Chief of Staff for almost twenty-five years."

I didn't know about Noah's promotion. He's not said a thing about it. "Well done." I respond, but I'm still thinking this through. "Isn't that primarily an administrative job?" I have to ask.

"It is." Noah acknowledges, "But I'll still see patients as time permits. Just not as many of them and probably only some of the tougher cases."

This move doesn't sound like Noah. "Why administration? I thought being with patients is what lights you up. Energizes you to be more than a good enough detective."

Noah grimaces, raises his wine glass and looks at the ruby red, tilts the glass to look through the wine, then tilts it back upright and gives it a swirl before taking a sip. We all wait for his response. "You're right. It was a very hard decision. Is now the time to make a move that reduces my patient contact? But Pediatric Oncology is a very difficult specialty. Even though we are much more successful in finding life extending treatments and surgeries, patients still die. And that takes a toll. I'm sure I could have continued in practice for a number of years. But at some point, I know that unless we find a way to save everyone, I will want to move on to that administrative job. To help indirectly, but not have to carry the memories and images of patients I was unable to help."

Noah takes another sip while we are all still absorbing this revelation. "As Mr. Wainwright mentioned, his brother was in this particular job for twenty-five years. Administrative jobs where you can have this much impact don't open up very often. And it's likely that when I would be ready to make the move someone would have just taken the job. Most likely that person will be there well past when I would probably retire from practice. It seems life always has a plan for you that doesn't match up with what you would design if you could."

"So, you're taking the sure thing rather than rolling the dice and seeing how a different choice would reward you." I don't know why I'm unhappy with his choice, but I am.

Noah looks at me quizzically. I don't know what he's thinking, but somehow, I think it has something to do with the conversation we were having before Mia joined us. "Aren't you working for the same thing? A partnership? Where you have a brotherhood of peers helping you find and groom clients to ensure your survival and growth as a firm?"

Stevenson answers this question, "A law partnership is different than a hospital. A partnership is a meritocratic society where the most able assist those who are more junior to gain experience and insights that will assist our clients in pursuing their various economic and community pursuits."

"You use that elevator speech often?" Noah seems to have heard it before.

"Not often, but I do enjoy summarizing our mission in the community. I'm the firm's ambassador, if you will. I have responsibility to ensure our clients know we are here for them as advisors and confidantes in their endeavors. And also, to let potential clients know how we can be of assistance, with our broad experience across industries and types of businesses. To say nothing of our unparalleled litigation prowess."

"That's an interesting way of describing your experience in litigation." Noah is still exploring the concepts of right and wrong that seem to bother him about what we do.

"Prowess?" Stevenson looks at me. "You're sitting here with one of the best litigators in Dallas. Was able to arrive at a favorable outcome for our client just today. On Friday she gave herself only about an equal chance of winning or losing the case. But she dedicated her weekend to uncovering any evidence that could influence the outcome. Her hard work paid off. What more can I say about her than she simply will not permit herself to lose. You know there are hundreds of attorneys in this city and nearly as many in Fort Worth. But I would put Miss Wilcox up against any of them in a trial situation and be confident we will prevail."

"Does that mean she's on the short list for partner this time around?" Noah launches out of nowhere. I almost drop my glass of wine. I can't look at Stevenson knowing he probably thinks I put Noah up to this question, or at least had been talking about becoming a partner before Stevenson joined us. I hear Stevenson shift his weight in the leather chair. He clearly would prefer to not answer this question, particularly with me present.

"We haven't put our list of partner candidates together as yet." Stevenson finally wimps out. "There are many factors that must be considered besides..."

"Prowess?" Noah interrupts. "How many other trial lawyers in your firm, who are eligible for partnership, would you use that term to describe?"

I know Noah is trying to help me. He's got his promotion and apparently thinks I should get one too, even though I'd never asked for this help, and never would have. Just the same, even though totally embarrassed by his actions, I'm glad he is thinking of me and of trying to help.

Stevenson has a decidedly uncomfortable look on his face. I catch just a glance and then look away again.

"I can't comment on personnel matters of the firm. But let me assure you the Partners know who is representing the firm in such a manner that they deserve to join the ranks of our partners. It is an annual evaluation of our talent. An annual evaluation of our clients and their needs. And an even more frequent evaluation of where there are opportunities to serve new clients with needs we are particularly well-suited to address."

"Am I wrong, or are you saying the decision to join the Partners is more about bringing in new business than serving your existing clients?"

Stevenson shifts in his chair once more. "All partners have a responsibility to bring new business to the firm. We sponsor their memberships in clubs and organizations where they have opportunities to meet potential clients and build personal relationships. Is that somehow unbalanced? Do we decide who becomes a partner more on how many new clients and how much they contribute in terms of new billings than on how they exercise their professional duties? I would say no. We are counselors. We provide services our clients value. That is why we are able to bill for those services. So, I would say the delivery of professional services has to be the most important factor in who becomes a partner."

"Please excuse my ignorance of these matters." Noah responds. "I may be wrong in my assumptions but there seems to be a long history of many worthy women not being chosen for partnerships in every law firm in the city. Just look at the demographics. How many men are partners and how many women? The numbers are greatly skewed towards men even though the number of law school graduates have been nearly equal. In some years the number of women has been greater than the number of men. And still there doesn't seem to be any real growth in the number of women partners. Why is that?"

Stevenson has a ready answer. "Your observation about the number of women graduating from law school is correct. What you're not seeing however, is a greater number of women are taking positions in government agencies and non-profits. We find fewer women who have an interest in corporate law, patent law or litigation. And many of those who do specialize in these areas are swept up by corporations that have equal employment requirements or internal targets for hiring women and minorities. So, to find qualified women who want to join our ranks is a challenge. To find enough to have balanced incoming groups is even more difficult. You see, we like to have our staff look like our clients. If the client legal staff is mostly women or one or another minority, we will attempt to find within our ranks someone who looks and acts like them. We want our clients to be comfortable with the person who is serving them, advising them, intervening on their behalf. Does that answer your question, Dr. Williams?"

"Thank you for the explanation. I'm pleased to understand you take gender and racial equality serious as you contemplate your partnership ranks."

Stevenson nods without commenting further. He finishes his drink and rises. "Ladies and Dr. Williams. Again, congratulations on your new position with Baylor. I'm sure you will find it both challenging and rewarding." He then looks directly at me. I can't read his expression but it's not one of fondness. "Goodnight."

Noah shakes his head, "He doesn't get the world has changed."

Elijah

Next case. I'm in the law library at work reading through the background material and prior case law summary. In this case I'm defending my client in a suit brought by a supplier. My client has provided a thick file of quality findings that required them to return the components to the supplier. The supplier rejected the returns based on their inspections, saying that the components met the specifications provided by my client.

I hear Mia coming my way. "Morning." I offer as I hear her arrive at the door. A moment later she is seated across from me looking like something the cat dragged in the night before. "What's… this?"

"Rough night."

"What's his name?" I have to ask. She's married, but I hear there are problems.

She brushes it aside. "So, why are you on this case? This is so way below what you usually do."

"The hand Stevenson dealt. Probably because Noah put him on the spot. But this has nothing to do with Noah." I try to assure her.

"I know, but you need to take him up on his invitation. Someone has to poke you twice a day or you'll shrivel up and turn into an old crone who has never had a loving experience in her life."

"You really see me ending up like that?" I've never thought of being alone forever. I shake off the momentary feeling.

I'm up at the usual time, going through my morning run, more asleep than awake. I've gotten past looking for anything to be unusual. If the blonde ponytail shows up, I'm going to stop her and find out who she is and what the deal is with her disappearing. Got to be a rational answer, I just haven't been able to figure it out as yet.

While I shampoo my hair, I suddenly get a panic attack that I've taken this case too lightly. That it's so straightforward I'll get caught in some trap I've not considered. Is that what Stevenson is doing? Setting me up for something I'll not see coming. That I'll go in to it too confident and not have done all the homework that's needed? Could easily be. I quickly run through all the assumptions I've made, trying to find something that could come back to bite me. I see nothing. I think through all of my arguments. Is there any that's not air-tight? Any that are made on an assumption that could be pulled out from under me? Again, I see nothing that should alert me to a need to go look at something else. Then what could it possibly be? What requires my personal attention?

While drying my hair I consider another issue I've not explored. What if the real dynamic that's playing out here is that my client is trying to put pressure on the supplier because my client wants to buy the supplier? Is my client hoping a lawsuit might drive down the value of the firm by calling into question, quite publicly, the quality of their products? Would fit the facts as I know them. Is certainly a possibility given there had never been a dispute about product quality in any shipments received over a decade. Could be why our client was willing to pay up for me.

At the court room, as I review my briefing papers, my client joins me at the plaintiff table. "Morning. Have we supplied you with everything you need?" he asks.

"I think we have submitted a very strong case." I respond. "There are always surprises, but I think they're covered."

"That's what I wanted to hear." My client glances at my dark suit offset by my long blonde hair. It is a strong visual I've used to my advantage on more than one case. We sit. Within a minute the judge, Horace M. Steppenwolf, enters the court. I've argued before him. He's fair and objective. Before he even sits, he calls from the bench. "Would counsel for both parties visit with me in my chambers?"

As I follow him, I realize Judge Steppenwolf has reviewed the case in detail. When I close the door to his chambers he instantly begins, "I see Miss Wilcox is dressed for success Mister Abrams. Having reviewed the briefs, the record of evidence and endless boxes of records, I feel compelled to suggest it may be prudent for you to simply negotiate a settlement with her client."

"Your honor…" Mister Abrams begins, but Judge Steppenwolf holds up his hand.

"Consult with your client, but so far I don't see an adequate defense."

"Yes, your honor."

I follow Abrams out of Judge Steppenwolf's chambers. As we enter the courtroom something seems strange. I blink rapidly as I continue to walk, although slower than usual. The room seems distorted in my view. Everything seems to be as it should be, but it's like a thin nylon curtain some theaters raise at the beginning of a play or performance is between me and my clients.

I feel my forehead. No fever, but the image won't clear. As I get closer to my table I notice what looks like a family sitting there. Man, woman and teenage son. I raise my hand and feel an electric pulse, just like the other morning. First on my hand and then over my whole body as I apparently move through that screen. I look at the family, not recognizing them, then turn around to look at the court. Now the distorted image is behind me. The judge takes the bench, Mister Abrams looks at me. And then they melt away to reveal a woman judge just looking at me as if she is waiting for me to finish saying something. I look around but realize I'm no longer in Kansas or maybe not even Dallas.

Disorientation

"Miss Wilcox." Judge, Honorable P. Lamoreaux, a large woman I've never appeared before previously, intones my name with a distinct southern lilt. "Please take your seat so the government's counsel may present their opening arguments."

"Of course, your honor." I'm disoriented but do as instructed. What's going on? Where's Mister Abrams? Where is my client? Who are these people? What case am I arguing? This has to be a dream.

The other counsel, an athletic looking black haired man I don't recognize, probably mid-forties, rises. "Thank you, your honor. The government petitioned to obtain custody of Elijah Mohammed Mason from his parents in order to adequately protect national security interests this young man represents."

I'm in a custody case? I'm not prepared to argue a case I know nothing about. And what's this about the government petitioning for custody? I've never heard that the government can take custody of a minor from his parents if they are competent. These people would appear to be. This is wrong on so many different levels.

"What kind of National Security interests does this young man threaten, Mister Spencer?" The judge sounds skeptical. At least I have that working in my favor.

"May we approach?" Mr. Spencer asks.

The judge nods and I follow the government's attorney.

"Your honor, Elijah Mohammed Mason, is not a threat to National Security. However, young Mister Mason is a prodigy in science, math and theoretical physics. He has the potential to unlock secrets of the universe that could substantially change our perceptions and understandings in many areas. It has been deemed by the Defense Department that young Mister Mason needs the protections and security that only the government can provide to free his mind to tackle these extremely important approaches to accessing the secrets we have been unable to understand from other approaches."

"Mister Spencer," the judge shakes her head. "You are going to have to do better if you don't want to see me simply dismiss your petition."

Spencer is very nervous, "Your honor, I really can't discuss what I need for you to know in front of someone…" Spencer gestures absently for a moment and then finds the word he's looking for. "Someone who doesn't have either a need to know or the proper security clearances. Your honor, you have a need to know."

"His parents have a need to know. As their representative and counsel, Miss Wilcox has a need to know."

"Thank you, your honor," I nod to the judge.

Mister Spencer looks about nervously, but plunges ahead realizing he's made a serious mistake in how he has approached this case so far. "Your honor, Elijah Mohammed Mason, the subject of this hearing has postulated a theory about a multi-dimensional universe beyond anything we can currently comprehend. The various dimensions of this universe are kept apart by a magnetic field powered by dark energy. However, young Mister Mason has written about an approach that could theoretically permit transit between these different dimensions. If such a device were to be built, if it were to fall into the wrong hands, it could disrupt our very way of life. That's why the government, in this instance represented by the Department of Defense, is petitioning to take into custody young Mister Mason. The purpose is to either demonstrate the plausibility of such a device or exhaust, with the help of a cadre of scientists and engineers, approaches that might enable dimensional transit."

I know I have to wait for the judge to respond, but I have an overwhelming desire to ask Mister Spencer to explain that again, in English.

"Mister Spencer. I graduated Cum Laude from Emory University. With distinction from the University of Texas Law School. I have been a serving judge for over ten years. I am not someone you might think of as uneducated, or unable to grasp complex concepts. But I have absolutely no idea what you just said."

I smile in relief.

"Take another crack at simplifying this concept or I will find I have no recourse other than to dismiss."

Mister Spencer looks back at the other attorney at his table, but evidently thinks better of his initial thought. He lowers his head and resolves to give it another try. "Your honor. The Department of Defense has come to believe that Elijah Mohammed Mason could potentially build a weapon of mass destruction the likes of which you have never even contemplated. His middle name raises concerns that he may have sympathies towards certain terrorist factions. For that reason, to protect him from himself and ensure terrorists cannot kidnap him for the purpose of exploiting his theory, we wish to place him in government custody."

"Mister Spencer, now that you have given me the Fox News version, what would my friends over at NBC have to say about young Mister Mason?"

Evidently Mister Spencer pissed the judge off by going too simple minded.

"Your honor. Einstein was only a few years older than Mister Mason when he developed the Theory of Relativity. In the next few years young Mister Mason could fundamentally change what we know of the universe. No one saw Einstein as a security threat even though his theory eventually led to the atomic bomb. Today we are much more cautious about revolutionary theories. As a nation we have to protect young Mister Mason. Enable him to prove himself either in the Einstein category or not. If he is in that category, we will all be better off if he develops his theories and potential weapons for our government than for a group of terrorists or worse the Chinese or Russians."

"Very good, Mister Spencer. Now that I have a better understanding of what's at stake you may proceed to make your case."

"Your honor." I register my first protest of many I'm sure I'll be making before this is all over. "What evidence has the government provided the court that would substantiate any of the claims Mister Spencer just made?"

"It's in the materials the government provided in discovery, Miss Wilcox." Spencer delights in pointing out.

"And how, Mister Spencer, would I know what document to look for if you don't identify it for me?"

"Mister Spencer. Miss Wilcox is making a reasonable request." The Judge responds.

"You should ask young Mister Mason. But I'll tell you. It's a paper he wrote and submitted to the National Review of Theoretical Physics."

"Didn't know they were reviewing articles and submitting them to the Defense Department before publication." I shoot back not sure they are and wondering how they got a copy.

"We have people who review anything that appears relative to certain subjects based on metadata searches." Spencer tries to deflect my real question.

"But something that hasn't been published won't show up in a metadata search." I push back.

"I can't discuss this further with someone without a need to know or proper security clearance."

"Are you going to hide behind national security for this whole trial? You seem to use it every chance you get." I note and wait for the judge.

"Miss Wilcox. I require appropriate decorum in my court. No more cheap shots."

"Yes, your honor." I walk back to the table and lean over to Mr. Mason who is sitting next to me. "She's going to let him present the rest of his case. I've noticed the government has already made a shift in how they are presenting it. Originally, they simply wanted to make Elijah a ward of the state, now they used the term 'government custody.' That's usually a temporary state. We'll have to wait and see how they play that."

"Can they really take him away from us because they think he needs protection?" Mister Mason asks. His voice shows confusion, anger and fear.

Now I'm on the spot, I search memories that are more than a decade old. "The government has the right to put someone into protective custody when so ordered by a court of competent jurisdiction." I recite from memories I thought were long lost. "This court would be considered of competent jurisdiction. So, the answer is yes, the judge could so order."

"But don't you have to request protective custody?" Mister Mason asks.

I really don't know enough, so I suggest, "Let's see where Mister Spencer thinks he's going to take us."

"Not where Elijah wants to go, I assure you." Mister Mason is emphatic as he turns back to look at Judge Lamoureux.

Crucial

Mr. Spencer reviews his notes before coming forward to make his case. "Your honor. This is a simple case, really. We have a child prodigy who has grown to a young adult. He has shown himself to me more capable than his peers. He thinks thoughts you and I could never comprehend on a great day of illumination. He sees a universe in his mind we do not. He sees a world that can emerge from a different way of thinking about the natural sphere we inhabit and the rules that govern how it exists within the universe. The child prodigy I'm referring to was Albert Einstein. At age twenty-seven he published a brief paper that fundamentally changed the way men look at their world. The point I'm making is that age is not a determinant of when someone can offer something earth shaking to mankind. We know of others besides Einstein who have made substantial contributions to society at very young ages. Men and women who process information differently than those in the same room around them. Men and women who have the ability to transform the world by solving problems we all see as insolvable at the moment. They make different connections, follow different logic paths, and see different relationships than the rest of us. Such individuals are national treasures. They bring the rest of us along with them on their rocket-propelled rides through life. They clear the way for those who come after to advance the state of the art in whatever domain of expertise. And in an open world, where information and knowledge are shared for the benefit of all mankind, such individuals can be citizens of the world. Much as Einstein and others like him have tended to be."

The judge decides to intervene, "Mister Spencer. If this is your doctoral dissertation, I suggest you present it to your dissertation committee. If this is the opening of your case, I suggest you get to the point and let us decide what we will with your request."

"Yes, your honor." Poor Spencer is sweating profusely now. He clearly is trying to figure out how to proceed when the judge has on three occasions asked him to simplify or clarify or simply get on with his case which still isn't evident from what he's said.

"Your honor, the point is we have brilliant people who could easily be targets of foreign operatives in this country. And to prevent it from occurring again, the Department of Defense has established programs for prodigy talent. These programs ensure young individuals such as young Mister Mason have special facilities where they can conduct experiments with teams of scientists and engineers. Working with people capable of translating theories and ideas into reality. Bringing about new capabilities in the defense of liberty. Ensuring that foreign nations seeking to reduce the ability of the United States to protect our interests around the world will not succeed."

"Mister Spencer." The judge shakes her head once more. "There is no need to elevate this discussion beyond what it is. A custody case. You're asking the court to grant custody of sixteen-year-old Elijah Mohammed Mason to the US government. In particular the Department of Defense. What is your case for doing so? Protection from bad guys won't cut it Mr. Mason. We have police departments charged with that responsibility."

Mr. Spencer looks around the courtroom.

"There is no one from the press present Mister Spencer." Judge Lamoreaux notes in response to his look. "You will not be able to keep your actions here a secret for long. What you are proposing will have long legs."

"Then let me summarize my case, your honor."

"Please do, Mister Spencer. If I have any questions, I've never been accused of being bashful."

"Your honor. Elijah Mohammed Mason is a gift to our nation. He will do great things in his lifetime. He will change many things we take for granted. Just what those things are at this point in time we can only imagine. I would point out what we are proposing is not so different from the witness protection programs of the Department of Justice or gifted and talented programs conducted in public schools for decades. Not so different from the Olympic development programs that have prepared our athletic ambassadors for the world's stage. Those programs could be considered like the farm teams for the majors. And Elijah Mohammed Mason is a big leaguer. In Einstein's talent pool. If Einstein were an American and sixteen years old today, we would offer him the exact same opportunity."

I can't stand it anymore, "Objection your honor. Mister Spencer is describing the forcible removal of a sixteen-year-old boy from his family, a family that has done everything we as a community could ask of them, as an opportunity. This is not an opportunity."

"So noted Miss Wilcox. Mister Spencer. Please be more precise in your wording and descriptions of what it is specifically you are proposing to do."

"Yes, your honor. What I was trying to say, although less precisely than it came out." Spencer glares at me momentarily. "... Is that young Mister Mason will have an opportunity to demonstrate the depths of his talents and the brilliance of his insights in the program we will place him. Your honor, I'm trying to make the best of a difficult situation. I would give you all the information you would like if national security did not play a part in what can be discussed in open forums such as this. You would not want to be thought responsible for a spy in a foreign country being outed by a public disclosure of his or her role. For that reason, I can't make some of the information you are requesting known without it compromising ongoing efforts within our government."

"Mr. Spencer." The judge shakes her head. "You are asking me to take a leap of faith, that the government has the best interests of Elijah Mohammed Mason and the country both in mind."

Thoughts

When I get back to my firm, something is different, but I'm not sure what it is. My office is arranged differently. Louise, Stephenson's assistant comes in.

I look up, "Hi." I wonder what Stephenson wants. She looks at me strangely. "New suit? Never seen that one before. You look good."

What? I've had this suit for at least two years and worn it how many times? She's seen it before.

Then she approaches my desk, looks through a pile of documents and pulls out the paper Elijah Mohammed Mason wrote and drops it in front of me. "Heavily redacted."

How did she know what I needed? I glance through the black marker covered pages. A few words here or there, but nothing I can make a decision about other than his name on the front page. I shake my head.

"What else do you need?" Louise asks.

Why is she willing to help me? Where is Roxy my assistant? Maybe she's out sick or something. "Could you see if Mia could help me?"

"Mia?" Louise seems mystified by my question.

"Mastrangelo."

"There's no one working here by that name." Louise informs me.

What? Mia quit? That's not what Louise just said. It was as if she'd never heard of her. "Do you have time to see if you can locate what firm she's with?"

"Mia Mastrangelo. Sure. What else do you need?"

"An argument to counter the government's claim of national security."

"That's your forte." Louise nods to me and heads off to find Mia.

I've gotten into preparing the case and forgotten how I got here, which I still don't understand. One minute I'm going to negotiate a settlement and the next I'm defending a custody case. How did that happen? The judge knew me, the family knew me. Why didn't I know them? I buzz Louise.

"What happened to the Sunbird litigation?" the one I was working.

"I'll have to ask Oprah."

Oprah? What does she have to do with Sunbird?

I hear footsteps. I don't recognize them. Certainly not Mia. A slender black woman, probably early 40s, well dressed, stands in my office door. "Louise said you were asking about Sunbird?"

"The litigation with their supplier, Custom Kinetics. What happened?"

"There was no verdict. Sunbird made an offer, Custom Kinetics rejected it. They were later acquired by a hedge fund. The new owners held on to them just long enough to flip them, loading them up with debt. That, of course led to a chapter filing and reorganization. Custom Kinetics shed all the debt at which point Sunbird made another offer and they took it."

"No litigation." I'm trying to understand how a case I worked on didn't happen. "Aren't you a trial lawyer?"

"I'm the best trial lawyer in the firm, but since the first filing, it's all been mergers and acquisitions followed by bankruptcy. I've not done any work for Sunbird. That's why when Louise called about Sunbird litigation I was confused."

"As am I." I admit. "What about Atlas versus eTronics?"

"eTronics prevailed." I hear embarrassment in Oprah's voice. "We just couldn't establish a fact pattern the judge would accept. Said he was looking at all the precedential cases and none would have supported our claims.

"Have you heard of Elijah Mohammed Mason?"

"Isn't that the case you're working now?"

"It is, but he may have worked as an intern at Atlas. While he was there he could have built a prototype. I may be all wrong, but it's worth checking out. Might give you evidence for an appeal."

"Did the kid tell you about that?" Oprah is curious as to my source.

"No, just something suggested by someone who worked at Atlas about that time."

"We're getting close to the statute of limitations on appeal. I argued that case three years ago."

She argued it three years ago? What's going on? Where have I been for the last three years? And why did Oprah argue a case I remember I did? Or thought I did. Am I losing my mind? Having a psychiatric episode or nervous breakdown? This doesn't make any sense to me.

"Seems like it was just last week," I finally respond and look at the calendar on my desk. I'm now three years in the future. How did I get here?

Louise buzzes me, "Mia Mastrangelo works at MacArthur Partners over in Thanksgiving Tower."

Oprah asks, "You know Mia?"

I nod without giving any further information, not sure if I do or not. "Appreciate you filling me in on those cases."

Oprah gets the message that I'm done with her and want to call Mia. As she leaves I'm dialing Mia's number.

Preparing

I scour the sources for government custody cases and find the law very muddy. Every precedent is for child welfare. Ensuring the child has adequate nutrition, clothing and a safe environment. And a safe environment is one where the child will not be abused or endangered by their parent or keeper. In many instances the person providing care has no biological relationship to the child. But for the government to simply decide they need to remove a child from a normal and healthy family relationship because the child may be able to do something extraordinary, there is just no precedent. So, with no precedents I should be able to easily win this one. But something tells me this will not be so simple.

Mia looks the same, although her hair style is different. The color's not the same as I remember having seen her just yesterday, but I'm finding out that was three years ago.

"Hi, J'ne Wilcox." I extend my hand as she approaches my table in the back of Rainbows, the dark, wood and chrome bar half way between our offices in downtown Dallas.

"Mia. It's nice to finally meet you."

We sit, my glass of red wine arrives and her vodka tonic. Mia looks at the drink. "You ordered me a vodka tonic? How did you know that's my drink of preference?"

"I try to know a little something about the people I'm going to exchange thoughts with."

"How can I help you?" Mia settles herself.

"I'm just pleased you would make the time to chat with me. I know you haven't looked at the specifics of this case, but I was hoping you would have some general thoughts that might send me in a direction if you know what I mean."

Mia takes a sip of her vodka tonic, *at least some things haven't changed*. "You're talking the Mason case."

I nod.

"The government doesn't have the means to simply take the boy from his parents, so they are trying to establish such a right in this case. If they win, there will be case after case all litigating the same right of the government which today doesn't exist."

"You have a good grasp of the overall situation." I admit although I expected nothing less. "In his opening arguments counsel cited witness protection, gifted and talented programs in schools and Olympic development programs for elite athletes."

"All voluntary. The government doesn't take the athletes into custody, even though they pay all their living expenses while in the training camps."

"What about witness protection programs?" I come back to the one that bothers me.

"Given a new life to enable someone to testify against bad guys. Not even close. So, you're down to the national security argument. What's in that paper? Have you read it?"

"Redacted. I only have the summary the government's counsel provided."

"Which is?"

"A theory, really. He's comparing the kid to Albert Einstein. That's where he loses me. But the kid has a Muslim middle name and the government implied he might have jihadist sympathies."

Mia takes a deep breath. "You're in real trouble. It's going to be real hard for a judge to not respect a government request where they are trying to prevent a terrorist incident, even if it is tied to theoretical physics."

"But in a terrorist homeland security case, wouldn't the government be wanting to put the terrorist in jail? In this case the kid hasn't done anything to proclaim a religious belief."

"The government may be more afraid that the Jihadist cells in this country would kidnap him. Put him to work on some weapon of mass destruction for the Muslim world to put the world order into nuclear balance as a propaganda coup."

That's what I like about Mia. She's able to take seeds and play them out better than I do. I was aware of the terrorist connection, but had not thought through how the other side might play it.

"How would you defend this?" I put out there to see what thoughts she might have.

"Well, as you said I've not had time to look at any case law or precedents."

"Nothing there we can hang a hat on. It's all the absence of a precedent that makes the national security gambit a plausible reason for setting a new precedent."

Mia sips her vodka tonic, thinking about my question and the last new information. "I'd probably put the kid on the stand. Try to establish that he may be real smart, but he's just a normal kid, whose family loves, provides for him and treats him well. That his family is preparing for him to go to university where he will demonstrate his potential to whatever extent he can."

I nod just once and ask, "That's great insight. Exactly what I was hoping you could provide. How can I help you?"

"You could clear up something I've been wondering about. Why did you decide to call me to discuss this case with the deep bench you have at Victor?"

"I knew someone very much like you in a former life. So, I played a hunch and it paid off." *After all, I've known you almost a decade.*

If You Know What I Mean

Something doesn't seem right as I approach the door to my apartment. I search my purse for my keycard, but I can't find it. I wonder if I left it in the office for some reason. Then I look at the name on the mail slot. It's not mine. Someone else is living in my apartment? What's going on here? If I don't live here how do I figure out where I do?

Then I decide to check my driver license. 2500 North Houston Street, Apartment 2815, Dallas, Texas. That's right next to Victory Park and the American Airlines Center where the hockey and basketball teams play. Why would I be living there? It would be convenient, but I can't afford that neighborhood.

I take the DART train back downtown and walk from the Victory Park Station stop to my new apartment house, which is only two blocks. I look around as I make the short walk. I rarely come to sporting events here so why would I live next door? None of this makes sense. And worse yet is I have no idea why everything has changed on me. About the only thing I can hope is I'll go to sleep and wake up tomorrow in my apartment, go out for my usual run, see no ghosts and go into work to find Mia helping me with the Sunbird settlement.

Approaching the apartment house, I realize from this location I can walk to my office faster than I can take the train or even a bus. Is that why I moved here? Doesn't seem like me. I'm just not someone who wants to pay this kind of rent.

The doorman apparently knows me, nods and pushes the floor on the elevator for me. Twenty-eighth. Wow. I'm up there in the clouds somewhere. As I come off the elevator, I have to check my license again to be sure of the apartment. 2815. I walk towards it and hear a click as I approach. I have something on me that automatically unlocks my door?

That's convenient. I enter this strange apartment. Not at all like my apartment. Art objects, original paintings and prints decorate the walls. The lights are on. Either someone is already here, or I left them on the whole day while I was gone. Also unlike me. If the door unlocks automatically maybe the lights turn on when the door unlocks. Can't dismiss it but as I turn into the kitchen, I see someone sitting at the kitchen table typing away.

I step closer. Noah is wearing a t-shirt and blue jeans. Don't think I've ever seen him when he wasn't dressed for work. "Good day?" Noah asks without turning to look at me.

Noah. Why is he here? I look around again and decide, yeah, this is his taste. This is his apartment. I'm sharing it with him in some fashion. Are we married and I just didn't change my license? Or more likely are we living together? I moved in with him. We seemed to be moving in that direction on Monday. But that was what, three years ago? What's happened to me I can't remember three years of my life?

Noah turns to look at me like he's wondering something, just as I am. What am I supposed to do? Kiss him hello? Cook dinner while he works? Drop my things so we can go out and get something to eat? Sit down and have a 'debrief on your day' conversation? I have no idea what to do.

Noah finally gets to his feet, comes over to give me a hug and then a kiss. Not a long and inviting kiss. A distracted one that says I love you regardless of whatever happened today.

I decide to ask the question rather than stand here wondering, "What would you like tonight? Eat in or go grab something?"

Noah looks puzzled, turns back to his work. "I already ate."

I look at the clock. Already nine pm. I can see where he might have given up waiting for me. I look into the 'frig. Not much to choose from. A couple containers of left-over Chinese take-out, Korean barbeque, but only sides left overs for one, linguini with clams, half eaten and most of the clams are gone. Not much that's enticing. I close the 'frig and check out cupboards. A box of Cheerios cereal, herbal teas, a six-pack of high PH water, and two boxes of crackers. Not much to feed the soul let alone your appetite. I go back and mix the two Chinese partial take-outs and put the container in the microwave for a minute and a half. Probably too long, but not long enough to heat it all the way through. Just the way it is. You over heat the outer parts and mix it to warm the still cold inner parts. You hope you get to an acceptable level that won't burn your mouth and still be warm enough I can shovel it down. And yet I don't want to melt the Styrofoam container.

I bring it over and sit down across from Noah. "What are you working on?"

Noah doesn't look up, continues a thought he apparently wants to capture. When he finishes, I've had two bites of the lukewarm Chinese. I'm probably going to put it back in the microwave for another minute. He then responds, "What was your question?"

"What are you working on?" I repeat trying not to sound annoyed and hungry and confused about why I'm here. Or how this relationship we are apparently in, works.

"Thought you weren't interested in what I write anymore. You used to read them all. You made great suggestions that made them better. But as you've lost interest in me you also seemed to lose interest in my novels."

Hold on. I've lost interest in Noah, but I'm still here. He's writing novels I used to help him with but I stopped. Why would I have done that? "I've not lost interest in you or your writing."

Noah raises an eyebrow. "Must have been a hell of a day to drive you back to me."

I reach across and put my hand on his, but I can't look at him, shake my head knowing I've not been the person I thought I would be. "No. I just want you to know I'm here for you now, even if I haven't been recently."

Noah has a glass of red wine sitting next to the computer. He picks up the glass, takes just a sip and looks at me with one eye open and the other closed. "Electro-shock therapy?"

"No. I've just decided to erase the last three years and start over." What else am I going to say when I have no idea what's happened in the last three years. Have I been in some kind of hibernation?

Noah muses at my response, nods to himself, "Try this on. I'm writing about a woman who finds herself tossed between different dimensions."

"Dimensions?" I have to ask.

"Points in time. You know. Like now is a point in time. The turn of the century is another."

"Time travel. Okay. That's the premise, what's the story?"

"We get to see her in her normal dimension. Everything that's normal for her. And then she walks through this portal and finds herself in a world that looks and seems a lot like what she knew, but it's not the same time, years into the future. The people she knows are either gone or doing different things with one exception: her boyfriend."

"You." I guess. *This all sounds vaguely familiar but how would Noah know? It's just a story.*

"Could be, but I'm not going there just yet." Something comes to mind. Noah looks down at the page and quickly begins typing. I wait, nibbling at the Chinese. But he keeps typing so I get up and stick the Chinese back into the microwave for a minute, bring it out and return to my seat as he finishes typing and looks up. "Thanks."

"For what?"

"Normally you'd just get up and leave when I get an inspiration. I have to capture it before it leaves me completely." Noah explains. "So, thanks for staying."

"I want to know what happens to your heroine and her lover."

"That's what I'm working out now." Noah looks off and picks up his glass of wine for a sip. "She's moved into the future but she's still denying anything has really changed. She's trying to excuse why things are different expecting she'll go to sleep and wake up to find everything's back to normal. It was all just a dream."

"Is it?" I have to ask.

"She meets the person with the key to the portal between dimensions."

"Is that her lover?" I wonder aloud.

"No. He will become her travelling companion, if you will, but he's not the one. As much as he might like that role, she won't give it to him. She's hoping to find a version of her lover who is perfect in one of the dimensions they travel. The irony I'm playing with is whether she finds him early on, but her traveling companion can't stay there. They have to go on. She may leave the ideal lover behind, not knowing if she will find him again."

"Why would you do that to her?" I'm compelled to ask wondering why he would do that to me.

"Because they aren't meant to be together. You'll have to wait for me to write that chapter to find out why."

"Is this autobiographical?" I ask. "That you don't think we will be together for the long term?"

"You've already started packing your things. What am I supposed to think?"

The Way I See It

Elijah and his parents sit stoically, looking straight ahead. Apparently not interested in what the judge may say or do in this phase of the proceeding. They are probably trying to imagine what life will be like where a government can come and tear their family apart. Elijah on the other hand seems to be amused by the proceeding. Maybe I'm just reading too much into his demeanor. Maybe he's where he seemed to be yesterday. Resolved that he's about to be a prisoner of the US government courtesy of his paper. A paper he wanted to publish because he thought he had something important to share. And the US government only wants to make sure he can't share it.

Is there more to this whole story than Mister Spencer has been sharing? He's not confirmed that they have taken anyone else into custody. Said the data was classified. Nice way of not having to say 'zero'. We've never done this before. But having read Elijah's paper we know he's solved some issues we've been dealing with.

Holy Shit. If there is something to Elijah's theory? Maybe I better spend a little more time understanding it rather than just dismissing it as a government fantasy. What did Spencer say about it? Dimensions. Something about dimensions. What does that mean? I thought there were just three dimensions. What are they? Length, width and height? I'm not sure. If we're talking about dimensions how do you move between length, width and height? This doesn't make any sense.

I move over behind Elijah. "Can you explain your theory to me?"

Elijah looks at me as if I must be a Martian or something. "You want a simple explanation of my theory?"

I nod.

"Think of the universe. Endless space, right?"

I nod, "Empty space with a few galaxies between."

"Glad you were listening in Earth Science. What if… there was more than one universe."

I don't think that's the case, but I nod following that concept.

"And what keeps them separated is a massive magnetic field. Magnetic forces push things apart when they encounter the same charge."

"Or pull them together when it's the opposite charge," I complete his thought.

"Exactly. Well if these dimensions are floating out there, kept in balance by the magnetic fields and something draws the universes together."

"Opposing magnetic fields." I suggest.

"If something pulls them together," Elijah ignores my suggestion. "Why couldn't something from one dimension cross over into the other? It would only require passing through a strong magnetic field which wouldn't harm you."

"And the government thinks you built a device that permits moving between dimensions."

Elijah looks away.

"Got it. Thanks." I return to my seat waiting for the judge to enter. We rise. She enters the room. "Alright Miss Wilcox. We have the government's arguments. What are yours?"

"Your honor, we all know the case law on this particular case doesn't apply. We know all the precedents Mister Spencer would have us embrace from witness protection to Olympic Training Camps don't apply. We know the government is trying to greatly expand its powers to seize any child from any family in America all to further National Security. I don't know if you have any children, your honor, but I feel confident you would strenuously object to the government coming into your home. Even more strenuously object to them taking away a child of yours because someone believes her or him to be 'too smart'. A child capable of developing what Mr. Spencer described as a purported weapon of mass destruction when most adults couldn't."

I retreat to the table where the Mason family waits. A nod indicates Elijah should come forward. "You honor, I call Elijah Mohammed Mason to the stand."

"Are you sure you wish to do this Miss Wilcox? You haven't established the defense premise you would have us seek to confirm from Mister Mason."

"Your honor, I'm glad you asked. The foundation of my argument is Mister Spencer has attempted to build a case against a faceless threat to our national security. I believe meeting Elijah Mason you will realize there is no threat to anyone except those seeking a full ride scholarship to MIT."

The Bailiff swears in Elijah.

"Mister Mason." I begin, "What is your middle name?"

"Mohammed."

"Who gave you that name? Your mother or your father?"

"My mother always said my father did. It means praise worthy in Arabic."

"And they both wanted you to be 'praise worthy'." I follow.

"I suppose so." Elijah looks to his parents who don't react.

"Are you or either of your parents worshippers of Islam?"

Elijah shakes his head. "We attend a non-denominational super church."

"So, you are not fundamentalist in your beliefs and not a follower of Islam per se."

"I have read more Buddhist texts than Islamic."

"So, no one in your family is Islamist, has Islamist or Jihadist sympathies, or in any way supports terrorism as a preferred approach to a new world order."

"No." He is definite in this answer which is what I hoped for.

I change direction now having established his non-affiliation with Muslim causes. "You developed a theory which the government thinks is a threat to the world order."

"I don't see it as a threat to anything," Elijah protests

"Is there any way you could see your theory being weaponized?" I watch the judge's eyes.

"That's not what my theory is all about."

"Elijah, you suggested there may be a means of transiting between different dimensions."

"And the Moon may be made of green cheese. Until someone goes there and brings back rock samples any theory is as good as another."

"So, you don't understand why the government is so interested in your theory?"

"Not really. It's just a theory. The one thing about a theory? It's wrong no matter how well it's constructed. And I certainly don't want to have some ignoramus like your buddy Spencer here, who knows nothing of what I'm suggesting, telling me I have to do research on flea farts."

I see the judge smile for just a moment. "So Elijah, as an American citizen, born in this country with the inalienable rights to life, liberty and the pursuit of happiness, if the court were to grant the government's petition the court would be violating two of the inalienable rights you were guaranteed at birth: liberty and the pursuit of happiness."

"If you say so."

Unhappiness

I complete my closing arguments. Spencer repeats the same points. It seems to me he was asleep during the whole defense presentation. Not interested is my guess. Thinks the government's interests will be the determining factors, not individual liberty or any of that bullshit.

The judge retires to her chambers to consider the merits of the case. Elijah's parents head off to the rest rooms, but Elijah hangs back.

"I thought you were going to mount a completely different defense." He seems confused about my tactic. "Why did you change your mind?"

"I decided that if the court is going to trample on an individual's rights, they need to know who that individual is. What that individual thinks of the whole proposal. I thought you did a great job. You made yourself memorable."

"And you linked in everything including the Declaration of Independence, which I'm not sure will have the intended effect since it was in essence a declaration of war with England. Not sure that was the greatest image to be invoking," he chastises me.

"You want to argue this yourself?" I regret almost as soon as the words leave my mouth.

"I would have done some things differently." Elijah considers.

"Like what?" I really wonder what his perception of the defense is.

"You only went after two things. I'm not a Muslim terrorist and I'm a normal kid who only wants to go get laid in college and see how many beers I can consume before falling down drunk. I get all that. It was necessary. I'm just not sure the judge was buying it. She studied me. Studied my reactions, my choice of words, and my humor to show I'm not all serious. I don't know. I guess I doubt she could see me falling down drunk. Too serious. Now getting laid? I can hope."

"You haven't told me what you would have done differently? Just what the judge probably thinks of you."

"I guess I would have spent more time on civil rights. You know. Locking up a kid who hasn't done anything wrong certainly is a bad precedent to set."

"What you haven't apparently grasped yet is that this case isn't about you." I inform him. "But that's what I tried to change. The government is looking for carte blanche to take any kid who might someday develop the next pop tart away from his or her parents. That may sound crazy but if the judge finds for the government that is exactly where this whole thing could end up."

"No, I get that." Elijah responds. "But I'm not sure your strategy will work."

"The judge has a son just about your age." I reveal.

"Why didn't you use that?"

"I did, by saying I didn't know if the judge has a family. If I had been specific, she would have reacted negatively. Probably called me to the bench for a dressing down about bringing her into the discussion. But saying I didn't know if she did, she couldn't react negatively. But I'm sure she personalized what's going on in her court."

"So, what happens now?" Elijah seems to be losing interest.

"We wait. Like I told you yesterday. This is one of those cases where the factors that will decide it are outside my control. The government has the cloak of national security and a complex theory no one in this court room other than yourself understands."

"You read my paper." Elijah confirms.

"It was so heavily redacted by the government that the only thing I was sure of when I finished was your name."

"Redacted?"

"The government took a black magic marker and blanked out anything they thought was a risk for anyone else to know. That was basically your whole paper."

"So, how many people have actually read what I wrote?" Elijah seems to be grasping what has happened for the first time.

"I doubt more than a dozen. And maybe only half of that. For sure someone at the publication and someone at the Department of Defense. How many more at the publication is anyone's guess. Probably not more than three to five. On the government side, the censor may have actually been the only one to have read it. Maybe a couple experts to confirm what the censor thought."

"If that's the case, then this whole thing is really a farce."

"I'm just trying to make sure your head fits inside your hoodie," I pat his head.

Elijah's mother and father join us. "What do you think?" his father asks.

"I think the judge would rather not approve a precedent that the government will use to run rampant over families. But she could feel constrained about the homeland security concern."

"I thought you settled that right up front." Elijah's mother reacts confused.

"I tried to. Even consulted outside experts to make sure I didn't miss some aspect of that argument. But I don't know if it will carry the day. That's just not a defense I run into very often."

"Watch the evening news. We're seeing it used as justification for all kinds of government actions that never would have stood before." Elijah's father jumps on the topic.

"We are, but I don't see many places where the court has pushed back. And most of those abuses are in regards to the economy. I'm hoping the family will be a different story."

"I for one am glad it's a woman judge," Elijah's mother informs us. "She ought to be more sympathetic to keeping families together. No mother wants to see her boy go off to war. Fathers for some peculiar reason seem to think every boy needs to serve just so he will learn discipline."

"I'm disappointed." Mr. Mason comes back to me. "I was expecting fire and brimstone." *Where have I heard this before?*

"The government isn't the issue here." I push back.

"What do you mean?" He asks incredulous I could see it any other way.

"The issue is whether the courts give the government authority to break up families. Without the court's permission they can't."

"What does that assumption on your part have to do with how passive you were?"

"You thought I was passive." Now I'm the one who is incredulous. "I wanted her to see your son for the individual he is, to make her ask, would she want the government to come into her home and take away her child?"

"You said yourself you didn't know if she even has children." Mrs. Mason was listening.

"Her son Trayvon is fourteen and named after a young boy who was shot to death by a white civilian security guard in Florida. At the

time it was seen as an extreme case of racial profiling and injustice."
There's Noah's word again. It keeps coming up.

Template

The Bailiff opens the court room door signaling the judge has made her decision.

"It's time. For better or worse we will know whether we all go home or start the appeals process." I inform them.

"Appeals? What good would that do?" Mr. Mason asks gruffly.

"It will give us time to build allies and bring more resources to the table. ACLU, Child welfare organizations, private foundations. I'll bet with time we could build a formidable collection of interests who would all contribute to reversing a bad decision at this level before it becomes precedential nationwide."

Mr. Mason is having none of it. "That will all be too late."

The judge enters the court room. We all take our seats. She looks about the room to see who is present. She addresses her comments to both sets of counsel.

"Before I give you my decision, I would like to make a few prefatory comments: First of all I am unhappy that neither the government nor defense counsels prepared a thorough or exhaustive case review and briefing for me."

Good grief. I had a whole day. But that's not an excuse.

"You both left considerable ground unexplored and forced me to do what should have been your task, namely, to prove beyond a shadow of a doubt what is the right course of action for this court. What is most distressing to me is that this has also been the hardest case for me to decide in my career on the bench. I fully understand the civil rights of families and minors. I would not tread on those rights without an overriding societal outcome of not acting. This case presented both extremes. On the one hand, a family that has done everything expected of them by society. They raised a delightful and intelligent young man who will do well in life if given even half a chance. On the other we have the government asserting the need to safeguard this young man from evil forces we can't identify, but unfortunately we all know are there waiting for an opportunity to strike against us."

The judge takes a sip of water. I can see this is a decision she really doesn't want to release.

"To grant the government a hunting license, to find bright young people and remove them from their families would be a travesty of the greatest proportion. Therefore, I must make a determination that is as narrowly constructed as possible. A decision that only pertains in this one case. A decision that cannot be used as a precedent for widespread social engineering. My decision is as follows: The government shall be granted the right in this one limited instance to relocate the Mason family, intact, to an unnamed community where Elijah Mohammed Mason will be enrolled in a university degree program of his choice. Mr. and Mrs. Mason shall be provided jobs by the government for the duration of Elijah's affiliation with the government research program which Elijah shall intern with and become a full-time member of once he graduates. If Elijah elects to pursue an advanced degree, he shall be employed by the national lab part-time until completion of all degrees. In no instance shall Elijah remain a member of the national lab research team one day past the tenth anniversary of starting his internship, unless Elijah freely elects to do so. His election must be without coercion of any kind from the government, and without regard to national interests that would be served by his continuation on that research project. What I'm saying Mister Spencer, is this is a time-limited offer. You will not have the ability to direct more than ten years of Elijah Mohammed Mason's work on your various national security related research."

The judge takes another sip of water and looks first at the government's counsel. "Do you have any questions Mr. Spencer?"

"No, your honor." Sounds like he's happy with the result even though not what he asked for.

She looks at me. "Miss Wilcox?"

"No, your honor." I respond but my voice is barely audible.

"This verdict is so ordered. Court dismissed."

She threaded the needle.

Mr. Mason looks at me and asks, "Did we win or lose?"

"She kept you together, isn't that the most important outcome?" I respond.

"But she basically made Elijah a government slave for ten years." Mrs. Mason reacts.

I feel someone behind me, turn to find Mr. Spencer and his associate waiting to talk to me. "They need to be ready by Monday morning."

"Ready for what?" I'm amazed by his instruction.

"To make the move. We'll have a house for them so all they need to do is to assist the movers. Who by the way will arrive to begin packing their possessions and furniture on Friday."

"The day after tomorrow." I clarify.

"Yes."

"Will someone from your office call the Mason's employers and explain why they were unable to provide a two-week notice?" I ask trying to make this more difficult for them than the Masons.

"Won't be an issue. They will have steady employment for the next ten years. No one should have a need to go back to earlier employers if the Mason's elect to change jobs."

"So, you're happy to let them burn bridges." I shake my head. "Will you guarantee they will get promotions equivalent to what they would have gotten or could get elsewhere?"

"I see your point. We'll talk with their employers." Spencer concedes.

"And you'll ensure Elijah gets his high school diploma in addition to being admitted into the university program of his choice as the judge ordered?"

"Don't worry Miss Wilcox, we'll take good care of Elijah."

"This is not your precedent, Mister Spencer." I push hard by my tone of voice.

"We got our man. The next one will be someone else's problem. But we shouldn't have to come back through the courts in the future."

"Why not?" his tone catches my attention more than the words.

"We developed a useful template the judge could accept."

"You worked with the judge?" *That's not how the court system works.*

Spencer realizes his mistake, backpedals. "We didn't work with her like had back room meetings without you present or anything. But if you read our brief…"

"I did. I can't tell you how many times," *I'm tired of reading it.*

"If you read our brief, we cited several cases of witness protection. We built the case that the family got a guaranteed new life in return for service to the government. The only thing I didn't see coming was the ten-year cap. Makes the whole proposition expensive. But if this kid is what we think he is, in ten years you won't recognize things." Spencer gestures to the whole world.

Shit. I dismissed the linkage to service to government in exchange for relocating the whole family and giving them a new identity. I even dismissed it in my opening statement. At least I won the day in that she didn't break up the family. I succeeded in part, if not completely.

As Spencer walks away I turn my attention to the Mason family.

"What did he have to say?" Mr. Mason asks immediately.

"Movers come on Friday to pack up your possessions. You'll be picked up and sent to your new home on Monday morning."

"That quick?" Elijah seems the most taken aback. "I can't possibly…"

"As you think of things, we need to clarify write them down and give me a call. I'll work them through Spencer until someone else appears."

"You talked about an appeal." Mrs. Mason now.

"I've already started working out the strategy. The judge basically made it hard to appeal because it's so narrowly written. Interest groups won't get on board because it's non-precedential. It keeps the family together. So, we have our work cut out for us. We will have to win it on the merits but I'm working the strategy now and consulting with the experts to make sure it will hold."

Legal Advisor

The next day I visit with the Masons at their home. They have already started packing things and going through the many items they will leave behind or donate. It's sad to see how much their life is going to be disrupted because I was unable to stop the government from taking Elijah. Yeah, I know the judge kept the family together, but the government got what it wanted which is access to Elijah's understanding of the universe. At least that seems to be what this is all about. I guess I shouldn't feel bad that I really don't understand what his theory is or why it puts our security at risk. The judge didn't understand either. If I'm right about how many people have even read his paper only a few really have any idea what he is postulating.

Elijah comes out of his room deep in thought. I'm sure if he shared those thoughts with me, I'd probably have difficulty following him, but I give it a try. "Morning."

Elijah looks up at me and motions for me to follow him out to the patio off the kitchen. He points to a chair and sits next to me.

"I was right about you," he begins, then stops leaving me wondering.

"I don't lose." I inform him. "That's why I started on the appeal last night."

"You'll never get the chance to file it," he seems to dismiss my determination to win.

"Why not? Is the government going to hide you away where even I can't find you?"

"That's all behind us." Elijah looks around as if trying to decide if anyone could hear this conversation. "We need to think about the alternatives."

"What are you talking about? Running away?"

"More like choosing a different future," he almost whispers now, leaning closer as if concerned people we can't see may be close.

"I have no idea what you're talking about and as your counsel..."

"I brought you from your world to this one, from a dimension you have known your whole life to this dimension you've known since you found yourself in my courtroom a few days ago."

"You brought me here." I have to repeat because I know he may be a genius, but they talk about mad scientists and maybe he's one of them. Someone so smart he hallucinates or something.

"What the government really wants isn't what I will figure out in the future, but a portal I've already built. That's why they weren't concerned with the verdict. They think they got what they want."

"Hold on." My head is spinning. Some things make sense, but it just doesn't seem possible. Three years I lost somewhere, but now he's saying he brought me to this place in the future through a portal he built? A sixteen-year-old kid? "You're asking me to suspend my beliefs that there is one and only one Earth, one and only one time, and one and only one me and one you."

Elijah looks happy, like a tutor who is finally getting through to a recalcitrant student. "Yes. Because that is the real world, or should I say, worlds. I have been through the portal to your time and place. You see, the you that was here is very smart and works very hard. But I wasn't optimistic about her. So, I went to a different world at random, which proved to be your world, to see if you were any different. I was in the courtroom that day when you were certain to lose. And yet you somehow found a way to win that case. The fact my science fair experiment helped you could not have been a coincidence. The significant thing for me was you found it. You never gave up. You made sure your client received the justice due him."

Noah would not agree with that assessment. "You came to my world to see if I was any better than the version of me assigned to your case here." I'm trying to follow him, but my mind keeps racing, trying to comprehend what he's telling me.

"I did."

"So, you opened your portal and brought me here, to your world, which just happens to be three years in the future from my world."

"Yes." Elijah is becoming more and more enthusiastic. "I haven't been able to verify much as I've only been to your world and another, but none are at the same point in time."

"Inhabited by different versions of the same people?" I have to ask since I'm a different version of his counsel here.

"Only three data points, but that would seem to be the case."

"So, what happened to the local version of me when I came over?"

Elijah frowns, "I can only speculate on that. And speculation is never a good thing. It's like a theory, only based on a whole lot less thought."

"I'm a big girl. I can take disappointment if you're wrong. But should I be waiting for her to return from wherever she went when I came through into your courtroom? Since she wasn't there when I arrived, she had to go someplace."

"That was a gamble on my part. You see, when I went to your world, I went looking for me. I never found him. So, I speculated that my self in that world must have come here to mine. And when I returned, so did he."

"You're telling me the version of me who was here has been back in my world mucking up my cases? That I'll have to go back and straighten out who knows what?"

"Hold on." Elijah reaches out and touches my shoulder to get my attention. "Don't worry about that. You don't have to go back to that world. You can choose another. It just can't be this one because I can't stay here. I want you to come with me wherever I go. I need someone like you who can see things I don't. Keep me out of trouble until I can get established."

I listen to his plea. Then an insight comes to me. "You're afraid you're going to be pursued by the government in any world you go to."

"I need to get somewhere I can decide what I research. Free to follow the trail nature has laid out before me."

I'm still back on the fact that someone else has been working my cases for the last several days. I try to catch up. "Let me see if I can summarize this conversation. First of all, you built a portal that has allowed you and me and at least two…"

"Three. I went to another world, but don't worry about that now."

"…Three others to move between time dimensions or whatever you want to call it."

"That's correct so far." Elijah is hopeful I've understood him.

"In each of the three worlds where you either live or have visited, the government is trying to take away this portal and lock you up to do more research for them."

Elijah nods his agreement.

"Now you want me to come explore the worlds or time dimensions out there looking for one where you can be free to research what you want."

Care Less

I spend a little time with Mr. and Mrs. Mason at their house, although they clearly would rather continue going through their things.

"Have you thought of anything else I need to be clarifying with the government?"

"The house." Mr. Mason asks. "What's the deal with the house? Are they taking this one in exchange for one wherever we're going? Do we have a choice of homes? Can we upscale if we want? But since I don't know how much I'm going to be paid, it's hard to plan out any of this."

"I'll ask." I respond, making a note on my pad.

"And Elijah." His mother begins. "Does he finish high school when we get there or is he going directly into college? There's the tuition. I expect we will have to pay his tuition, now. All this time we thought he'd get a scholarship so that wouldn't be a burden."

"Good question." I start making another note.

"If the government is going to pay it that would help so much." Mrs. Mason wrestles with one more change. "The tuition these days is just unbelievable, especially at the schools where Elijah should go. MIT or Berkeley, Stanford or Chicago."

I don't have the heart to tell her the decision of school will be the government's as the court decision was written. Will they put him in any of those schools? It's hard to tell. Dimensional transit, as Mr. Spencer referred to it, doesn't appear on any of the specialties of any of the labs. Does that mean they will have to stand up a whole new research group around Elijah? If so, it could be anywhere.

"Will I be working directly for the government?" The reality of the situation seems to be slowly sinking in for Mr. Mason.

"Depends on what the government is able to find for you." I respond to put him at ease. "My guess is unless they've been working this plan for a while, which I doubt, they probably are going to have to create a job for you within the government."

Mr. Mason nods, "What you're saying is no one knows. Until we show up wherever it is, they're taking us we can't expect any answers."

"Probably a good way to look at it." I acknowledge. "But if questions come to you, I'm going to ask them. See if we can get answers to at least a few before you go. Ensure they're working the other issues you identify so you'll get a quicker resolution once you're there."

"What about our families?" Mrs. Mason suddenly gets quite agitated. "Are they going to cut us off from our families like the witness protection families? Make us change our names and have no contact with my mother?" she looks to her husband.

"That's not how it was described by the judge, nor was there any reference to that in the decision she handed down, but it's another good question." I muse aloud.

"This whole court case is going to draw attention to us." Mrs. Mason goes on. "Tell the world Elijah has discovered something fundamental. Something that will change our way of life."

"Elijah is only sixteen." I begin to point out the legal issue. "The court can seal these records since the case involves a minor. No one needs to know about Elijah through this case. The ruling will be made public, but the specifics of who was involved will be redacted."

"Oh. I didn't know that." Mrs. Mason calms down a bit. Continues thinking about other things that will happen in the move.

"You didn't answer the question about our identities." Mr. Mason pulls us back.

"I told you what I know. It could go either way."

"How can a court just uproot us like this without our having any say in it at all?" Mr. Mason is looking for answers and bitter about his feelings of powerlessness, helplessness and despair. He most certainly isn't looking forward to a new experience.

"Tell me about your job." I ask, trying to get him to flesh out what he's feeling.

"I've been with an auto parts manufacturing company for twenty years this fall. Chief Accountant now. Worked my way up from inventory clerk. I know the company inside and out. The owners know that. I'm sure I'll be the next CFO when old Davidson retires in a couple years. At least that was the plan until this happened."

"You have to start all over. Learn a new company or organization. But accounting is accounting, isn't it?"

"That's a real simplification." Mr. Mason almost seems insulted. "Accounting's not easy."

"And I'll bet you're real good at it." I hope he will come to understand that he shouldn't be too concerned with the move. "It's not likely the government will ask you to do anything you either can't do or would be illegal. After all, they are the government."

Mr. Mason looks at me like I'm taking the government's side of the argument. "You seem to be trying to get us to just accept what's happening here."

"On the contrary. I've already started putting together the appeal. Plan to file on Friday. I think this is a terrible outcome for you. I will find a way to change it."

Mr. Mason shakes his head. "Forget the appeal. I've contacted another attorney. She's already started working on it. You had your chance. The outcome kept our family together, at least that's what the court said, but you've uprooted the entire family in the process. Don't you see this is worse than if they'd just taken Elijah from us? At least in that outcome they would have left us alone."

I'm stunned. I never thought the Masons would take me off the case. Particularly since Elijah tells me he traveled across the universe somehow to find me and bring me to his time to be his counsel.

"Who did you retain?" I ask although I know he is under no obligation to tell me.

"The person I wanted in the first place, but Elijah had other ideas."

"So, you're telling me Elijah chose me to represent your family in this matter and now you're ignoring his wishes and going a different way."

"I'm his father and I can damn well do as I please since your incompetence has now dragged me into this whole mess. I was happy to go along with his wishes as long as it was just him."

"So, you didn't care if you lost so long as it didn't affect you?" I accuse him.

"Look Miss Wilcox. I have to give up my job and start life all over again because of you."

"You were going to do that anyway," Mrs. Mason interjects. "Start over with your girlfriend."

Mr. Mason won't look at his wife. "I was going to be the CFO and have the money that goes with it. Now I'm stuck. For a decade probably. I'll never be what I could have been. Don't you get it? Elijah will be fine. I'll never recover from this. Never. So just go back to your tidy life, sucking life savings from people like us and not having to suffer the consequences of your incompetence."

His wife glances at me and simply says, "My husband has been running his whole life – from ghosts that have haunted him forever and now from me and Elijah." She glances at him then continues. "Mia Mastrangelo is the attorney he hired."

The Gossip Bird

I wander down the hall to Stevenson's office, but he is not listed as in that office. I walk back up to Louise, "Where's Stevenson?"

"In his office, where he always is." Louise lets me know what she thinks of Stevenson.

"And where is his office?" I know I shouldn't be asking this question, but the only other option is to wander the halls until I find him.

Louise looks at me over her glasses as if I'd lost more than just my mind. "He's in nine, where he's always been. Ever since he made partner. What was that? Twenty years ago? More probably."

I wander down the hall to nine. Stevenson sits in his office, buried in his computer screen. I have no idea if he is looking at pornography or legal briefs. Frankly I could care less what our managing partner does since he is nominally my boss. In that role I need to keep him up to date on what I am doing. I've actually been surprised not to have had a visit after the perceived loss in the Mason case.

"Morning."

Stevenson looks up. There's something about his suit I notice instantly. Not the tailored look I've become accustomed to. His hair. That's not right either. Too much die probably. I don't see the grey peeking out that I normally see below the black toupee. It's almost like he recently re-died it to make sure everything lines up. If you didn't know about the toupee, you probably wouldn't think twice about his hair. Oh well. Not my concern. "Do you need something?" He's clearly disoriented by my appearance. Normally he would direct me to a seat across from him. Today, nothing. He just waits for me to tell him whatever it is that's on my mind.

I just wanted you to know we are appealing the Mason case and expect to win on appeal."

"Why are you personally telling me this? You're the Managing Partner. You trying to manage damage control? I heard the family removed you. You at liberty to discuss that?"

I'm the Managing Partner? What's he talking about? Better answer his question. "The father sought independent counsel. He wants out. The decision keeps him together with Mom for ten years."

"Then you're still on the case?"

"I am, representing Mom and the boy."

"Good to know. When the gossip bird flies by I can correct the conventional wisdom that you blew that one."

"So, that's what the gossip bird is saying?"

Stevenson nods just once. "People are trying to interpret what happened and the effect on you. Now that you've lost a case for the first time in what? Ten years? Maybe you will be more tolerant of those of the rest of us who lose one once in a while. Somebody has to lose if you've forgotten how the court system operates."

"I didn't lose, but it wasn't a clear victory."

"Not how the government views it from what I hear." Stephenson puts me in my place. "It's tough being perfect." Stevenson muses. "Maybe you need to be more selective in the cases you accept. Maybe we all need to be more judicious in our early reviews and not be so reluctant to walk away from fees when we're staring at a clear loser."

"You think Mason was a clear loser?" I'm surprised at his characterization.

"I wouldn't have taken it. David and Goliath. The everyman kid whose rights are being trampled by the government? How often does David win those encounters? The government lawyers tend not to be up to our standards, but they have a lot more of them to call on for any given case than we do. If they lose, they turn around and appeal and bring in the second team which is all much more experienced attorneys than the first team who are all just learning the ropes and often have sympathies with the plaintiff."

"Didn't know you had taken so much interest in Mason. Given where we are, how would you proceed if I were to assign it to you?"

"Me? I'm hardly the litigator you are." Stevenson tries to dodge the bullet. "You're probably the only attorney on our staff who has the resume to stand up to the government on appeal. And as I remember your resume, I don't think you ever have gone up against the government on appeal."

"Thanks for the journey down memory lane. But if you don't want to find Mason in your job jar tomorrow, I would appreciate your analysis."

"Appeal. Custody of a minor. Protection. National Security. Hmm. As I understand it, the decision was a modified witness protection scheme. The boy goes into government custody. They put him to work in a government lab in exchange for putting him through school? That right?"

"Close enough." I respond.

"What would I do? I would go after the imperfect model the court accepted. In witness protection the individual is compensated to prevent retribution for coming forward and removing a threat from the community. In the Mason case the kid did nothing wrong, didn't finger anyone for the government. Hasn't done anything of note, has he?"

"He wrote a paper and submitted it for publication."

"Lots of people do that. Not advocating government overthrow, I suspect."

"No."

"So, no trigger. Do you see what I mean? The kid hasn't done anything that would warrant a government intervention."

"Someone thinks the paper is. Suggests there might be a portal to other worlds."

"Has the kid built one?" Stevenson goes right to the core of the matter. If I say no, he doesn't have perfect knowledge of the situation. If I say yes, I've revealed something that was discussed with me in confidence, even though apparently Elijah's father is openly discussing it with Mia.

"That's what the government is trying to understand." I finally sidestep the issue.

"So, this is a fishing expedition. The government is willing to pay for a new life for mommy and daddy to find out if the kid has something that might be of interest?"

An interesting way of putting it. I should come talk with Stevenson more often. "That would appear to be an accurate assessment."

"If it's a fishing expedition, cut down the period of exclusivity and protection. Argue that if there is something of value in this boy's theory the government should be able to find it in say three or four years. You said the kid is bright and should graduate college in three years. Let the government pay for mommy and daddy for three years and then cut them loose. If the kid is what he seems the government will have to come back and pay up to get him, but at least the period of exploration of his value is now equivalent to his undergraduate experience. At that point he's what? Nineteen or twenty? The government hasn't destroyed the kid's life. In fact, they've given him some real world experience he can claim on a resume. And if daddy really wants out of this family?

Three years isn't so long to wait."

"I didn't say anything about daddy." I point out he has a lot more information than he's claiming.

"The gossip bird." Stevenson dishes off the responsibility.

"A good strategy of where I want the court to go if I can't get a full reversal. But reversal is the objective. How do I do that?"

"I would file the appeal and try to settle out of court. Present a settlement where the parents agree to let the kid work for the government while attending some university on a full government scholarship. They agree that any inventions during the period of employment would revert to the government, including theories and devices. If the government wishes to provide protection for the kid, that's solely up to them. Make it voluntary. Get the involuntary servitude specter off the table."

"Gossip bird? What is the law library bugged or something?"

Stevenson shrugs. "You note I never have conferences there."

The Ending

Coming home to this apartment just seems so foreign. Not me at all. So, how did I get here? I decide to reminisce with Noah to get some insight. I approach the door. Again, it recognizes me somehow. I'll be real disappointed some night if I come home to find the door doesn't recognize me. What do I do then? Hope Noah is home so I can get in? Or do I call the guy on the desk downstairs? Would he come up and let me in? I have to assume he would or tell me where I've moved.

I open the door and enter the well-appointed apartment. I realize it is actually smaller than the one I used to have. But it seems more spacious because of the floor to ceiling windows that look out over the city. I don't know if I will get to a point where I'll not see this art anymore because I'll just assume it's there. I drop my purse on the table near the door as I hear the door locking behind me.

Noah looks up from the kitchen table. "You're home early."

I look up at the clock. I'm surprised. Only seven-thirty. "Just one of those days." I respond.

"You don't have many of them. Seems you've been coming home closer to ten than seven for… I don't know what it's been, but it's been a while."

"You eat?"

Noah looks back at the page he has been writing. "Inspiration doesn't wait for anyone."

"So, that's a definite no." I confirm. "Why don't you come out with me? We can do something fast and you can get back to your novel."

Noah looks at the page. "Let me finish this chapter. Shouldn't take long."

My cue to be quiet until he gets his thoughts down on paper. I go look out the window at the lights of the city. I'm constantly amazed at how many lights I see from here even though I'm only looking in one direction. Towards the DFW airport. If I look sharply right, I can see Love Field and the airplanes taking off and landing there. Some of the planes come over downtown but they are on the other side of the building, so I don't see them.

Below us is the American Airlines Center. Huge Jumbotrons illuminate the plaza with constantly changing images. I could go outside and stand on the deck, but I'm not comfortable out there. I'm up twenty-eight floors. No. I'm just not going to do that, even if Noah were to come out with me. I look at the red tail lights of cars on the freeway below. Not a thread but a dashed line of lights that variously shine brightly and otherwise just glow red.

Noah mumbles to himself. I turn to look to see if he might be directing that mumble in my direction. His head is down, and he types furiously. I notice that he looks at his hands periodically. Apparently, he's not completely comfortable just looking at the screen as most of the fastest typists tend to be. I guess I can't be too critical of him since I do the same.

Another glance out the window, this time in a different direction. Towards Reunion Tower and the Union Train Station. The tower has a ball on top that encloses a revolving restaurant that I've never visited, assuming it's there for the tourists. The tower ball lights up at night and displays multiple different patterns of light that send messages about winning sports teams or memorials to special people who have passed on or concluded iconic performances. Always Texans. Preferably people from the Dallas area. Although they make a lot of exceptions for people from other parts of the state.

"I'm good." Noah announces. "Got this to a point I can leave.

Come back later and not miss a beat. Where do you want to go?"

"Let's walk over to Savor." This is a glass walled restaurant within Klyde Warren Park. The park was built over a freeway that runs through downtown Dallas, reuniting the upper and lower parts of downtown. The park has always been a favorite. Food Trucks line up at lunch time and bring out the office workers in the tall buildings that surround the park. Benches line the sidewalks providing places to sit and enjoy both the sun and greenery of the park itself. A suspended structure over a freeway, it seems crazy that trees grow out of the deck. But it provides a limited amount of shade, a music pavilion for concerts from Booker T. Washington High School for the Arts, which is also within walking distance, and both a playground for young kids and a water grid where streams of water leap from the ground to attack unsuspecting kids and even adults who aren't paying attention to where they are walking.

We are led to a window side table overlooking the pavilion. No performance this evening, but the pavilion has been attacked by kids climbing up onto the stage to give their mock performances.

"What made you decide to come here?" Noah asks as we take our seats.

"I've just always liked it." I offer to avoid a faux pas about its significance to him and me and decide I need to challenge him if I want to avoid him asking me all kinds of questions about it. "Do you remember the first time we came here?"

"That's what I was just thinking about, but thought it curious you would want to come back."

Obviously, I should know what that means and I don't. Must have been after we moved in together since it's so close, but it must not have ended well. "Just trying to make new memories."

"Memories." Noah raises his eyebrows as if that's not a good subject either.

"What do you have against memories?" I push him to get him talking. I need to know more about what's happened between us.

"It's not my memories, it's yours. Whatever happened you have to believe me that I'm never going to treat you that way."

"But I see the darkness in you. The pain of loss you carry about from the patients you've not been able to save. How do I know you won't succumb at some point to something to help you deal with that pain? Something to erase the loss you carry with you every minute of every day?"

Noah considers my comment, nods once and then continues. "There are many ways to deal with loss. I was hoping my relationship with you would be enough. But after that first year when everything seemed to be perfect, you suddenly started withdrawing from me. I don't know if we can come back together or whether we've just drifted too far apart. I know I'd like to give it another chance, but I don't know where you are. Last week I wouldn't have given us a snowball's chance in hell. But this week? It's like you're different. Like you've put all that aside and come back to me. Decided maybe we can be helpful and significant in the life of the other. But you scare me. Changing that dramatically that quickly. How do I know you won't be back where you were next week? Or next month. I hate to plan my life around you because I'm not sure of what to expect. You've been the only person I've loved for almost a decade. I can't devote another decade to a relationship that's never going to work."

I hear the pain, frustration, and regret mixed in with the continuing love in his voice. What have I done to him? Does it have something to do with constancy? About always being there for someone? He said we were good for about a year and then it all started coming apart.

"What do you think changed after that first year?" I have to ask.

"You." Noah thinks more about my question. "That was about

when you became Managing Partner. That changed you. Suddenly you had to be perfect in everything. Your image, the clothes you wore, whether your teeth were white enough. All of a sudden you were distracted from us. Seems you felt a need to be someone other than who you are. I tried to convince you they knew what they were getting when you were selected for that position so, why would you want to be someone else now? I never got a satisfactory answer to that question."

Managing Partner? I was surprised to find out from Stevenson that I was what he had been in my world. But only two years here. Apparently, someone else got the job ten years ago. That person only stayed eight. I was elected even though I'm relatively junior in the firm and must have only been a partner for a short time. Must have had something to do with my trial prowess. *Another term from my other world.*

"I'm sorry," is all I can think of to say to him.

"Why are you saying this now? A bit late, don't you think?"

"Things have been a bit strange for me recently…"

"Like losing a case?" Noah notes. "That's not happened since I've known you."

"I didn't lose it, just going to appeal."

"Sounds more like the you I've come to know. Denying reality to make yourself and your firm look better. I've come to the conclusion you're married to the firm and you are both very happy together."

"No." I try to protest but see the light of interest receding in his eyes. I reach across and put my hand on his. "Believe me, I'm not the person you've written off. I do love you. Very much. And I can't imagine how unhappy I would be if you weren't in my life. All I ask is you suspend your disbelief of my love for you and give me a chance. If I can show you how much you mean to me will you let me stay? Let me be a part of your life? And learn the ending to your new novel?" I smile hopefully.

Winspear

I run as I've always run each and every morning. The adjustment to a different start and ending wasn't hard because I just jog up and catch the Katy Trail. There I'm able to pick up my old course with only minor modifications. I look for the blonde ponytail runner, but no one resembles her among the few out this early. I look for the shadows and fog I'd seen before, but no evidence of them either. If Elijah is behind what has happened to me, he hasn't turned on his portal this morning.

Back in for a quick shower, shampoo and dry my hair. I pick out the appropriate outfit from my more extensive closet. I wonder at some of the outfits I find. Not what I would have worn before. They make me look older. I never thought that was a good idea. I push those back into a corner and find something that must have been here for the last three years. I remember having worn it that last week before everything changed. The problem is shoes. Do I have a pair that goes with this? Sure doesn't look like it. Too early for a shoe store to be open. I don't want to wear those old person's clothes so I'll have to mix and match until I can find time to get to a shoe store. A few new outfits would help.

When I breeze in to the office Louise takes a glance at me and remarks, "Haven't seen that one in a while. You going through your closet for some reason?"

"Trying to change my image and that of the firm." I suggest. "Younger. More vigorous."

"That because you lost a case?" Just hangs in the air.

"We're going for the whole enchilada on appeal," comes out

without thinking.

"That's going to be the new mantra. You just wait." Louise turns her back to me.

"What are you suggesting?" Don't think I like what I'm hearing.

Louise looks at me as if she is deciding whether she can tell me the truth.

"I'm not going to be mad. What is it?" I try to be completely open.

"You set the tone for the whole firm. We've done so well since you became Managing Partner because you led by example. You always won. If your new example is excuses, that's what you can expect to get from the staff. Better to just own up, admit you're human and you're going to do everything possible to ensure you don't have another loss."

"You don't think winning on appeal is a better way to go?"

"If you were absolutely confident you will win on appeal you could chance it." Louise muses. "But from what I've heard your chances of winning are slim and none. Better to have owned up to your loss than point everyone to a possible salvation that doesn't appear. Then you're dead. Someone else becomes Managing Partner. Someone who can restore the firm to its winning ways. Someone else for me to break in. And that takes a toll on me if you haven't noticed." Louise shakes her head.

"I take it the Gossip bird has been by to see you." I decide to test her reaction.

"Everyday." Louise is completely deadpan.

"If this is so clear to you, why aren't you Managing Partner, Louise?"

"Because you have to be a lawyer to be a Partner. You have to be a Partner to be Managing Partner. A silly tradition I think actually does a disservice to the firm. If you're a great trial lawyer why are you worrying about what everyone else is doing?"

"Do you think you could have been a better Managing Partner than I have been?" I test.

"Have been? You throwing in the towel so soon? No. You have been exemplary until now. But from your recent behavior, it looks like that's all about to change."

"What are you saying?" This honesty is beginning to hurt.

"A Managing Partner must always demand the truth. Must always tell the truth. No matter how painful, embarrassing or harmful to the image of the firm. If your partners don't trust you, how can they expect their clients to trust them? The other thing a Managing Partner must never do is hesitate to take action. Cancer grows exponentially. It must be cut out before it spreads."

"How many Managing Partners have you shared this exact same analysis with?"

"You are the third, with the exception of the cancer part. That's new."

"So, you said this to Mr. Vetro when he was Managing Partner?" I realize how far back she goes.

"I did, because I learned it from Mr. Victor who was a masterful Managing Partner for the few years he managed the firm before turning that role over to Mr. Vetro."

"Why didn't Utley ever want it?"

"Mr. Utley was the finest trial lawyer to ever occupy an office at this firm."

"Really?" *She has to know I think I am. What's she saying to me?*

"He was better than you because he didn't think he was a great lawyer." Louise reads my mind. "And because he thought that, he worked harder at being a good lawyer than anyone I've ever met, including you. In the days when all cases were recorded in books and kept in law libraries, Mr. Utley would set up in there. He would stay for days until he knew everything about every case that could possibly be cited. He could rattle off facts any opposing lawyer could cite. He was able to point out the errors in the opposing counsel's knowledge of the facts and do it all from memory."

"Sounds like he had a photographic memory." I observe.

"If that's all you remember about Mr. Utley than you missed the point entirely. He could remember everything; but he took the time to understand it, put it in to context and describe how the law treats any given situation. He was a great trial lawyer. That's why after he lost his first case, he never lost another. He was always in fear that if he didn't put in the work the opposing counsel would make the firm look foolish. And it was the reputation of the firm that was most important to him."

"What you're saying is that's the tradition I need to uphold."

Louise doesn't answer me apparently glad I've heard what she had to say. Then she seems to remember something, "You have a visitor waiting in your office. The younger Mr. Mason."

As I enter my office Elijah looks out my window. "Do all lawyers have views like this so you can look down on the world you're trying to rape?"

I instantly stiffen at his language. "Everyone has the right to represent him or herself in any court in the land." I try to defuse his word choice. "Those who chose to pay an attorney to represent them do so expecting to take advantage of their subject matter expertise and procedural knowledge."

"Is that worth all the money we pay you?" Elijah is toying with me.

"In most cases." I decide to sound conciliatory. "It's Monday and you're still here. Was that worth what you paid me?"

"We haven't paid you yet. But if you hadn't intervened neither of us would be here."

I shake off the nonsensical statement. "I'm filing the appeal today." I inform him.

"I told you that was a waste of time. But go ahead."

"Why are you so negative?"

"Do you remember I told you I went to a third world, time dimension, whatever?"

"Yes." I remember his comment.

"Well that dimension is two years ahead of this one. In that world you filed the appeal and it was denied by the Appeals Court without a hearing. So, if I don't change things I know what will happen. It's not good for me or you."

"What do you mean?"

"In that world you're no longer Managing Partner here. In fact, you're no longer practicing law. You separated from your doctor boyfriend and took a political appointment to become a member of the International Trade Representative's Office in Washington."

I half turn to see if Louise is listening to this.

"That world is not viable for either of us." Elijah continues. "And that's why we need to leave this one. Tomorrow. Your self from the next world we visit will have to deal with the appeal here. That's why I said you don't need to worry about it. Tomorrow it will be someone else's problem."

"Why tomorrow?" I'm overwhelmed once more by what he has to

tell me. "We have time."

"You weren't listening. The Appeals Court issues its decision without a hearing. That decision will come at 4:43 pm tomorrow. The car taking me and my family to the airport arrives at 5:00. They have this thing wired. There's no time to wait and see what happens. Once I leave Dallas in their custody I'll not be coming back if I don't leave on my terms."

"What's your plan?"

"When you go for your morning run, come to the Winspear Opera House. Be there at 5:00."

Sounds Like

After Elijah leaves my office I sit in my chair for a long moment, wondering, what do you do on your last day? It's a last day in that tomorrow I will leave this time/dimension/whatever-it-is. It all depends on what world or time dimension we cross over into. I have no idea how Elijah knows where we are going. I actually assume that he doesn't. That we just take the luck of the draw. But he deliberately went back three years to find me. And then he went forward two years to find out what happened. Does that mean he knew when I stepped into his court room that I would lose the case? That he knew we would have to leave here? Why did he let me find out what I did to Noah? What I did to myself? That when things don't turn out as I would have them, I make excuses rather than making it right? That I have to be an example of the behavior I want from my teams. Or did he set this all up so I could learn some important lessons about myself before we head off into the unknown universe awaiting us?

Who is this sixteen-year-old kid who knows so much? Who can conjure worlds no one sees and bring the lessons of them back to guide his life? A sixteen-year-old who will readily abandon his parents to a life neither wished or wants? Am I ready to flee a fate he has presented to me? A fate whose seeds I can't see forming about me? A staffer to the International Trade Representative. Really? Not a career I ever considered. If I were to be the Trade Representative that would be one thing. But to just be another member of that person's staff? Someone who can offer opinions, but whose opinions can as easily be swept aside as a snowflake on a car's windshield? No, that's not me. But I haven't been me since Elijah came into my life before I even knew he was there. Why is it you never see the people and things that will most change your life until well after they have seen you?

Oprah knocks on my door. "Have a minute?"

"Always." I respond and rise to talk with her.

"I have a case I'm stuck on and would like some advice."

"Sure."

"It's actually a trade case, and even though I know you've not been to trial in such instances I thought you might have some insights that could give me ideas where to go look."

Trade case. Is this where it starts? "What are the specifics?"

"A Dallas company bought a California company that is in the same product areas, but serves different market segments. The now parent company has been buying components for their products from various contract manufacturing houses in China and Korea. The California company set up operating divisions in China, Vietnam and Thailand. Since the companies build similar products the parent company has decided to rationalize the supply chain for both firms."

"Makes sense." I agree although not sure where this is going.

"The issue at hand is after having done an extensive analysis of costs at all locations the company has decided to terminate all suppliers and move all production to a new hub in the Philippines where they can achieve lowest total cost of delivered products into global markets."

"I understand. So, what's the trade dispute?"

"The Chinese government has brought suit against the company to block them transferring all production, patents and supply purchases out of the country. The government is claiming that under transfer of technology agreements the company cannot move the Intellectual Property that the production equipment, processes, bills of materials and system software represent."

"What do those agreements say? And what is the governing law?"

"The second issue is the crux of the problem. The agreements are being interpreted under Chinese law even though the agreements specifically set Texas and California as governing law and place of dispute resolution."

"So, the Chinese government has chosen to simply say that possession is governing law."

"Well it doesn't stop there." *This doesn't sound good.* "The company planted bombs in each of its factories and moved everything out of the contract manufacturers without notice. They destroyed all equipment, documentation and removed all inventory which they have flown out of the country on chartered aircraft. The Chinese government has declared this a full-blown international incident. So, now we have Department of State, Department of Defense as well as Commerce and the International Trade Representative's office calling us."

International Trade Representative's office. Hmmm. "The Dallas company is our client." I try to affirm.

"We just picked up the California company as of last month, so we have the entire company."

"But none of the history of the California company." I note. "Do we know anything about whether the orders to destroy the equipment and documentation were given by company officers or representatives of the California entity?"

"The California firm is currently a wholly owned subsidiary but the paperwork to merge them into a single entity is in work. And the answer to your question is no one is talking."

"So, in this instance we are being asked to defend our client before what court?"

"The Chinese government had initially insisted that it be heard in the Intellectual Property Court of Beijing, even though none of the plant locations were in that district." Oprah explains. "It's now insisting that since a criminal act was committed the case must be heard in the High

District Court of Beijing because the plant locations cross several provinces. In other words, this is going to be a show trial to put US company executives in prison in China as a warning to any other company that may contest the government's seizure of intellectual property."

"Sounds like we are going to need to find Chinese speaking associates who know Chinese commercial and criminal law as a first step." I muse aloud.

"Do I have the authority to start that process?"

I hesitate. "I take it you have been discussing the case with the company and they are intending to defend their interests even though they burned bridges behind themselves, so to speak."

"They have confirmed their intent and they most certainly did burn bridges." Oprah nods.

"Let's set up a war room." I decide on the spot. "This is going to take a lot of expertise from a lot of our team as well as outside counsel. We need to make it all visual. We can't afford to make a mistake that enables the Chinese government to detain any of the companies' or our staff in their country."

"Understood." Oprah beams. "This is so exciting. I was afraid you were going to back away and say we aren't prepared to deal with something like this."

Is that what happens to me? We take on this case, we lose badly, and in the process bankrupt our client who then can't pay us and the firm takes a big hit, dumping me in an attempt to right the ship?

"Oprah." I call before she is out the door. "We have to be judicious on this one. We have to know when to turn it over to someone with more experience if we're getting in over our heads. We can't just add experts and think we have any idea how to win a corporate criminal case in a foreign country where we haven't been practicing. If you're right and this is a show trial with the intent to lure corporate executives into their country and put them in jail, well we have to be smart enough to wave them off before that happens."

"This isn't supposed to be a cakewalk, J'ne." Oprah responds. "If we aren't prepared to deliver results for our client we should say so right now."

"Think about that for a moment, and before you answer, this case could cost tens of millions to defend. What's the upside for our client? Is it worth that much to them? They've burned the bridges. They're not going back into China. Never. So, why spend millions they will never recover?" I puzzle aloud.

"You're saying we could spin this all up, our client could walk and then refuse to pay us for all the expense we've taken on to defend them?" Oprah sees where I'm going.

"Think about that. If you had shareholders expecting you to deliver profits, you just torched any possible relationships in the world's largest market and you're getting ready to defend yourself in their courts with no possible reentry into that market. Why do it?"

"Maybe they're only thinking of defending themselves in Texas Court since this is governing law." Oprah considers. "Clear the IP charges but let the criminal charges sit over there since they have no proof who actually set the fires from what I'm told."

"Talk to them and make sure it's very clear what they want us to do, give them an estimate of what it will cost to do that and make sure we have a written acknowledgement of how they want us to proceed in light of the probable cost to do so."

"Why are you suddenly getting cautious?" Oprah reacts to my tone. "A minute ago you gave me permission to start looking for Chinese speaking Chinese law experts. Now you want a signoff of probable cost before we do anything except make an estimate. This doesn't sound like you."

"You're not the first person today to have said that." I observe.

"And what's with the outfit? Those shoes certainly don't go."

Impressive

The rest of the day is one crisis after another for members of my team. I sort of take Louise's advice and simply don't talk about the Mason case. I let my morose attitude speak for me. Everyone I come in contact with can see that I hold myself to a higher standard than I performed at on this one without having to say a word.

About seven I decide I need to head home, to see Noah, this Noah, and make a decision about whether I show up at the Winspear Opera House, just a short distance from Cirque where we live. If our apartment was on the other side of the building I could easily see the whole Arts District, which includes not only the Opera House, but the Meyerson Center where the symphony plays, the Wylie Theater for stage plays, the Booker T. Washington High School for the Performing Arts and a variety of museums, including the Nasher Sculpture Garden, the Dallas Museum of Art, and the Trammel Crowe exhibits which change frequently but include a great deal of Asian Art and artifacts.

So, why does Elijah want to meet at the Opera House? I have no idea. Hopefully his portal is not far from there. He was able to have it appear at the courthouse. I think he had it operating along the Katy Trail where I do my morning runs. All within a couple miles of the Opera House as the crow flies. I don't know if Elijah is into symbolism or anything mystical, but I'll have a chance to ask him if I show up. I just don't know. He paints a bleak picture of my future here. My relationship with Noah is so tenuous I don't know if I can save it now. So much water under the dam that I never saw or experienced. Can I jump into his life now, without those shared moments and feelings and pick up the pieces? So many conflicting thoughts, feelings and simply incredulity to a large extent. I still don't know if I believe what Elijah has told me. It all just seems so…

As I close my door, I see Stevenson's light is on. I remember how he used to make me feel in my last life. I decide now that the roles are reversed, I need to show that it's not the role you're in that shapes your behavior. I can make a choice about the kind of leader I want to be. Thanks to Louise I'm a little more aware of that than I was before.

"About time to…" I begin but Stevenson waves at me to wait a minute. He is deep in thought and recording those thoughts in what would appear to be a brief he is writing. I wait and watch him craft his submission to a court. I don't know which one since Stevenson is working on multiple cases at the moment, none of which, he has made it quite clear to me, are up to his standards. I'm not quite sure what those standards are, although they probably should be the firm's standards. And if that were the case then if the firm accepts the client, we by definition accept the work they send us, unless it would put us in a position to break the law in order to enforce the client's rights.

Stevenson smiles. His head bobs up and down. I'd never noticed that before. But then I don't think I'd ever seen him working on a briefing in his office before. As Managing Partner Stevenson chose not to take any cases. Everything was assigned. Said he couldn't do justice to both the firm and a single client at the same time. Personally, I think it was a way not to be embarrassed when he was not successful. Maybe I would have been better off if I'd not taken on Mason. But I already had by the time I got here, according to Elijah. The fact I have no memories for the last three years would tend to be a powerful validation that something unusual has happened to me. Do I believe Elijah is responsible as he claims? Well, I think the jury is still out on that because there must be other plausible explanations for a memory loss.

Stevenson stops typing, looks toward his window, but I don't think he is looking out so much as opening up his vista to conclude the thought. Again, his head bobs, and then he turns back to the keyboard and furiously types with a flourish, raising his hand high to keystroke in the final period.

The smile Stevenson radiates is a new perspective on him I've never had. He seems truly happy about whatever he just wrote, as if it were Huckleberry Finn or something grand and majestic. A classic, if you will. "Thank you for waiting. It was worth it to me to finish that thought. I'm afraid if I'd broken just then I would have lost it, probably forever. Now I'm done with a draft I can review tomorrow and then submit to the court. So, what's on your mind tonight?"

Stevenson slowly rises since I'm standing.

"I'd like to read your brief." I start. "You seem very proud of this one."

"Would you? You never read my briefs." Stevenson is wondering why I would make this offer.

"You never impressed me as a maestro before, the way you conducted the computer and ended the piece with a flourish. Quite impressive."

Stevenson raises his eyebrows and glances at the computer, "Oh, that. I guess you could have that impression although I really wasn't thinking Maestro so much as a composer recording the notes of a symphony for the very first time. Hearing the music in his or her head, although they were all men back then. I often wondered if a composer hears all of the instruments playing together. Hear them playing off each other when the first draft of the music is composed. Do they write the piece and then decompose it for the individual instruments? I don't know since I've never met a composer. I'd like to someday. So, I could ask that question. How does he do it? That question just fascinates me."

"I didn't know you were in to classical music." This discussion is a revelation to me.

"We haven't talked much, you and me. You've been busy climbing the ladder and now managing the firm. That doesn't afford you much time to socialize. But I'd like to take you to a symphony some time. Not as a date or anything, I know you're with Noah, but just so I could show you classical music. How an orchestra organizes to coordinate all those elements into a single integrated sound that moves an individual and an entire audience."

"I'd like to share that experience with you Stevenson. I'm sure I could learn so much from you. Not only about classical music and symphony orchestras, but about your view of the law, our firm and our clients. You've expressed frustration about some of the cases you've been assigned. Given the results I can understand that. Maybe it's time we sat down and took a hard look at our clients. Review which ones are core and which ones actually cost us more to serve them than we make in fees and forgone opportunities with other potential clients. Cull and expand our non-core. Build a growth platform around the core that keeps us viable long term. Does this sound like something you'd like to help me with?"

"I certainly have some opinions," Stevenson laughs. "But you're suggesting a more fact-based review. You know I've never really thought about our clients that way. I'm thinking of my current client list. You know there are probably five I would say are core to the firm. Companies we would want to do everything we can to keep them and ensure we provide the best service so no other firm could take a run at them. The rest? Well, as you say it would be instructive to put all the data we have on them together. Then we could decide who we keep and who we either reduce our efforts to only provide specialized services or let others take from us."

"You would have some good insights valuable to such a review." I straighten my stance. "Louise will let you know when we are getting started on that project. I need to talk to a few others who I'd like to participate. Get a cross section of views. Make sure it's a balanced review and not just driven by revenue numbers, although revenue will need to be one component of the analysis."

"Oh, absolutely. I agree with that one-hundred percent."

"There is one more thing I wanted to mention." I continue. "I had a conversation with Judge Freeman. He was extremely complimentary about how you handled the Washington versus Board of Education case. I know it was out of your area of specialty, but we really don't have a section devoted to those kinds of cases. Judge Freeman said you defused what could have been an ugly racial aspect of the case. You came prepared with relevant case law, precedents and facts and data. You calmly and professionally drew out the relevant facts of the matter. At the same time, you deflected the racially explosive testimony some of the interested parties were trying to get into the record by insisting on only facts and data. Thank you for representing your clients and our firm in such an exemplary fashion."

Stevenson looks at me like I'm a Martian or something. "Am I hearing praise? I don't think I've ever heard a Managing Partner of this firm make a special effort to recognize the good work we do. It's always been implied threats of not being selected for a Partnership if we don't do better. And once we're partners, we seem to be punished by the next case assigned when we don't win. Does this represent a change in how you're going to lead this firm?"

"It does." I confirm.

"You have to know that the Board of Education case? I couldn't have done it without Bri-nay Wilson's research. As a legal researcher she has to be among our best. What she came up with I don't think I would have found if I'd spent a month going through all the prior case law. But she found everything in a few days. It was organized so it was logical to follow the progression of opinions, and decisions. She also showed me where I had holes in the briefing I intended to file. She helped me find relevant cases that made the briefing air-tight. I can't say enough about her work. I hope you'll stop and give her an atta-girl."

"She's impressive, although I guess I didn't realize just how impressive. What you're saying is I need to get to know the team better. Thank you for that insight."

The Toy Room

My mind is still on Stevenson and just how different he is here from what I've known of him previously. He actually seems to be a nice man. Not a slave driver. He even noted what he characterized as a counterproductive practice of driving folks without recognition, which he is famous for back three years ago. In another time and place. Does that mean if I wake up tomorrow and I'm back in my own time and place that I should try to break down Stevenson's façade? Let him know he can lead us much more effectively by getting to know us and supporting us, rather than threatening us?

The door to our apartment recognizes me and unlocks. I open it and find Noah head down, just like I found Stevenson. Is there something in the air that tonight is a night for producing great works? Maybe I should sit down and see what inspiration overtakes me this evening. I go up to Noah from behind and kiss the back of his neck, putting my hands on his shoulders.

"Been a while." Noah mumbles as he keeps writing.

"It's not late, only about eight." I respond to what I thought might be a comment about how late I'm arriving home.

"Since you kissed me." Noah clarifies. "Or showed any kind of affection for that matter." The tone is one of weariness and wariness combined.

I come around front and kiss him on the lips, softly, slowly, lingering only the right length of time. Noah looks at me suspiciously.

"Does this mean he threw you out?" Noah accuses me.

I stand up, almost repelled by the tone of his comment. "What are you talking about?"

"Whoever it is you were planning to go live with next."

"There is no one but you." I counter, hurt by the accusation, confused that he would make it and trying to understand how I respond to his suspicion.

"I've known you a long time. You always have a backup plan. Where you can go if things crater here. What you can do if you get fired from the firm. Who you can go hang with if your Friday night friends decide to exclude you from their conversations."

I don't know how to respond to him. And why is this all coming out tonight? Is this all because I kissed him? Showed a little – not too much – affection? I've spent the whole day looking at who I am, here in this time and in this place. I'm different than I was last week in my time. But it seems people here are reacting to who I have become here, three years in the future. I've spent much of the day trying to change those perceptions and the future they imply. But I can't tell Noah about this. He would never understand. I don't understand.

I go around the table and sit across from Noah. He looks at his computer and not at me. "How does your novel end? Is she alone and forgotten? Cast out by those who love her because she just seems incapable of expressing love for anyone else?"

Noah looks over the screen. I see those guarded eyes assessing me, considering my words, reflecting on what his experience with me tells him. He looks down a moment, gathering the words he wants to say to me. "Is that how I should write it? Because that's what you're going to do to yourself and those of us who love you?"

"I so much want you to write a happy ending. Where she comes to accept the love of those who support her. Finds a way to get past the images and memories that haunt her to show love again."

"I can write that, but I'll need a little help." Noah pulls the computer screen down and leans forward. "I have to know what those memories and images are that haunt her. I've been in love with her for a decade, or so it seems, and yet she has never shared them. How can I help her get past them, how can I write about them if she won't share them?"

"Your character is a strong woman." I begin to answer his question without thinking.

Noah nods to confirm my opening premise.

"Her strength was forged in the crucible of a failed relationship, but a relationship she was totally committed to. An individual she was totally committed to, because that was the kind of love she had, the kind of love she had sought her whole life. It was there, engulfing her, serving as the prism of the light that shone in her heart."

Noah listens to me as I write the pages for him in the air, only neither of us are recording this, but that's all right. "Sammy was his name. Tall, dark hair, the deepest blue eyes she had ever seen. Those eyes sparkled in the sun and in the moonlight both. If he looked at you, it seemed you were basking in his admiration. He didn't have to say a word. You just knew."

I stop for a moment to gather myself, not knowing if I can continue doing this, but I have to let it out, have to stop holding on to the fear that paralyzes me. "At first I was just one of the girls that Sammy regularly talked up. He would get real close and whisper something obscene in my ear. But then he would walk away and do the same to another girl on the other side of the room. It was all foreplay. But it was also a means of seeing who would overcome their own inhibitions to spend a wild weekend with The Man. That's what we called him. At least I did. I seem to remember some of the other girls picked that up as well. It wasn't a competition amongst us girls to see who would sleep with Sammy first, although at one time or another all of us did. The challenge was to get Sammy's sole attention. And that was the competition we were in. Who would win him and take him off the streets?"

Noah seems to picture what I'm describing. No expression. Hard to tell if he's making judgments about what I'm saying or just creating the mental image so he can see what's happening. "After he'd done us all, which took him about three months as not everyone was as eager to do the deed with him, he came back to me. I don't know why. Some of the other girls were a lot prettier than I am. Some of them were known to be well experienced in the arts of love making. I wasn't. Some of the other girls had much richer daddies than I had. But for some reason he never explained, he came back to me. Don't know if it was to see if I was as good after he had lots of comparisons, or he thought he might be in need of a lawyer someday even though I wasn't one yet. But he came back. And this time he wanted me to come to his place rather than do a weekend away like he had with all of us individually."

Noah makes a few notes on a pad he is keeping next to his computer. I'd seen him organize things there before he would write about them. Sequence things, make notes about when things happened or the names of minor characters that might only appear once or twice. I don't know what he is writing and don't wait for him to finish. "I got an entirely different impression of Sammy when I saw where he lived, how he lived, who the real Sammy was. His external persona was an act. When he slept with us on those weekends, that wasn't him. When he was home, he was relaxed, he was funny, and he talked about all kinds of things. Fantastical things. Adventures he'd either had or hoped to have. Maybe I could be part of those adventures. Books he was going to write, just like you, but he wasn't going to write the Great American Novel. He was going to write a book about something no one knew about. He was going to bring new knowledge into the world. Inform everyone about something important they'd never heard of. He was going to get a job acting in movies, he was clearly good-looking enough. And he showed he had the acting chops. Sammy offered to bring me along for the ride. Unfortunately, I bought in. There was never a question about would I. It was always 'what adventure are we going to have today?' Every day was a new experience. Every day just a look from those deep blue eyes and it made me feel more alive than I'd ever been. He brought me to life."

I stop for a moment. Noah looks up from his notes. "What happened?"

"At the time it seemed to go on forever. I never knew from day-to-day where I would wake up. One day in Memphis, the next in LA. Sometimes we would explore Copenhagen until midnight and have breakfast the next day at the Ritz in London. But if it was raining in London, we'd do the Ritz in Paris instead. Life was a blur wrapped in a cloud of love so deep just his touch remained electric for me the entire time we were together. You talk about two people becoming one? I don't know where I started and he left off. We weren't two people. We were a couple that was inseparable, loving life and each other every moment of every day wherever in the world we were."

"When I looked back, I discovered our cloud of love only lasted about six months. I distinctly remember the first time he hit me. It came as such a shock. When he became angry about something, I would touch him and calmly put whatever had upset him into perspective. He always regained his composure immediately and we would put it behind us. But one of his friends offered him acid. He was already coked up. When we met, he did coke once in a great while and only a small amount. He never reacted with anything other than more energy to keep the party going. I guess I hadn't been paying attention. He had apparently gone to the edge of overdose on coke when he added the acid. He was flying around the room at this hotel in Casablanca. There were all these people there. I had no idea who they were or where Sammy met them. I heard the one guy say something about Sammy had taken a double. At the time I had no idea what they were talking about. But suddenly he came flying across the room and landed on top of me. He just started beating the shit out of me. I was screaming for him to stop, but no one stepped in to help. No one did anything. They were probably all drugged up. Still there was blood all over my face from my broken nose. I had two broken ribs. Have you ever been in a Moroccan hospital? It's not an experience you ever want to have. They gave me pills for the pain, but I had no idea what they were. I wouldn't take them. So, I had to just deal with the pain."

Noah drops his head and shakes it. "You were taking drugs that whole time and that was the illusion you were living?"

I don't respond to his question. "I had to walk to that hospital. Sammy was still flying about. No one else would help me. Just the blood on my face and the pain. I can't even begin to describe the pain. It pulled me out of whatever state I was in. The hospital wanted to admit me. But I didn't have insurance. They discharged me after taking all the money I had. So, here I am in Casablanca. A city I know nothing about, without any money as I had to do a cash with drawl of all the money in my account to pay the hospital. I'm basically fucked in Morocco because I couldn't even remember where Sammy was. The only thing I could think of to do was find the US consulate. Of course, no one spoke English, so I walked into a hotel. I finally found a person at the front desk who spoke broken English. She took one look at the bandage across my face and the way I stood stiffly indicating I had broken ribs. She wanted to send me to a hospital. But I convinced her to direct me to the consulate. She showed me where it was on a map, but said it was too far to walk. I told her I had no money as the hospital took it all. She spoke to her manager and he called and paid for the cab."

At this point I assume Noah is sorry he asked what had happened, but then I notice his eyes are red and moist. He's feeling my pain as only a doctor can. "The consulate arranged for a flight to get me home with the promise I would repay the ticket as soon as possible after getting back. It took two weeks for Sammy to show up at his place. I was there, of course, because I had nowhere else to go. Sammy was apologetic, but didn't seem to be the least bit sorry I ended up in the hospital. All he could talk about was the new experiences he'd been having. I asked when he realized I wasn't there. He didn't remember. Thought I was with him the whole time, getting high too. I thought of leaving then. I should have. But like I said every time he touched me it was electric from the first time to the last. We made love that night and I was right back in."

I get up and take a glass down. Fill it with a red wine I find open in the 'frig. "Want one?" I hold it up so Noah can see. He nods and I fill a second glass. I need a sip before I can go on. A long breath. I sit back down, take another sip and continue. "A couple weeks later Sammy decided to try for a new high. This time I don't have any idea what he added to his coke and acid diet. I wasn't taking anything at that point. I'd been desperately trying to keep him clean. I may have been one with him, but somewhere along the way he'd lost me. He was fine most of the evening. I let him sit in front of the big screen we had in what I called the toy room. That was where he kept all of his toys which included old pinball machines, early videogame arcade versions, air hockey, billiards and a wet bar. He spent a lot of time there when he was high or when people would come by. At first, I didn't realize it but in retrospect they were mostly dealers selling him different drugs. It must have been about midnight. I'd fallen asleep on the couch in the family room across from the fireplace. Something hit me, I didn't know what it was until I opened my eyes. Sammy is throwing billiards balls at me. Two of them hit me in the face before I could turn away. He then leapt across the room like he was trying to fly like Superman or something. He came down on me hard. If I'd been on the floor, he would have broken a lot more bones than he did with his fists. This time I drove to the hospital. They discovered he'd cracked my left eye socket, broken three fingers on my left hand and thankfully a different rib. If he'd broken one of the ribs he'd broken earlier it would have been much worse."

I stop and take another sip. "Is this enough for your novel or do you want the details of the third time? When it was particularly bloody. Even then, I went back to him." I take another sip to calm myself.

"What happened that you finally left?" Noah asks, apparently deciding two horror stories is enough.

"He brought home an automatic rifle with a bump stock he got from one of his drug dealers. Hung it on the wall in his toy room. Kept it loaded."

7:30

Noah is overwhelmed. He just sits there thinking about what I'd told him for probably an hour. Of course, I'd not had anything to eat so tonight is the left over Korean Barbeque sides since the meat was gone. Not what I'd say is a delicious meal. But between it and the calories from the wine I should live to see another day. I just hope it is a day I never got to see three years ago. But that has to be wishful thinking at this point. I go to bed about midnight. Noah is still up working on his novel.

When 4:30 arrives, it brings an alarm clock ring I hoped to sleep through. But, of course, I don't. Being awake at this hour is ridiculous, I decide, even though I do it every day. I pull myself out of bed, throw on a clean running outfit, my running shoes and head out the door. When I get to the street I have to decide. Do I go up the Katy trail as usual or go meet Elijah at the Winspear? Decision time. I stand there just looking across the street at the backside of one of the Victory Plaza office buildings.

This is one of those decisions I will be living with for the rest of my life. If I head up Katy Trail, I'll be trying to figure out how to fix my relationship with Noah. I took a big step last night, but it won't be easy from here. I'll work to lead my law firm better. To avoid the leadership problems I so resented before becoming Managing Partner. I'll be working the appeal to keep whatever Elijah shows up here out of the clutches of the government. I'll also be trying to figure out how to get to know my team as people, not as just lawyers. Or I can turn left and head over to the Opera House. See where Elijah takes me. He said this time and place isn't good for either of us. There has to be a better one out there for both of us. I don't know enough about his portal thing to know if that's possible, particularly since this one wasn't necessarily better or worse for me. Just different – managing partner. With different challenges and issues. But all related to the life I was living before. I look in the direction of the Opera House for a long time. It holds different possibilities if, in fact, it is what Elijah represents it to be.

I turn left and head for the Winspear. It's unmistakable. It has concrete walls with a jewel red glass riser sitting on top. A huge metal canopy covers just an incredible amount of the waiting lines that surround the building during an event. It is that metal canopy that makes the building unique. As I come out on Akard Street and the Freeway I look across Klyde Warren Park and see the distinctive building on the other side. I walk past Savor where Noah and I had dinner just a night ago, cross through the park and am coming up on the back side of the Oprah House when I see fog rise. It envelops everything. It's not a dense fog but it's just enough to create shadows under the limited street lights. I keep walking. Out of the fog and shadows Elijah appears.

"Take my hand." He reaches out for me.

I close my eyes, take a deep breath and do as he asks. His grip is not tight, but firm. He leads me into the fog. I feel that electric impulse across my skin. It's the same as the one I felt in the courtroom. *What was that? About a week ago?* Elijah leads me behind a wall where diesel generators provide emergency power to the Opera House. We go around behind one of the generators. A green metal cabinet, among many there, appears to be Elijah's target. He opens the cabinet, pushes a button and a light changes from green to red.

"What did you just do?"

"I closed the portal behind us so no one else can come across."

"Why would you do that?" I'm confused.

"We are in a different time and place than where you were when you left your apartment only a few minutes ago."

"This looks the same." I respond, confused.

"By time and place I'm referring to a timeline. You are in a different time, but the place on the timeline is different as well. That's why I talk about time and place. You can be in the same city, in the same house, but it will be a different 'place' than the one you left."

I have no idea what Elijah is talking about, so I let it go. "But who do you think might be following us? Who else even knows about this?"

Elijah looks around nervously, "The government suspects I've built something. They've been all over me like a wet blanket. I don't think they were out there, but I can't be sure. I don't want them coming through and following us now."

I look around as well. No one followed us back here. Not a guarantee that no one was watching, but I don't feel a need to flee. "Let's assume you're right and no one got through. It looks exactly as I remember it out there. So, when are we?"

"Five years in the future. I'm twenty-one and you're…"

"Five years older." I consider my answer and continue. "In every sense except biological if what you're playing with doesn't change my biological clock."

"Good point. You can actually say you're eight years younger than your local self would have been." Elijah is smiling but I'm not sure he appreciates it quite the way I do.

"So, how do we check this out?" I look for direction. "Determine if it's right for us?"

"Try going home, see what you find." He suggests.

"After last night I sincerely doubt I'll still be living there," I realize aloud glumly.

"You can try your cell phone. It might register if you didn't upgrade. Five years is a long time, but if that doesn't work you can try the public library or go back to your old office."

"I don't have my badge. I left it in the apartment. Besides you said I wouldn't be there now."

"Only in the other world I visited. I have no idea about this one. In fact, I'm hoping none of what I saw happened here."

"Hold on a minute. How do you get to select how many years we go into the future or past?"

"Harmonics." Elijah answers, clearly hoping that will forestall a need for greater explanation.

"That doesn't make any sense." I push back.

"Nor should it, but it won't help you find yourself in this time and place. What I suggest is we split up because we're looking for different things. Let's plan to meet back here at 7:30 tonight. That should give us enough time to get a feel for what's happened to us."

I look at Elijah dubiously. He brought me along to help him and now he's saying we need to go our own way this first day. "If something happens to you, they pick you up and send you somewhere, how am I supposed to, first of all, help you? And second, even know what happened. I have no idea how, in this time and place, I'd be able to trace what happened to you. Particularly if you're in a witness protection-like program where nobody is supposed to know where you are or who you are."

"You have a point." He sounds embarrassed he hadn't thought through the implications. "I've made certain assumptions, but I don't know if they're accurate. I could be walking into a trap and off to a gulag where I'll disappear for the rest of my life."

"Exactly." I'm glad he's finally thinking this through more than he has so far. "If your two-year dimension is correct neither of us are still here." I point out.

"Were you on LinkedIn or Facebook?" Elijah asks as he pulls his cell out of a back pocket.

"LinkedIn, but not Facebook." I respond.

"LinkedIn. Here you are." He reads down my profile.

"Damn, you're still here. But you're a judge. State Supreme Court. You certainly made the most of your contacts."

"Does it give an address?" I ask hopefully.

"Email. Damn. I'm surprised anyone is still using email when there are better ways of communicating."

"Great. I can send an email to myself, but I won't be there to pick it up," I note ruefully.

"Hold on. Since we know you're still living in the twenty-first century let this post millennial see what other media would have a physical address. Whoa. What's this? Place.com? Never heard of it. But then maybe it didn't exist five years ago. Place says you live at 2815 2500 North Houston Street."

My heart skips a beat. That's the apartment I left this morning. The one I share with Noah. Are we still together? I can only hope my overtures and explanation helped turn the course of our impending split. But how did the version of me from now handle it all? Was she grateful I'd made her life a little less lonely? Or was Noah correct that I'd had someone else on the side five years ago? Someone I was unware of? I wonder what that person thought when first I didn't and then my successor in that time frame didn't show up. But maybe she did. I can't keep going on with the endless possibilities of what I might encounter at the next turn all because I made one different decision. And I know I've made a lot more than one different decision than my first life made.

"What about you? Are you on LinkedIn?" I push back at Elijah knowing he's about to dump me by simply telling me to go home.

"No, but I might find me on Instagram. And here I am. That's an ugly t-shirt. Where the hell am I?" Elijah enlarges the image, "Oh." He goes quiet.

"What? Where are you?"

"I'm wearing an MIT t-shirt, but I'm at the Particle Physics Lab at the University of Chicago."

"Isn't that good news? You're not at one of the government labs."

"No." A big exhale. "Chicago means I'm in the wrong area of science. I'd only be there if they didn't stand up a team to work with my ideas. Means they didn't know what to do with me."

"I'm sorry." I touch his shoulder in comfort. "Should we just leave now?"

"Wait." He continues scrolling, looks at additional images. "Never judge a book..."

"What are you finding now?"

He shows me an image of the current version of himself in the arms of a gorgeous woman also apparently in her early twenties. "Apparently I haven't done so badly."

"Willing to go check it out?" I ask, "Given that you were only concerned about intellectual freedom."

"I wonder if she does sleep overs?" Elijah asks himself more than me.

"Only one way to find out." I suggest. "What I've learned in the last few days is there are some things that are worth more than anything else, and they have nothing to do with breakthrough science accolades, or professional kudos. At the end of your life when you are at the Pearly Gates or whatever is there and you look back, what did you do that was most rewarding to you and most meaningful to those who knew you?"

"You had me until the end." Elijah observes. "Why limit to those who knew you? Why not most meaningful to the world and those who will inhabit this world once you have left?"

"Probably because I can't think in those terms. When I'm gone no one will truly care. Others will have stepped up to fill in for me at work. So, then what?'"

"Why are you so cynical?" Elijah sounds confused. "You weren't like this back in the beginning."

"Back in the beginning, as you call it, I wasn't cynical because I hadn't met you, hadn't seen the world as only one possible future and hadn't tried to understand what my impact is on others. But you started that by bringing me here. I was happy where I was. Why am I having to push myself through your keyhole just so you and I can both be happy? Maybe. Whatever happy means."

Elijah has continued scrolling on his Instagram page. "My other self is never gonna speak to me again."

"What are you looking at?"

Elijah shows me the picture of what is apparently his lab team at the University of Chicago. The women are all beyond exceptional in appearance. And the team is all women. It would appear that Elijah has surrounded himself with a very appealing work group. What occurs to me and apparently hasn't to him is who is the team leader? He may not be even though he has assumed he is. If this isn't his area of expertise, I wonder why they would put him in charge of the team. I'll bet, but I could be wrong, that he's the team genius to help the rest of the team produce something that they wouldn't alone. Then the most likely recipient of the team member affections isn't in the picture.

"You still want to meet up at the end of the day or are you on the next flight to Chicago?"

Elijah puts in an input to answer a question. He looks at the answer. Gets quiet. "My parents are in Boston. Stuck there for five more years. My father hating every day and probably screwing his lady every chance he gets. That is if she followed him. Guess I can't assume she did."

"You're on your way to Chicago. So, call me at 7:30?" I'm already thinking of what's next.

Lectures

The door lock recognizes me as if I'd just left, even though it was five years ago. As I take the last steps towards the door, I wonder who I'll find on the other side. If I'd not thought it through, I'd have gone in expecting to find Noah. But maybe not. Funny how a cue is so easily ignored. But if it's perceived to be what it is, it can save so much confusion.

I open the door and smell coffee. Did the me from this time put it on for Noah before I left? I hear the shower running. Someone is definitely here, but until he comes out, I won't know who it is for sure.

A cup of coffee will get me started since I didn't do my usual run. I need something to get me focused, although I still don't know where my office is or whether I'm supposed to be in Austin for a hearing or what the story is. I go to my computer on the kitchen table, back to back with his. The computer is not the one Noah had five years ago, but I shouldn't expect it to be. I sign in with the passcodes I've written right next to the machine in violation of every security protocol. I'm not happy I'm that careless, but I'm also happy I did so I don't have to go searching everywhere to find them.

My schedule shows me in the Dallas office today. Only where is that? I go to the bottom of the webpage and find an address. 5201 Fountain Place. Not so far from the apartment. Still walking distance. Guess I really don't like public transit. Or I'm making enough I can afford to live close to where I work, whereas so many can't.

The bathroom door opens, and I hear a familiar voice, "Morning. Have a good run?"

I'm afraid to turn to look, but I do anyway to see a tanned and naked Mia walking towards the other bedroom. Or is that the other bedroom now? Noah and I shared the one closest to the door. I'm disoriented. I have to go to the bedroom I used with Noah.

I find my things are in there. What a relief. Mia is my roommate. What happened? She had a husband, but no kids that I was aware of.

I look around for the artwork from before. Gone. I didn't even notice. Apparently, my confession to Noah didn't change the inevitable. Whatever happened in those three years was too much for me to overcome with even the best of intentions on my part and honesty about what I was trying to overcome.

I go into the bath, shower and shampoo my still long blonde hair. In fact, I haven't had it cut in eight years even though it's really only been about a week. My stylist would wonder about me. Something different about the shampoo. Not sure what it is, so I look at the bottle. Same brand, but new enhanced formula that will ensure my hair shimmers and falls back into place every time even if badly windblown. What will they think of next?

Mia pokes her head into the bath as I'm blowing my hair dry. She does a double take. "What did you do? Get hair extensions? Wasn't it that long when you were with Victor? But that's been what? Two years? You said you'd never grow it out again because people wouldn't take you seriously with long hair. What made you change your mind?"

I look at her and ask, "Would you like to ask one question at a time?" and smile back.

"I just never expected long hair again." Mia pulls her brown hair forward and looks at it. "Do you think long hair is back in? Should I grow mine out again? What do you think?"

"One question." I shake my head.

"Yes, your honor." Apparently, she calls me this when I get too formal with her. "Is it the opinion of the court that long hair is coming back?"

"It is the opinion of the court that one should not hide or downplay one's best features."

Mia looks at me standing there naked. "If that's the opinion of the court, then I think you need to ditch those robes. You've got nothing to hide. By the way, did you lose some weight since like yesterday?"

I look down and give her a shrug. "Diet wine?"

"Perish the thought." Mia is about to close the bathroom door, but then looks back in, "You doing Friday night with the old gang?"

"At Sambuca?"

Mia seems confused I'd ask this question. "No. They're still at the Flora Street Café. They haven't met at Sambuca in years."

The office? Did she move back to Victor, Vargas and Utley or did she never leave in this world? I'll have to wait to test that later today. "What time?"

"Probably start drifting in about six."

"You want to catch something to eat afterwards?" I ask, having no idea who I would eat with.

"Let's play that by ear. I never know who might call during the day. I have so many admirers as you well know."

I'm not sure how to interpret her response so I let it pass, thinking to myself I need to see if there are any power bars in the cupboard here. I had them in my original world, but never checked to see if they were here when I was living with Noah. I didn't find any, but who knows? I have no idea what strange things I might have started doing in the last eight years. In any event, I might need one tonight if I don't get dinner, but have a glass of wine before coming home.

I arrive at my office on the top floor of one of the tallest buildings in Dallas to see a panoramic view of the city looking north. I go to the window and look around. I hear someone come to my door. I look around and find Louise watching me curiously.

"Contemplative today?" Louise asks.

I smile at Louise and come back away from the window. "Just thinking about what a strange journey it's been getting to this point."

"If you might permit a personal reflection."

"Of course."

"There has been several times in our relationship when I've looked at you, what you say and do and I have no idea who I'm talking to, because you seem to constantly transform yourself."

Oops. She's noticed I don't look like I did yesterday… again.

"Joseph Schumpeter, an Austrian economist talked about creative destruction, a concept he borrowed from Karl Marx. Basically, he said you have to burn down the old to make way for the new. Think of all the forest fires in California. They burn down great swaths of forest lands. But what happens? Seedlings grow in the now open spaces. In a few decades, which I know is a long time in our lifetimes, but is short in world history, a new forest emerges. Stronger than the last. More able to withstand the ravages of diseases, insects and the next forest fire. The trees are green and less undergrowth serves as kindling."

Louise frowns at me. "Why is it every time I make a simple observation about your hair or your clothes or your bone headed decisions you give me this long intellectual lecture about something I could care less about?"

Deer-In-The-Headlights

I Google myself to see what the public record says about me. I find mostly references to the many social endeavors I supported as Chairman of one event or another during my short tenure as Managing Partner at Victor, Vargas and Utley, the most prestigious law firm in Dallas. I apparently was what is known as a bundler for the current Governor. I raised a lot of money for her election campaign and bundled it into a single contribution. Millions of dollars it says here. I find another article that says I would have been a Lieutenant Governor candidate if I hadn't been a woman. Seems Texas wasn't ready for women in both of the top two positions. So, I declined to run. My reward was an appointment to the State Supreme Court, easily confirmed by the Texas Senate. Still another article attempts to assess my 'Judicial Temperament', a vague concept that tries to interpret the trends or meanings or leanings, if you will, that my decisions would imply. According to the article I am perceived as a conservative judge who leans more towards the middle ground than the extreme right. Not what the article author would prefer from the tone of the article. Seems that being a centrist in Texas politics is just short of a crime in the eyes of some factions. At least they appear to be losing credibility from other articles I read.

Okay. I know what I'm perceived to be, I know how I got here, but I haven't found out what happened between me and Noah and how Mia came to be my roommate.

I Google Noah. I find him as a Vice President, Pediatrics of Hospital Corporation of America. HCA, as it is known, owns hundreds of hospitals and urgent care centers all over America. Guess the Baylor job got him good visibility in the Industry. Says he's living in Nashville, Tennessee now. I wonder if the job found him and took him from me since I couldn't sit on the Texas Supreme Court and live in Nashville, or whether we had split and this was a good way of starting over. In any event, it appears our interests and careers took us in different directions.

What about Mia? First article that comes up says she is a trial lawyer at Victor, Vargas and Utley. Either she came back or in this world she never left. Hard to tell which. I keep searching and find a picture of her and her husband, Tom. Article was about five years ago, about the time I just left. She looks happy in the picture. He is a good-looking guy, athletic, thinning hair, but warm and broad smile. I wonder what happened there. Why did they split? Why did she end up here? I read through the article. Her husband owns an automotive dealership. Seems his father started a chain of them and then gave one each to his five kids. Tom owns the BMW dealership so he's doing all right for himself. Still doesn't give me any indications of their reasons for going separate directions.

Now the question is what can I find out about Elijah Mohammed Mason? He is listed as graduating from MIT two years ago, Summa Cum Laude. Guess he decided he didn't want too much attention, although the article says he graduated with a perfect cumulative grade point average as did the Valedictorian. He just had fewer extra-curricular activities, so she was named Valedictorian of the class. Quibble, quibble. That's the only reference I find on him. Appears his self from this time was careful. Puts out Snapchat pictures, but they're gone after they're viewed.

Guess I need to get to work and see what the call at seven-thirty brings. Could this be a comfortable life for me? I don't know, but it seems more suited to me than International Trade Representative staff member. Particularly since I saw the seeds of where that came from. Did I change my future based on the decisions I made that one day? And did the J'ne from this time, who cut my hair, follow that direction to avoid getting too deep into the international scene which would have brought me to the attention of the ITR? Seeds. Decisions I made in one day changed the whole direction of my career. I just wish the decision to tell Noah about what happened to me had changed the nature of our relationship. I only had a few days with him at Cirque, but those have probably been the best days of my life so far. Basking in the glow of someone who loves me, but not feeling the drug fueled compulsions Sammy brought out.

I dive into the briefings for the next case that will be presented before the court. It's really an interesting case, but my mind keeps wandering back to Noah, Elijah and occasionally Mia. I need to get focused because if this world works out for Elijah, I'll be hearing this case on Monday in Austin.

A knock on my door and a young woman, probably in her mid-twenties enters. Long brown hair, shy eyes and smile. She seems to be uncomfortable coming in to see me. "Good morning, your honor."

I wait for her to continue, since I must know who she is, hoping the context of her request will help me figure out who she is and what I need to do for her.

"Did you have a good evening at the symphony?" she asks.

Small talk, will have to wait a bit to figure this out. "Very nice. Have you been?"

"No, but I do like Chopin." Again, I wait, *it must be making her nervous. I suspect the J'ne that was here before was much more engaging with her. My behavior is putting her off.* "What did you do last night? Something in the Arts District or around town?"

"Same as usual, studied until Midnight and then went to sleep."

"What were you on last night?" is the best question I can come up with that might tell me more. *Is she a law clerk having passed the bar or is she a college intern still working on her degree? I can't tell.*

"The law of conservation of energy."

"Engineering?" I'm surprised she would be studying something technical.

"Adding patent law as a specialty requires me to get that degree too."

"It's certainly an area in need of good minds." I suggest as a compliment without really knowing anything about her. "So, I couldn't talk you into corporate law?"

"You've tried, but my parents… well, my Dad in particular, thinks patent law is one of those disciplines where you'll always have work in good and bad times."

"Being a judge is another good way to weather the storms of the economic cycles," I offer as a counterpoint.

"I'm sure you're right, but what you have to do to become a judge? I just don't think I could do that."

"What? Put in some volunteer time with a political party. Stuff envelopes, ring door bells, get people out to elections. And then tell the leaders of the party you select that you'd like to be a judge."

"That's not how you got…" She starts to say something, but apparently thinks differently of it.

"I got here because I did all those things, but never identified being a judge as an ambition. I just helped the party. I wanted to see another woman governor in the state. It had been a long time. So, I joined her campaign as a volunteer advisor. She got comfortable with me. I raised a lot of money for her. That's how I got here. The people who were in the position to appoint me got to know me."

"People help you along because they see what you're doing?" is her timid response.

"It's real important for you to start talking with conviction." I point out to her. "If you come across as if you're not sure, people will look in a different direction when they need someone to go do something for them. So, that's why you always speak with conviction. This is the answer. If someone points out that you're wrong? What do you do?"

She acts like she's startled by the question, apparently hoping I'd just give advice. "Say I'll go check that out." She tries to respond with conviction. *Better, but still not there.*

"Why do you want to be a patent lawyer?"

"Because my Dad…" she changes her mind. "Because patent lawyers do some of the most important work in the legal profession, safeguarding the value of intellectual property in the global economy."

"Better." I smile at her to hopefully get her to relax. I notice she's standing up straighter. "Chin up. You're getting it. You want to greet the world as an equal, and if you're always looking down, you'll not see the world that's coming to meet you."

"I can do this," she remarks. Voice is stronger, but her eyes betray her timidity.

"So, what can I help you with this morning?" I ask to get us back to the reason she came in.

"Oh, I'm here to research and help draft your decision on Peterson versus the Texas Department of Transportation."

"Okay. And where are we?"

Deer-in-the-headlights, I realize.

Hopping

About six o'clock I walk up the street to the Flora Street Café. Local celebrity chef Stephen Pyles owns this Dallas hot spot, which is located directly across the street from the Meyerson Symphony Hall in the Arts District. Small, it is one of the hardest reservations to get in the city when there is anything going on in the Arts District. There is at least one performance nearly every night now.

When I get to the café, I see familiar faces at the bar. Mostly from VV&U, my old law firm. A few others from firms I used to argue against from time-to-time. As I walk in nearly every head at the bar turns to look at me. I'm not sure why since it seems I come join this group frequently.

Oprah is the first to come greet me. A hug and she holds me at arms-length. "You haven't looked this good in five years. What did you do to yourself?"

"Went back to my old hair stylist," seems to be a safe response. "Are you keeping everyone in line at the firm?"

"Not me." Oprah smiles and holds her hands up to show the firm is not in her hands. Mia is talking with Stevenson at the end of the bar. I nod to each person but head down to chat with the two of them.

"Are notes of Chopin dancing in your head?" Stevenson asks.

I remember my conversation with him… yesterday in my time, but five years ago, where he talked about taking me to the Symphony and teaching me all about composing, composers and performance of symphonies. "Great fun. Thank you."

"Great fun." Stevenson responds. "Not an appropriate symphony lover's response. You still have so much to learn about being a music snob."

"You're not a snob, you just love music and marvel of the mystery of it all," I suggest, to keep him talking.

"Au contraire, Madame. J' le grand snob." Stevenson responds in horrid French.

"But Chopin was what? If my memory serves me, he was Polish. Do you know any Polish music snobs?" I kid him.

"A better question is: do I know anyone who is actually Polish? That would be a no. But you're on the symphony board now..."

"With a little help from you," Mia points out.

"True, but she has served with distinction. In any event, since you're on the board, I would suggest you request more French symphonies. I need to practice my snobbishness by attempting to communicate in that language, before, during and after the performance."

"It may be better if I not make that suggestion to spare me your snobbishness, before, during and after each performance." I laugh.

Mia asks an interesting question of Stevenson, "Why doesn't your wife attend with you since you're such an avid supporter?"

"She likes plays. So, she's on the Board of the Wylie Theater and the Dallas Theater Center. She attends the plays with our son. He's acted in a few productions and hopes to get into Julliard in New York when he graduates."

"Is he at Booker T. Washington?" I ask, although if I've been attending the symphony with him for five years, I should probably know this answer.

"He plays concert piano in addition to acting and stage design.

Likes lighting and sound, but his forte really is on stage. He has presence. Your eyes just follow him as he moves about the stage."

"I think that's a proud papa speaking," Mia responds taking a sip of her vodka tonic.

"Not at all, ask his mother." Stevenson grins and sips his red wine.

I'm still standing there with no drink in my hand, so I turn to the bartender, who I don't know, but he evidently knows of me because he hands me a red wine without having to ask. "Thank you. What is this?"

"Malbec. Argentinian," and he winks at Mia, who apparently clued him in what I like.

I make the rounds of the other attorneys, asking about their families and what interesting cases they're handling. I finish asking whether they are working cases that might make it up to the State Supreme Court. None are. About seven fifteen I make my excuse and walk back towards Cirque. Elijah should be calling soon since I didn't hear anything from him during the day.

At 7:30 I'm walking up to the front door of my apartment house when my cell rings. A quick look and I see it is Elijah. "I'm just walking into my place, can you hold until I get upstairs?"

"No problem."

I hustle to the elevator and wait impatiently for it to reach my floor. I don't wait to get to my apartment before I continue the conversation. "How is Chicago?"

"It took a while to get here."

"It's only what, about a two-hour flight?" I'm puzzled it took so long.

"If you have a ticket on the next flight out. I had to wait until 1:30. So, I got here about 4:30. Only have a superficial sense of things. By the time I found his apartment, located his badge and got to the lab there were only a few people still here."

"You have a roommate?" I ask now being sensitive to this issue with Mia sharing mine.

"It's a two bedroom. Didn't really check it out because I was focused on finding the badge, which he'd left in the kitchen on the countertop. Whoever the roommate is, I didn't meet him. Looking through some of the files on his computer I can see what he's doing. It's alright, but I can see I'm going to have to work hard having not attended MIT. "

"What are you saying?" I'm not sure if this is positive or not.

"First thoughts only. I just think it's going to be hard to pull off replacing him on this project when he has five years of history with this project that I don't. I'm going to have to really dig in just to keep up at least for a while."

"What about the people?"

"RayAnn is real nice. She's the particle physics theory guru on the team from what I can tell. I haven't gotten a handle on who does what just yet, but that should all become clear tomorrow."

"You going to hang there for a while tonight, reading through files to get yourself oriented and ready for whatever you need to do tomorrow?"

"That's my plan. RayAnn wants to go out and get something to eat. I'll probably do that. Get to know her better. Find out what the issues are on the team and with the work. I think she'll give me a pretty good idea of how to approach tomorrow."

"One day at a time?"

"For the moment. It should get easier," Elijah seems to be okay with things.

"What about the government?"

"Don't know. I haven't seen anything of them yet. But since I still owe them five years, I bet they're keeping an eye on me. Wait. Hold on."

"What?" I'm not sure what's he's reacting to since I can't see what he's doing. I can just barely hear him mumbling something, something he's apparently reading.

"I'm going to have to think about this." Elijah says into the phone, although I can't tell if he's talking to me or himself.

"What?" He drives me crazy when I don't get enough information to understand him.

"I'm reading a theory he wrote. It's a redefinition of a theory I wrote about a year ago, well, that would be six years ago here. So, this represents six years of evolving thought, informed by an MIT education and national lab experimentation. I'm going to have to consider the implications."

"Good or bad?" I look for a directional indication.

"Too early to tell. Initial reaction is there might be more order to the multiverse than I recognized. Might allow me to simplify the design of my portal device. Move more functionality to the client and the host becomes more of the power source and ground reference. Might permit a greater range of operations."

"Greater range?"

"May permit going further back or forward from the base without hopping."

Roommate

Mia comes home about nine. "Thought we were going to grab a bite to eat after. But you took off like you had some place to be."

"I had an important call I had to take, so I came back here to take it. Sorry, I forgot to mention it to you. Did you get something?"

"I did, with Henderson." Mia lets me know that wasn't much fun by the tone in her voice.

"He still at Ballard and Strauss?"

"He's trying to set up a pure litigation house with Tim Anderson. They're arguing about whether it should be Henderson and Anderson or Anderson and Henderson. Tim's trying to convince him that being first in the alphabet has its advantages. Henderson is trying to convince Tim that someone looking for a litigator is going to who has the best talent, not where you find them in a directory."

"And that was how much of your dinner conversation?" I can guess, but wait to see if I'm right.

"Too much. Henderson wants me to join them as a partner. Might even get my name on the firm."

"Henderson, Anderson and Mastrangelo. Has a nice sound. You'll never get your name on the firm at VV&U.

"I could use my married name, Henderson, Anderson and Sexton. That sounds more Blue Blood."

"If this were Boston, I'd agree with you, but in Dallas it won't make any difference if you're not married into one of the oil families."

"Tim's wife is a Hunt." Mia mentions. "That's our entre."

"Sounds like you're seriously considering making the move." I begin. "This a way of repositioning yourself after your divorce?" I'm trying to get insights to what happened there.

Mia looks at me strangely but then seems to consider my question. "Reposition. An interesting choice of words. Mia decides to come over and sit down across from me at the kitchen table where I'd been working on computer searches. "You offered to let me move in with you when Tom bailed on me. I've probably overstayed my welcome, although you've never made me feel like that. But at some point, you're going to want to have Noah come visit you or you're going to want your privacy again."

"Noah's getting married." I just lay out there what I'd just read in an email from him.

Mia is quiet considering this change of events. "I'm sorry to hear that. I know you were hopeful he'd come back to Baylor to a better position."

"He likes HCA. Apparently, they've been good to him," I respond, which is the impression I get from the email. Not how I would have thought Noah would have told me something like this. I can only interpret that he's given me an indication this might be coming the last time he was in town, but I have no idea how long ago that was.

"What are you going to do?" Mia asks sympathetically.

I shake my head and shrug, holding back a tear.

Mia reaches across and squeezes my hand. "You'll get through this just like you've gotten through every other adversity you've faced." Mia knows of Sammy. Not the details that Noah has, but the general nature of the relationship.

I pull it together. "Don't worry about me. You need to decide what you're going to do. I'm going to be sitting on the Texas Supreme Court for the foreseeable future. Living here because it's close to everything."

"But you need someone in your life. Without Noah, who is there?"

"I always have Louise." I half joke since Mia knows her well from the time all three of us were at Victor, Vargas and Utley.

"Yes, you always have Louise. She will keep you focused and let you know when you're off the reservation."

"So, what are you thinking about Henderson's offer?"

"It's not the first time I've thought of leaving. But it has the potential to be a good move in the long run. A more limited client list, for sure. Probably have to take a pay cut at least until we get established. I'd be a senior partner day one. Make me more responsible for my own work. There's a lot of appeal to that. But I'd miss the people at Victor, I'd miss the collegial discussions, the security of a big firm. The access to litigation resources and research, although modern technology has erased the advantage of the big firms in that regard. So, when it comes right down to it, the choices are pretty equal."

"Which way are you leaning?" I have to pull it out of her and I'm not quite sure why.

"You're aware of Henderson's reputation?" she asks cautiously.

There were unconfirmed rumors that Henderson was sleeping with one of the researchers at Ballard while he was still married. I'm not sure if this is what she's referring to as it was an unconfirmed rumor back then, what was that? Eight years ago? "I'm not sure."

"Part of the reason he wants to set up his own firm is Ballard has asked him to go elsewhere. Now this isn't what he's saying, but Tim made me aware of it. Said he didn't want me to make a decision about joining the firm and find out afterwards."

"I wasn't aware of that." I confirm.

"Seems he got one of the researchers there pregnant. She had an abortion at his insistence. But she regretted the abortion afterwards and committed suicide about a month ago."

So, the rumors were true, unfortunately for everyone, especially the woman. "How did it all come out? His involvement and the abortion?" I wonder aloud.

"One of the other researchers was aware the mistress was pregnant. She couldn't hide it from someone who sat right next to her and saw her every day. But then the other researcher noted her cubemate wasn't pregnant anymore. They talked about it. That was when it all came out about Henderson's role. Henderson's mistress's mother found her dead of an overdose about a week later."

"And then HR got involved." I advance the story. "Doesn't sound like a particularly good atmosphere to go into."

"That's the thing. Since it's all out in the open we can deal with his past behavior. We can make sure he doesn't get involved with the staff. If he wants to sleep with every woman who doesn't work for him in the whole city of Dallas, who am I to criticize? Why should I even care? So long as it's a consensual act, shouldn't be my concern."

"Was the sex consensual or was it a positional power thing where he could make or break her career?"

Mia shakes her head.

"If you don't know that answer I wouldn't get close to the situation."

"Tim's a good guy. He wouldn't go into this with Henderson if he thought there was an issue."

"Take this for what it's worth," I start. "In my experience, guys have less sensitivity to harassment issues. Some guys can be sitting right next to someone who is a serial harasser and not even notice."

Mia becomes introspective. "You know Tom was. A serial harasser."

I shake my head. "What happened between you?"

Mia looks at me, "I'm surprised you never asked before." Then she looks away, probably remembering things she'd rather forget. "Tom had the gentlest hands. His touch was so light you barely knew he was touching you. A caress he used to say. 'I caress you'. I can still hear him say that. When he was caressing me I loved it. The problem was he caressed most of the women who work at his dealership. But his caress is so light most of them weren't sure if he'd touched them or just brushed by. At least that's the story I got from more than one of them. Anyway, he focused in on Bonnie. Old fashioned name but from the stories I got before the divorce, she was a wild one in bed. Tom was all too willing to go along for a ride. Found out he paid for her fake boobs, and the nose job. Really changed her appearance. So much so she moved on to Mr. More Money. At that point Tom didn't have an outlet for all this extra happiness he wished to spread, so he went after the other hot women he hired. And women are attracted to BMWs to sell because the men who buy the expensive models clearly have the money." Mia shakes her head at a memory. "Janelle was next. She wasn't very smart and let herself get pregnant, but you know that part and what happened when I found out."

I nod even though I don't.

The Next Explosion

The next day I send a note to Noah. It is the hardest thing I've ever written. I tell him I am happy for him. Glad he has found someone worthy of him. Hope he will have a wonderful life with her and the children they will have together. The one word reply I get from him pretty much sums up my life to this point, at least as I see it right now. "Thanks."

There are so many ways I could interpret his response.

I'm sitting at my desk high up over Dallas, mulling on this one-word response when Louise comes in. No knock. No peeking in. She's just in front of my desk looking at me. "Are you more out of your mind than usual?"

"Probably. What did I do or not do this time?" I try to put a smile on it.

"You gave Fawn an impossible assignment for a brand new clerk."

"Fawn?" *who and what is she talking about?*

"Peterson versus the Texas Department of Transportation. Does it ring a bell? By the way, it's this pile…" she moves a couple files to reveal several more underneath. "…right here."

"Oh. You're talking about Miss Mouse." *Probably shouldn't have said that, but that is exactly what she reminded me of.*

Louise rolls her eyes as if I'll never get it. "Fawn is a very nice young woman. She may have led a sheltered life because of who her father is, but some things are crosses we must bear."

"Obviously I don't know who her father is." *I just might as well take my beating and get it over with.*

"Where were you that day? I know you were distracted but how can you forget a Hunt?"

"Hunt Oil." I toss out like I'm remembering, but I'm not since I wasn't here when the previous J'ne interviewed her.

"Okay Sherlock. Now that you have your first clue. What do you think happened when she went home last night and told Daddy Warbucks that she needs confidence?"

"He went out and bought it for her?" I suggest trying to be a smart ass since there is no redeeming this day.

"He called the Governor to complain about your attitude."

"Wonderful. So, when does the recall petition start? I'll sign."

"No. You don't get off that easy. The Governor had the temerity to tell Daddy Warbucks that the Warbuck stopped there. She is not going to discipline you or remove you or do anything at all. She told Fawn's father that he should hire Fawn into one of his companies. Let her practice patent law for the family. Then he can assess whether she needs confidence to do the job they assign, rather than expecting the State of Texas to do it for him."

"Oops," is all I can think to say. "So, why did you say I'm not getting off that easy?"

"Since you did such a stellar job with Fawn, who came in this morning and handed me her resignation, the Governor is giving you two more new grads for clerks for you to shape up."

Louise is about to leave when she gets another thought, "Oh, and the Governor sent you a personal message. It's in your inbox. Of course, you haven't read it yet or none of this would have been a surprise."

Then one more thought. "And Fawn also sent you a note that she won't be able to complete the assignment you gave her yesterday."

"Guess I know what I'm doing after I respond to the Governor."

"Copy me on that if you would. I'd like to see how you wiggle out of this one." And Louise is finally gone.

The Governor wanted to remind me that the Hunts provided a significant contribution that was part of my bundle. If I want to piss off those who are willing to donate much needed funds for campaigns that I need to find a replacement because the next election won't be cheaper than the last. My one-word response, since I learned from Noah, is simply, "Understood."

I pull forward the files Louise pointed out. I start reading through and detail a list of questions I need answers to. I start on that research which consumes most of the rest of my day. The issues aren't complex, I just need to understand how this case made it all the way to the Supreme Court.

I walk over to Café Momentum on my way home. It's a school for repeat offenders, designed to give them marketable skills working in a public serving restaurant. I always pay double the bill because the program behind this restaurant never has enough funding to serve the number of offenders who need the experience and job skills. The meal is always excellent, and I engage my waiter in conversation.

"What's your name?"

"LeVeon," is his curt reply.

"How long you been working here LeVeon?"

"Half a life-time. For me that's been about eight months. I'm a short timer. Another four months and I'll be working full time and making serious money. You know what I mean? Here I only get about half what I'd normally get. But they feed me and give me a place to stay. Half the time I'm in a class or something, people making sure I got the skills and habits to make it. The rest of the time I'm here waiting on folks like you."

"So, what's good tonight?"

"What I like is the New York Strip steak, but that's because I never had a steak in my life before I came here. These people take care of you. They want you to make it and keep out of trouble. You know? So, I'll always think of the people here when I have a steak. – oh, but I'm supposed to ask if you're vegan or gluten free?"

"Neither. But how is the fried chicken?"

"Best I've ever had, and I've had a lot of fried chicken where I come from."

"Gulf Shrimp?"

"I'm not big on shrimp. You know. Not all that much to them. Kind of rubbery if you ask me. But people who have them here say they're real good. So, if you like shrimp, absolutely. Do it."

"Okay LeVeon. You sold me. I'll try the Texas Pecan Salad and the Gulf Shrimp."

"Anything I need to know about how you want them shrimp prepared? Some people like them one way and others not so much. So, you got a favorite way of fixing them or something tell me now."

"Just make sure they're cooked. With shrimp that doesn't take long." I smile at LeVeon as he takes my menu and puts in the order.

I see Mack Henderson, the attorney trying to recruit Mia, sitting at another table by himself. I get up and walk over. "May I join you?"

Mack jumps up, startled. "Of course, your honor."

I point out to LeVeon that I've changed tables. He nods. "How are you Mack?"

"We're living in some interesting times."

"I understand you recently divorced," I push the conversation in the direction I want to go in.

Mack nods without saying anything.

"Transitions are always hard. But I'm sure you'll find your footing and get on with life."

"Thanks. You eat here often?"

"Once a week if I'm in town" I confirm. "They do important work with these kids."

"I come here for the food. You know us trial lawyers. We aren't trying to help anyone but our clients."

"I don't believe that, Mack. If you weren't interested in supporting these kids, you would be at McDonalds."

"They don't serve Texas Gulf Shrimp," he reveals his meal choice even though I didn't ask.

"I appreciate you're here and hope you'll keep coming."

My salad appears so, I begin to take bites during the conversation. "Mia tells me you've offered her a partnership in the new firm you're starting. Litigation only."

"Mia would give any new firm instant credibility."

I nod, "But one thing I've been wondering. You three are coming out of very large firms with strong multi-faceted relationships with their clients. If you are litigation only, how many of those firms will follow you?"

Mack shifts uncomfortably, "You were a managing partner. You spent your time looking for ways to lock your clients in. Everything from concierge service for the executives to complimentary home closings to get the bread and butter. We will only want to bill our clients for specific hours on a specific case. No fluff. No adding to bills to cover all the wrap-in services. Unbundling seems to be the trend these days. Everyone wants to eat Chinese. One from column A, and one from column B. Add egg rolls a fortune cookie and you're done. Each item is a la cart. You want to cut the bill? Don't order egg rolls. If you can get the best people at the lowest cost because our offices aren't in the nicest building, and we don't have expensive art work to study as we contemplate their case, well, that just means we're putting their hard earned money back in their pocket rather than ours."

"I see you've been working on your sales pitch." I acknowledge how smooth he has it down. "But what about the innuendos that follow you?"

Mack darkens. "What innuendos?"

I don't respond. I don't have to. Mack gets even more uncomfortable.

"Why are you bringing that up?" he finally responds angrily.

"From what I can see, your venture has a better chance of success without you."

"It's my idea." He drops his fork on his plate, making a ringing sound.

"Ballard and Strauss asked you to leave."

"Where do these rumors come from?" Mack looks around uncomfortably. "I wasn't asked to leave, I turned in my notice."

"Born of necessity since you are leaving Ballard and Strauss within the next thirty days."

"I've been thinking about doing my own thing for some time now. Been getting restless. You do the same thing for ten years the grass starts to look greener."

"How do you deal with the fact your mistress committed suicide?" I just lay it out there.

Mack stands up, not sure what to do, he finally throws down his napkin, "Excuse me." I watch him go to the men's room.

My shrimp arrive. While eating slowly I have eaten them all before Mack returns, shuffling and looking about the café.

He sits and picks up his napkin. "In life you make a never-ending series of decisions. Some turn out good, some turn out great and some just turn your life to shit." He hesitates before continuing, apparently thinking a moment about that last statement. "The problem is that when you make those decisions you can't see where they will take you. If I had a time machine and could visit my life five years from now, I would be able to decide what not to do when I came back. But that's not possible. So, we always have to flip the coin and hope we called the right side."

"Mack, you make it sound like every decision you make is made in a vacuum. It's not. You have all kinds of indications of how things will turn out. So, why are you struggling to apply the clues, the precedents and the cues you see to the decisions you make in your own life?"

"There was a time when life in this country was as simple as you just described. But we have the media that spews out this never-ending barrage overwhelming our senses. Buy this, try that. Life is good, life is bad, but can be better if you try and use our grand new product. And underlying all this media hype is a by-line. No one is responsible for your behavior. You can have it all. Hot and cold running sex? Come and take it. Drugs of any kind? Step right up. Don't worry about the cost or the consequences. Impulse control? That's so last century. Enjoy life.

Enjoy every minute of life. You don't need to leave anything behind. Spend it all right now. More will be there tomorrow. Someone will take care of you if it's not. There's this big long narrative that old fashioned virtue is dead. Live for now, not even today. This second. If it only lasts a second, well there's another right around the corner and you can catch that balloon and sail to the sun with the rest of us."

"Drugs?" I ask.

Mack looks at me like I'm crazy. And I have to interpret that as a 'well…yeah.'

"So, now that you've lost everything of value to you, your wife, your home, your job, your mistress, your response is I'm going out on my own where no one will hold me accountable."

"Hell no. If Anderson wants to be the Managing Partner that's okay by me. It's about getting back in the saddle. Picking up the pieces. Finding out if Humpty Dumpty can put himself back up on that wall. Yeah, I've taken a big fall. Flew too close to the sun like Icarus. My wings melted and here I am. Groveling on the ground like a broken dog. But I know where to find more wax. I've got the feathers in my head. All I need is a chance and I'll be up there flying again. Tim will make sure I don't get too close to the sun this time."

"Mack. Sex for you is a game. It blew up in your face twice now, but I've not heard one word about how you fix that in your life, other than you expect Tim to pull you off before the next explosion."

"Twice? How did you know about that?" Mack is almost in a panic.

Just Fine

On my walk back to my apartment I think about the discussion with Mack Henderson. It was disturbing to me that at the end he still had no more idea of why his new firm will crater than he did when I sat down with him. A waste of my time. I have a better idea of how to advise Mia about going over. Although she already knows I think it's a bad idea.

I walk down towards the Winspear Opera House, planning to cross the park to the other side of the highway tunneled beneath and down the three blocks to my apartment house. A pleasant walk this time most nights. But as I approach the Winspear I see shadows in a rising fog that looks just like the fog that brought me to this time. I detour towards the generator cove behind the massive structure and under the big metallic awning that I suddenly realize must be some kind of massive antenna for Elijah's device. As I step around the generator hiding his box, I find him standing there doing something, but I can't be sure what. "Elijah. What are you doing?"

I startle him. He jumps up about to fight me, I think. Recognizes me. "You shouldn't be here."

"Where should I be?"

"Not here. I'll come for you when I'm ready," he seems confused as to what to do with me. He's different, distracted, acting guilty about something.

"For what?"

"To make the next jump. I'm not ready."

Something's wrong here. And then I realize he shouldn't be here. He would have called if he was coming back.

"You sent him back, didn't you?" It suddenly becomes clear.

"What are you talking about?" I hear recognition in his voice, he knows I know.

"You're another Elijah who figured out how to override the portal closure on this end. The button Elijah turned off to keep anyone from following us. That was really for you." Great. So, now the Elijah I came here with is back in his old time, in the custody of the government, and the Elijah from this time has returned putting everything back where it was except me and the other J'nes.

"I'm not staying there so he can get a free ride on all the work I had to put in."

"What about me?" I have to ask since he's apparently locked out the Elijah who brought me here.

"What about you?" Elijah seemingly doesn't want to have anything to do with me.

"So, this is the world where I get off? The end of the line?"

"You're still you, aren't you? Getting to live a dream without having had to do all the hard work. Live through all the disappointments, all the annoying stupid questions, all the government types who come in and tell you they know more than you do about something they know absolutely nothing about. I haven't found one person here who understands my theory or has any idea how to build this device. You're free to go do what you're going to do. I don't need you. I'm doing just fine."

I pull my wrap around me trying to comprehend what has just happened. I watch Elijah walk away, apparently returning to his Chicago lab and the life he has made here, realizing my days of time travel are now over.

THE MOST SENSE

The door to my apartment recognizes me. That's good, I'm not sure I do at the moment. I open the door and find Mia at the kitchen table working. "Hi." I call as the door closes behind me. I touch Mia on the shoulder as I go by to the window to look out over the city lights that grow in intensity as the night takes hold moving the day aside.

"You look like you could use a glass of wine." Mia notes my unusual behavior.

I smile and nod. So, this is where I am. From this day forward, this is the life I have to live. No more excursions with Elijah. No life with Noah who's getting married in Nashville. A Texas Supreme Court Justice appointed by the Governor who isn't so happy with me at the moment because I tried to help someone.

I'm sure there are worse lives to live. I just need to bear down here and decide what I really want to do with this life now that it's mine for as long as I shall live. And that will be about eight years longer than I would have lived otherwise.

Mia brings the wine, clinks glasses but is still waiting for the toast. "To figuring out life." We clink again and each take a sip.

"I heard you had dinner with my new boss." Mia informs me.

"You turn in your resignation?" I have to ask to know how far down this path she's gone.

"This afternoon. I talked with Tim. Everything is under control. Tim is the Managing Partner and Mack is 'of Counsel'. At least that's his official title on the letter head."

"So, who really owns the firm?" I have to ask.

"Tim. Mack pretty much lost everything in his divorce and the payment he made to the family of his mistress."

"He made a payment to her family?" I didn't think Mack would part with a penny he didn't have to.

"Half a million, which just about wiped out all of his remaining savings after the divorce." Mia sounds like she at least respects Mack doing what was right.

If Mack isn't an owner… "Hold on. What's the firm's name?"

"Anderson and Associates." Mia informs me.

So, neither you nor Mack are Title partners?"

Mia shakes her head.

"So, why is Mack your new boss if he's of Counsel and neither a partner nor an associate?"

"What's on paper is to protect the firm. But in reality, Mack is the senior partner. I'll be working for him."

I turn away from Mia, look out at the night lights and take another sip of the wine. "Malbec?"

"Of course. That's your favorite at the moment, isn't it?"

I think about the conversation with Mack. All I can do is close my eyes and shake my head. After what seems a long time, but I realize isn't, I turn back to Mia.

"You seem to be struggling with the very idea of me going over." Mia notes.

"My discussion with Mack was often blunt and brutal, especially for me. You know how I hate to confront people."

Mia laughs since I have exactly the opposite reputation.

"Anyway. Mack said he expects Tim to keep him under control, with his sex addiction or whatever it is that drives his behavior. Only Tim doesn't know that's part of the role Mack is expecting him to play. This sounds like a recipe for disaster. Tim is going to have to be prepared to jettison Mack at the first indication he's gone off the reservation. He's going to have to be ready to fund the entire partnership until it's making money. This isn't going to be easy because the large firms, as you know, are doing everything to wrap up all the client's needs in a one price bundle."

"Mack has a counter to all that worked out." Mia responds convinced.

"I heard it. Some people will like the idea, others won't bite."

"Before you left Victor you did a strategic account review. The team identified accounts we were willing to let go elsewhere because overall, they weren't profitable for us. Those become our targets. Companies that don't want concierge service for the execs but want reasonable litigation costs when they need those services."

Here we go again. She's basing the whole thing on the Strategic Review Stevenson and the team did for me. Why does everything I did with the best of intentions come back to bite me and those I care about?

"That was five years ago. In that time the firms Victor didn't find profitable have made other legal arrangements. I doubt that many, if any, are still looking for legal assistance. And those that are will not be the firms you will want to represent."

Mia nods as she takes a sip of her drink. "We know that. By bringing on the best litigators in Dallas, we should be able to peel off work from the core accounts of the other firms. Particularly accounts that have used particular litigators in the past who have come over to us."

"That's always the theory. But in practice it's hard. You know the Managing Partners are always working the General Counsels of the big firms. Making sure they're happy and ensuring they believe they're getting the best teams to work on their needs."

"Lunch at the Club." Mia describes how it's done. "I'll be doing lunch at the club too. I'll have to if this is going to work. You got into the clubs. Thanks for opening the door for me."

I'm done with this discussion. "I still have reservations, but it sounds like you've decided. So, now it's time for me to drop the matter and wish you good luck." I hold up my glass once more. "To fulfillment."

Mia clinks again and we both take a sip.

"I wanted to talk with you about something related," Mia begins with a bit of trepidation in her voice. "But it's something I probably should have raised to you a long time ago."

I nod to continue.

"You and I have been good friends for practically our whole professional careers."

"We have." I acknowledge.

"When things got bad for me you took me in. You didn't have to do that, but the stars aligned. If you hadn't been here for me that transition would have been much harder. You were so supportive and helpful. The fact you didn't charge me any rent until I got my finances set was a godsend. No one else I knew would have done all the things you did and continue to do for me."

"But…" I say for her.

"It's time. I'm all healed up from those wounds. I'm ready to take on new challenges and make a name for myself apart from Victor, Vargas and Utley. You did. Two years ago. And look at you now."

"Yeah, a lot poorer on a government salary and a lot wiser because I won't make that mistake again." We both laugh.

"The point is it's time for me to move on." She finally gets it out. "Even though it's absolutely the worst time for me to do so since I won't even be sure what my salary is going to be until the firm gets stabilized. I need to get myself into the right mindset. Cheap apartment, cheap food and two buck chuck wines instead of grey goose."

I hug her.

"I understand why you're thinking this is the best thing for you." I begin my counter. "But let me give you another scenario. When you left your husband what you needed to establish yourself was flexibility. Even though you had a good salary, until you knew what your expenses were going to be having the flexibility not to have to pay rent had to be helpful."

"I know where you're going…"

"Let me finish. The choice is absolutely yours. If you decide to leave, I'll support that just like I've supported every other decision you've made. But if you decide that staying on here gives you the flexibility to invest in the firm, to pay the salaries due every week from your savings because the fee income doesn't cover it? That is absolutely fine with me too. I enjoy having you here. Someone to talk to after the day is over. Someone who is objective and not in the middle of what I'm dealing with all day. So, my proposal is: you stay on, I pay the rent and expenses and you invest your cash in the firm to make sure you can cover your bills. When the firm cash flow is continuously positive and you've taken a full salary for six months, then move out to your own place. I think that makes the most sense to me."

On Time

The night sky caps the street lights from below as I draw in and take strength from the Dallas skyline. Mia is deep into planning for her move to the new firm. Anderson and Associates. I'm glad Mia is willing to stay a bit longer. It may not be six months cash flow positive, but even if it's three months I probably have a year with a roommate to keep me from being lonely. And my offer was as much, if not more, for me as for her. It's crazy. A little over two weeks ago I was fine living alone, running each and every morning, going to work for ungodly hours and trudging home for a light bite before falling into bed. Now that I've had two different roommates, I find I'd much rather live this life than that one. Have someone to share my life with rather than live it alone.

Okay. The next problem for me is to figure out how I want this to be the launching point for the rest of my life. Elijah gave me two chances to find something better than where I was. This is the second. Now his older self has revoked the travel privileges to find something that might be even better. The Nirvana Elijah was looking for, although I doubt he had any idea of what it would take for me to find such a place for myself. We are such different people. I have to thank him though. He opened my eyes to what the world, life and decisions mean. And I've found that even what would seem an insignificant decision that I'm making can have dramatic effects on me and a whole lot of other people in this world and the others that inhabit the multi-verse as Elijah has described it.

Noah's gone and Mia is leaving sometime in the next year. So, I need to widen my social circles. Start looking for someone who will be willing to spend time with a woman who is at the top of her profession but still looking for the right person. One to explore life and the world we are living in as well as accompany me over the decades to come.

Not an easy project but I think it needs to be my top personal priority.

The second thing I need to do is start planning my post Texas Supreme Court career. What is it I want to do? Go back to Victor, Vargas and Utley? There are worse places I could go. I could stay right here with this same view of the city. But I could also look for a different challenge. Doing what? Going to Washington? Joining the staff of the International Trade Representative? No, that's not on the table. But what about a Deputy Attorney General? Having been a Supreme Court Justice in Texas that would seem a logical career progression. Unless of course I'm re-elected for another term. I still have four years on this term. If re-elected, I'll be on the bench for another ten years. At that point I'll probably want to do something else having served twelve years. That's longer than I practiced law before being appointed.

And then there's the whole legacy thing. What is it I want to leave behind that will cause people to remember I even passed this way once? That's really a hard concept to wrap my mind around. I've done a lot of things no one thought I could. Youngest Managing Partner at VV&U. Youngest Texas Supreme Court Justice. Is that my legacy? That I did things at a younger age than anyone else? What does that really mean? To me it means a lot of other folks did the same things I did, it just took them longer. That means I'm not so special. Just in a hurry. And when it comes to law that isn't necessarily a good thing.

Mia comes over and gives me a hug, "Did I tell you I really like your hair long? Makes you look ten years younger. And since none of us are getting younger, that's a good thing."

I kiss her on the top of her head. "I appreciate all the positive feedback I can get."

"I also wanted to say thanks." Mia gets quiet. "I know you have a lot of questions about this new law firm but you're willing to support me anyway. Not everyone would do that. And almost demanding that I stay here when I thought it would be better to go? You were able to show me there's no sense putting more stress on myself than I need to. You're absolutely right. This isn't going to work out as we planned. It's going to take longer than we imagine to go cash flow positive."

I take a sip of my wine, although the glass is almost empty by now. "You're my family, Mia. Together we can weather any storm. And when you leave? You'll still be family." So, is this the end? When Mia leaves, I'm all alone in this world? I'll still have Stevenson accompanying me to the symphony. I'll still have all the faces that talk at me from the many community boards I now sit on. I'll still have Louise chastising me for one or another failing. She is always right. And I'll have all the petitioners of the court who want to plead their cases. That should be enough for most people. But I still feel the vacuum that pulls me out of myself. And that vacuum is love. None of the people I've described other than Mia loves me. And Mia and I have a love of friendship. I never thought of our relationship in any other terms. If anything, I wish I had more friends I could describe the same way. Stevenson and I have a friendship based on common interest. We both love symphony. We love listening to composers who can change our mood, change our perceptions of the world and fill us with wonder at how highly skilled individuals can decompose works, write parts for different instruments and hear it all in their heads without a single note being played. Stevenson and I love something in common. We have built a friendship around that common love. Totally different than the love I'm looking for.

It's time to go to bed, but I'm not tired. I turn off the lights so Mia can sleep, but I return to the window to commune with the City of Dallas that has nurtured me and permitted me to become what I am.

My cell phone rings. Who would be calling me at this hour? I go look for the phone. It is on the countertop near the sink where I had washed out wine glasses over an hour ago. I look at the number. It's Elijah. Why would he be calling and why at this hour?

"Hello?"

"I can't explain but meet me on the rooftop of your building at 5:00 am."

"Elijah?" He's gone.

5:00 am. Five hours from now. That means no shower. How can I possibly meet him then and why on the rooftop? He was very clear that I am extraneous to his plans. He is good with where he is in the greater scheme of things. I have no part to play in them. This is probably a hallucination. The Elijah I know is long gone back five years to suffer at the hands of the Feds as the Elijah of this era has. But there was something in his voice. Something – what was it? Optimism? Enthusiasm? It wasn't the jaded Elijah of this era. It was the boyish Elijah who has been dragging me around the space-time continuum to explore new vistas, new worlds and new opportunities to be more than we could be where we started.

The Elijah I met at the Winspear had been beaten down by diminished expectations. The one on the phone sees nothing but new horizons. I know which one I'd rather be with, although the one from this era didn't offer that as an option. So, somehow the Elijah I've known and traveled with is back in the game even though he was pulled out of his great opportunity to get laid by a jealous older version of himself who he somehow must have caught totally by surprise. But then since I'm dealing with different versions of the same intellect, it's an interesting match of wills to see who will succeed. At the moment the older and wiser version seems to be in the driver's seat. But somehow, the naïve and idealistic version of himself has found a way back. At least I think it's the younger version. What if I'm wrong?

So, the real question I have to answer is will I get any sleep tonight or will I simply sleep right through the rooftop rendezvous at five am?

I try to think about what I need to do to prepare. So far, I've shown up in running gear and cell phone. What should I be bringing since I really have no idea of what to expect? If I'd not been coming back to my known apartment I probably would have been totally out of luck since I didn't even have a credit card on me. This time I need to be at least a little smarter. I probably ought to go check out the route to the roof. What if it's locked and I can't get out? But for some reason I thought there was a pool or something up there. Maybe the pool is on another floor. Whatever it is, I need to be able to ensure I can get to the roof and if not be able to call Elijah at 5:00 to tell him. But which Elijah will answer if I call? And how did he work it so he could call me, and the local version didn't know it?

This is all way too difficult to understand. I'm sure there's a logical answer. I'm sure much of it will become clear once I've had a chance to talk with Elijah. But at the moment I'm totally confused about what I'm supposed to do, where we're going and how that will make things better for either or both Elijah and me.

I go out in the hall and look for the stairwell to the roof. I find it at the other end of the hallway, of course, and go into the stairwell to find the doorway up. There's a ladder and a door at the top. I climb the ladder and finally reach the door. There's a sign, FIRE ESCAPE ONLY. If it's a fire escape it can't be locked. So, I check the door, it opens; although it's clear it hasn't been opened often or recently. I step out on the roof and look out at all of Dallas around me. A brisk wind blows in my face. This is why I never go out on the balcony. Too windy. Too far down. Hopefully Elijah will be on time.

Crater the Future

5:00 am comes when it promised. It finds me making my way up those same stairs with trepidation, having barely slept. This time I'm wearing work clothes since I have no idea where I'll come out, which Elijah may show up, and or whether an Elijah will actually be here. It may have been a dream, day dream or worse, a figment of my imagination. Entirely possible that my mind is trying to cope with all of the whiplash changes of the last few weeks. When I left the Winspear after having met this era's version of Elijah I was pretty deflated. Focused only on how I make it with this hand I've been dealt. But the more I dug in, the more I knew I could succeed. It was only a matter of deciding, even though I am unhappy with some of the things I learned about others I care about and myself.

I push the door open. The stars are twinkling. Thankfully, the wind has died down a bit, but is still strong. I'll need to plant my feet carefully to make sure I'm not blown about. I have my purse this time and have a store of things that will hopefully be helpful no matter where Elijah takes us. One thing that keeps coming back to me is that he said something about he had figured out from the new theory updates how to extend the range of worlds we could access without hopping. What did that mean? I don't know. Hopefully I won't find out now. So far, all movement has been within five years. How much further can we go? Will it be forward or back?

I let the door close behind me. I stand the best I can into the wind on the landing by the door access. I look around for the fog. For the magnetic field that enables me and him to cross into another time. But why here? Why an inaccessible point by other than those of us who live in this house? But the more I think about its Elijah could be trying to arrange a meeting at a point where his current version would not be able to interfere. I can hope that's what this is all about.

I think about Mia sleeping below. I hope if I do leave this time and place, the version of me that comes will respect the deal we made last night. Mia seemed so relieved that I had her back.

It occurs to me I should be able to see the Winspear from here if I but climb around to my right. I do so in hopes I might be able to see the beginnings of the magnetic wave, if that's what the fog represents. I do so. As I get to the right place, I see a fog rising from the metal awning that covers the exterior of the Opera House. A little late, but I could easily have been late as well. The fog seems to rise, which I don't remember from my one previous transition where I could actually see what was happening. Elijah hasn't explained how he pulled off the court house exchange, but then I've not really pressed him on it either.

The fog seems to be coming in this direction. Rising higher. And unlike the previous fog I can't see movement within. Can't see shapes or figures moving about in the fog. What's different this time? What has Elijah learned from his older self to enable this different approach to inter-dimensional transit? Wasn't that Spencer's term?

I find myself fascinated by the rising fog, following its rise. Suddenly I realize I should look around to see if there is anything that might put me in peril up here. I see the lights of Reunion Arena, the more distant lights of broadcast towers and even further off the runway lights at DFW airport. But nothing up here would make me concerned for my safety. So, I go back to watching the rising fog. In only a few more minutes it seems to engulf Cirque. Now I can't see more than a foot from me. But then I feel a strong hand grip mine and pull me forward. Do I go or stay? Is this Elijah or some sinister force leading me to my doom? But then I see Elijah's face turn towards mine, feel the electric pulse on my skin. I seem to be some other place as the wind no longer presses against my face or causes me to stand into it.

"Where… when are we?" is all I can think of to say.

Elijah doesn't answer, but rather waits for the fog to lift. I stand quietly with him. He's now wearing an MIT t-shirt. Must have found it in his other Elijah's apartment. I assume it is the same one who left me for the airport two days ago. I have so many questions for him, but I know now is not the time to begin asking them.

"Welcome to a different time, a time when no one will ask us to do as they please, but a time when we can do as we please.

"I'll ask it again, when are we?"

"1956."

I don't know what to say. I let that scenario run through my mind. It takes only a second for flashing lights to start sending out the questions. "There is no me or you here yet."

"Correct," Elijah happily responds.

"So, there's no one to replace me in the future."

"Solves a major problem for both of us doesn't it?" Elijah has no idea what I'm talking about.

"I need to go back. I made commitments to people. They're counting on me. I can't just disappear and never return without being replaced with another me. I'm a justice on the Supreme Court of the State of Texas. If I suddenly disappear and another version of me doesn't show up that's going to create all kinds of issues. Bring attention to what we're doing."

Elijah seems stunned by my reaction.

"You have to take me back," I demand.

Elijah shakes his head, "Or we can send someone from a different time to that future and let them deal with it. Come back here afterwards."

"What if we return the version of me who was there originally to that time? Just as the version of you who lived then restored himself?"

"We could try it." Elijah removes a device from his pocket and starts entering code. The fog soon appears and wells up around us. "I will have to leave you there when I pick her up and then I will return for you. It shouldn't take long but be prepared to wait if it's not immediate."

I nod and feel the electric pulse on my skin, covering my body from head to toe. Elijah is gone. It seems the fog resides around me for a long time. Occasionally I see a shadow moving, but no one comes near. No body appears out of the mist.

I hope the fog will remain in place. I wonder what happens when there is a hole in time. When someone who was there is suddenly transited elsewhere and no one else comes to replace them? If this version of me, who had been a Supreme Court Judge, came back to be a Managing Partner and I replaced her there is a linear chain. But if a link is missing, what happens? How is the chain continued when a person appears in the future who was in that role in the past without someone in between?

Elijah would say 'don't worry about it. That's mother nature's problem to solve.' But I'm worried. I've made promises to people. I can't just leave without a plan for how those promises will be kept. I'm allowing friends and the people who put me in a position of trust down if I don't provide a plan for how the duties I've assumed will be discharged.

The sun is rising. The dawn of a day I was never to see because Elijah had ripped me from the time continuum before it and returned me five years later.

I'm at the Winspear, near the generators, waiting. Apparently, Elijah doesn't believe anyone will come here looking for him since in this time only he knows it is here. But what about his future self? Having been here, will he decide to return on his terms knowing so much more? Knowing how to manipulate things to his benefit?

The sun is starting to rise. It will be light soon. Elijah doesn't like to do this in the light. Too many witnesses. But then again, he did switch me in the middle of a court session. So, there's more tricks up his sleeve than he wants me to realize.

Is it possible Elijah really isn't the prodigy he would have everyone believe, but someone who grew up to control dimensional portals? Someone who benefitted from what someone else developed?

I'm not liking what I'm thinking because it could fit the known facts. But what I'm most concerned about are the unknown facts of this matter. The ones I can't see. The ones that could crater the future of people who are important to me. If I was there, I could help prevent that. But being back in 1956 I can't do a thing to help them.

Bubbles

I'm sitting on the portal box, as I've come to think of it, when Elijah hurriedly peeks around the corner of the massive generator. He seems to be in a hurry, but I am not. "I need to know about this whole time, place, timeline, whatever it is that you're playing around with."

"You want to know the theory behind our movement between dimensions now?" Elijah clearly doesn't think he has time to go through all this now.

Elijah makes a puzzled face, like he's trying to figure out how to put this so I'll understand it.

I interrupt his concentration, "Think horsy ducky."

Elijah laughs. "Okay. Horsy ducky. Think of a bubble bath. You have a tub. In the beginning there was one bubble that contained the universe as we know it."

"One universe, but now we're in a bubble." I try to follow this.

"Early man thought the earth was carried about the universe on the back of a turtle, so there are stranger concepts or theories people have had in the past."

"A turtle or a bath tub. Think the bath tub more probable, but what do I know? Go on." *Interesting, but not terribly relevant*, I think.

"In my theory, just like a bubble bath, that one bubble splits and now there are two bubbles with a universe in each one. The second universe is just like the first at the point where they split. But since universes are populated with people who have choice, the individuals in each bubble may make different decisions and get different results.

The important thing is the bubbles keep splitting, moving forward in time and each bubble is at a different place in time when the new bubble splits off. So, there are bubbles out there at all different points in time independent of any change that might take place in the source bubble's past or future."

"Hold on. Let me explore one thing at a time. So, in one bubble I'm a trial lawyer, in the next I'm the Managing Partner and in still another bubble I'm a Texas Supreme Court Justice."

"Correct."

"But all three of me could have been the same person making the same decisions and getting that one set of results."

"Yes, that's entirely possible." Elijah prefaces, "But in one other bubble I visited you had gone to the International Trade Representative's Office in Washington. So, there are other outcomes based on decisions each of your selves make. An example was your friend Wainwright. He was the managing partner in your original world but a trial lawyer in the other two. In his case based on a different decision that others made about him."

I nod, "Got that. So, talk to me about replacement. Up until this last transit, when I moved from one bubble to another, the version of me in the bubble I'm going to is exchanged for me. I go into her bubble and she goes to mine. I don't see her at the exchange, I can't talk to her, nothing."

"Correct. The bubbles are in equilibrium until a portal opens. When a new element enters, if there is a corresponding element already in the bubble, it is moved to the bubble from which the exchange in made."

"That's why you got sent back when your future self figured out how to access the portal in your original bubble."

"I outsmarted myself on that one." Elijah seems embarrassed.

"Does this help?"

"I'm getting there. But what about the J'ne who was here you took back to five years from now, which was her original bubble. What happens here now that there's no J'ne here? I'm assuming the one who was here is still in the bubble I came from."

"She is." Elijah confirms. "We could bring her back, but since the Texas Supreme Court Justice J'ne is in a different bubble, the fact that the J'ne who was here isn't won't affect her future in that bubble."

"How many bubbles are there?" I ask trying to understand how many different futures may be out there.

"I have no idea. Billions maybe. It all depends on when the bubbles started splitting. No one knows the answer to that question." Elijah answers simply.

"So, a bubble starts from a point that comes from another bubble."

"Right."

"So, if I'm not in one bubble, that doesn't mean I won't be in another already in the future."

"Correct." Elijah is getting anxious to move on.

"What you're telling me is if we leave here and go back to 1956, that won't affect the bubble we left where I was the Supreme Court Justice, because you moved the version of me who was there back there. That leaves this bubble with no J'ne Wilcox. And that won't be a problem to the people here."

"If we go back before we were born, there will by definition be at least one bubble without us."

"And others splitting off from that one." I observe. "Not a very horsy ducky explanation. I think I understand what you're suggesting, but I still have no idea how this all works."

"The only question is are you ready to move on?"

A thought reoccurs to me that I had while waiting here for him. "You're intent on going back to 1956. Wouldn't you rather get your university education in the future, where what you learn will be so far advanced from what you would learn in 1956? Why not go twenty-five years in the future when you would be well past the government's custody?"

Elijah shakes his head, "I saw what I had learned at MIT. My future self was well ahead of where I am. If I were to go into the future, I would have to step into the shoes of a me who knows so much more than I do. I'd struggle to keep up, let alone contribute as I want. In 1956 there would be no one my equal. I could be the next Albert Einstein."

"I've heard people say that about you already. I'm still not sold that 1956 is the time for us. I'd be about the same age as my grandparents. Why 1956?"

"That was the year Marty McFly went back to in 'Back to the Future'. It was a time of innocence, a time when people were open to new ideas, willing to share, to help people succeed. It just seems like a welcoming time."

"You can be Doc Brown tinkering in your garage with your very own time machine," I suggest, to complete his fantasy.

"I don't exactly have the hair for it."

"And you know, it wouldn't be at all like the movie." I try to be gentle ending his fantasy. "That bore only a mild resemblance to the world at that time. The Civil Rights movement was just gaining steam. The first advisory forces were sent in to Vietnam. The Brits and French tried to seize the Suez Canal from Egypt with the help of the Israelis. There was a lot going on in this country and the world. And all that was bubbling up, if I can use one of your terms."

Elijah sheepishly admits, "I don't know much about history. I've had my head into the science and math books since I can remember. That's why all this government wanting to take me into custody and turning me into a lab rat, well, it's just a bit overwhelming. I never thought about the government as anything other than the people we elect every fall."

"We have to make a decision." I inform him. "We are several days now past the point where the government moved your family. You're not supposed to be here."

"You may not have noticed but we're not where you think we are. We're a year earlier."

Herniated Rattlesnakes

"Are you saying you'd rather stay here than go back to 1956?" Elijah asks although it is clear he would rather just go back.

"Can you live without your cell phone?" I respond looking at the device in his hand.

"What does that have to do with the decision of now or then?"

"There were no cell phones then, no Google, no Facebook." I point out. "People had to talk to each other face-to-face because the only telephones were land lines. You often found there were other parties on your line, and you had to wait your turn."

"1956? That can't be right."

"Cell phones didn't become common until the early 1990s." I inform him.

Elijah looks at the cell in his hand. Apparently thinks about all the things he uses it for. "Let's make a deal. We'll try here first. See what happens. If we need to pull the plug, then we go all the way back to prehistoric times."

"1956 isn't pre-historic, but it was certainly pre-technology. That's why I asked you about going to school back then. There's so much you take for granted that just wasn't invented yet."

Elijah looks unsure for probably the first time since I've known him. "You need to get to work and I need to go to school." Elijah realizes. "Talk at 7:30?"

"That should work."

Elijah surprises me by giving me a hug, "Thanks." And he's off to school. At least I'm dressed for work so I can go right in and not be obviously late.

Of course, Louise is in. She looks the same no matter which year or which role she's playing for me. She looks up as I pass by her desk. Obviously, something about my appearance catches her attention. She follows me into my office. As I bring up my computer, she just looks at me like I should know something, but I don't and don't want to admit it to her.

The computer comes up. I check my calendar first. And of course, the first thing I note is I'm supposed to be meeting with the management committee and the meeting started half an hour ago.

"Do you have a copy of the agenda?" I ask Louise who is clearly marveling at something.

"On your desk." Of course, I have no idea where. So, I start looking and immediately Louise goes to the other pile and pulls it out.

"Thanks. We're in…"

"The client conference room."

I walk past Louise, who stops me. "You were sitting on something dirty." She wipes down the back of my skirt and then releases me. "You can thank me later."

As I walk into the meeting, I see there are little groups talking amongst themselves, I take my seat and, "Pleased to see we've gotten through most of the agenda items in our private discussions, so would someone like to inform me of which ones still need our attention?"

Stevenson understands my intent. "I think we can skip down to the hiring freeze."

"Thank you. Glad to see you've used your time together productively. As I understand it the hiring freeze has had the desired effect of stabilizing our cash flows and restoring the target partner equity. So, do we take the freeze off?

Charles Utley Junior is the grandson of one of the founders. He is the firm's only ERISA attorney, which is a federal law on employee retirement income security, essentially pensions. And since the firm's only expert retired as Charles was reaching the minimum time to be considered for partnership, it became an easy decision for the partners. Bring young Charles up, since his grandfather was the most senior partner at that time. "Yes Charles?"

"Of course, I believe in keeping our powder dry for the storms periodically plaguing us, but I just happen to need someone to help me do research. As the only partner in the practice in my field I don't get to ask for help from any of the rest of you. So, my staff associates must be out of proportion. It's just the nature of what I do."

It doesn't come across as a complaint, really. More a whine from a guy who feels he doesn't get the respect he deserves given the revenues he brings in month-after-month from a stable of clients who have to keep up with annual changes from various Federal oversight agencies. I understand why Charles is making this request. And it really has nothing at all to do with his workload given the data we have started to collect on billable hours in each area. It's all about respect from his partners. And respect is a major issue for the grandson of one of the founders who decided to pursue a niche passion rather than the bread and butter contracts, oil and gas, and utilities work.

"Does anyone else feel they simply must start replacing retiring individuals?" I phrase the question in this manner because, again, going back to the data we are collecting on billable hours and retirement dates anticipated no one should be in a crisis if we keep the hiring freeze in place at least through the end of the year and quite possibly into next spring.

"I understand the hiring freeze only affects support staff, but this might be the right time to discuss a strategic hire opportunity." This comes from Colton Reynolds Jr. a mid-tier litigator who I know for a fact was not in agreement with making a woman, much less me, the Managing Partner. He felt as qualified and a better developer of new clients from all the community involvement leadership roles he has taken on.

"I understand Ballard and Strauss just announced their new partners. One of their best young litigators was overlooked. I happened to have drinks with him last night to discuss him joining the board of the Heart Association. I think if we were willing to consider offering a fast track to partnership, we might be able to pick him up. That would give us entre to several companies we've been working for years."

I instantly think of Mack Henderson, but I can't reveal what I know that happens in a different bubble. Besides if I were to try to explain any of this I'd probably be taken out in a restraining jacket.

Of course, Charles Utley asks the question, "Which associate do you think is one of their best young litigators?" The condescension is dripping as Charles doesn't have much respect for Colton either.

"Mack Henderson." Colton responds without hesitation, apparently hoping to get support from the other litigation partners. But the silence is complete. "He has an excellent record of wins." Now Colton is having to plead the case which apparently, he didn't expect.

Sid Shelton, one of our oil and gas partners clears his throat. Sid speaks slowly. He also uses colorful language that everyone in the room breathlessly awaits. "Ah've been in a courtroom with yer Mister Henderson." Silence while Sid formulates his next sentence. "Ah've been more impressed by a herniated rattlesnake that can't raise his tail to rattle. Come to think of it, Ah have been more impressed by a blind roadrunner. Now that was at least amusin'."

"I take it you wouldn't be interested in talking with Mack?" Colton just can't seem to get out of his own way. He should be in full retreat after Sid's evaluation since Sid is the Chairman of the partnership committee. But it's also clear that Sid became chairman of the partnership committee specifically because his predecessor ramrodded Colton through.

"Ah wonder why ah talk with yew sometimes. No, most the time. No, all the time." Sid is just waiting to see what Colton does next.

"In that case would someone give me an idea how we can get business from some of Ballard and Strauss' better clients?"

"Yore brain must be 'bout the size of a gnat's. Don't yew get it? We like it when Ballard and Strauss' clients sue arrrs. Someone got to rep'sent 'em 'gainst us. Court don't let us rep'sent both sides."

Colton looks like he's gearing up for one more go at Sid, but I intercede. "As the partnership committee as represented by its chairman has indicated no interest, I think we should go on to the next item."

Bein' Yew

The day did not get any better. Charles absolutely had to see me about hiring an associate this time. Something about one of his primary accounts putting their ERISA legal work out to bid. This was immediately followed by Colton coming to see me about how to improve his relationship with Sid. I couldn't tell him to go back to law school and get A's rather than B minus on all his courses. But Colton is right. He's our community face because he's on every community board. Maybe I should remove his legal load and just name him VP of External Affairs. At least then Sid wouldn't think we would be embarrassing ourselves.

Towards the end of the day Louise comes by and waits for me to get off the phone. She then closes the door and sits down. Louise never sits down in my office. She looks at me like I'm a ghost or something. "I don't know how you do it. One day you look like Mother Theresa and the next you come in here looking like the current teeny bop singing sensation of the moment. What's the deal?"

"I take it you don't approve of my appearance?"

"I'm not your mother, although obviously you would benefit if yours was closer."

"And you think I'm irresponsible because I couldn't make it to my own meeting on time."

"This firm has always been led by example." Louise is resolute. "If you want your attorney's blowing off client meetings then being a half hour late may be acceptable."

"I think I turned that one around with the partners."

Louise rolls her eyes, like she's thinking 'here she is going off thinking she's found a way to dance around her own funeral pyre'. "Go on. I can't wait to hear this one."

"I asked Stevenson to advise me which agenda items they had not resolved in their small groups and we picked up there. Didn't go back over half of the agenda because they indicated they used the first half hour to work through them. Creates an incentive that they can get back to billable hours quicker if they use their time with or without me more productively."

"That's the message you hope they took away." Louise reminds me. "What's the message they probably took away?"

"It was a good use of their time?" I respond although I see where she's going.

"Don't think so. What they took away is half of the nonsense on your agenda can be done away with because no one cares about it."

I see the truth to what she's saying. After all, Louse has been here a lot longer than I have. She has worked for the last three Managing Partners. So, what do I do now? Find a more effective way to lead. But according to Louise I'm a walking disaster. Although the firm prospers under my leadership, so somewhere along the way I must figure it out. Or… just maybe the firm prospers despite me. Could events put us in the cross hairs of the major cases, and we knock them out of the park? Not because of me, but because I have the best and brightest counsel on my team? Is half of leadership just being in the right place at the right time? I'm convinced you can be the best and strongest possible leader, but if you're on the wrong team, no one will ever know.

"Louise?"

She looks at me without answering since I have her attention.

"What do I need to start doing right now to turn this all around?"

Louise laughs. "Do you have any idea how many of your predecessors asked me that same question?"

I shake my head.

"All of them. Do you know who asked it sooner than any of the others?"

Again, I shake my head.

"You have. I view that as a good sign. Means you're listening. Maybe you're not so full of yourself that you think there's only one way to lead this motley crewe of barristers. And I really think that's an accurate view of them, although if you repeat that to anyone, I'll deny it." Louse smiles at me and seems to relax. "What you need to start doing right now, and don't look back, is doing exactly what you want them to do. Walk tall. Walk proud. Never make excuses. Own your performance, but tell them immediately what you're doing to fix your mistakes and the lesson you've learned. Hold them and yourself accountable. Unabashedly sell the firm, sell them and sell what we mean to the community and our clients. Does that make sense?"

"What about delivering performance?" I have to ask, unsure how to phrase that.

"Every lawyer here, every staff member here, every subcontractor we employ has a stake in that. You can't deliver performance. All you can do is steer us away from disasters. At the same time, you need to hold everyone accountable to support their clients the best they can."

"Who taught you all this? You've got the language down."

"All of your predecessors." Louise reflects. "Everyone I've worked for has taught me something about what makes us great and what ensures our success. I've been fortunate to still be here to share that all with you."

"I take it you'll remind me of the lessons you've learned when you see I'm not doing it right?"

"Doing it right? That's not the issue. That you're not doing it. Now that will be the issue. Leading the performance you want, by doing the things they have to do to achieve it. It's simple."

"But I'm not in the court room that much anymore. I'm not researching cases, which is most of what they do. How can I show them what needs to be done if my day is very different than theirs?"

"You're not listening." Louise pushes back. She gets up. "I was so hopeful for you. First to ask the key question, but last to understand the answer."

"Wait, wait, wait. Are you going to just watch me sink if I'm really blowing it?"

Louise shakes her head with an enigmatic smile, "Leadership is active rather than reactive; it's walking the talk; it's accepting and assigning; enforcing accountability. Start there."

Louise walks out shaking her head, but somehow, I get the impression she's smiling all the way back to her desk.

Great. I know less than my assistant. So, where do I start to turn this ship? I decide to wander down the hall to see Sid. I know he will pass away about four years from now, so I need to treasure him while I have him.

"Knock, knock." I appear in his door. His office shows the thirty plus years of accumulated knowledge and experience in the oil and gas fields of West Texas. The wild rough and tumble of men who carved fortunes from some of the most inhospitable lands on this planet. And in that service, they fueled the rise of a civilization that would not look at all like what I see out my window without their dedication to purpose.

"Yo, Missy. Yew had yer come to Jesus with Louise yet?"

How did he know?

"Ev'ryone o' yer predecessors went through the same learnin' curve. So, now yer lookin' to find out what yew don't know."

"You're a wise man, Sid." I come in and sit down since he hasn't told me to go away yet.

"That's why every one o' yew come see old Sid."

"First of all, thank you for handling the Henderson issue."

Sid closes one eye to look at me, "What yew not tellin' us?"

"You confirmed my estimation of the man. I just didn't want to try to influence the partners when my view may be diametrically opposed to what you all know."

"Yew ain't listenin' to Louise."

Oh god, I've screwed up already and it's only been twenty minutes.

"Yew know somethin', yew need to stand up and tell ev'ryone of yer peers what yew think and why. If yew're arrr leader we'll listen. If yew have good reason we'll be with yew. But if yew're just on an ego trip. Forget it. We'll have no trouble tellin' yew to get yer head out yer ass."

"Noted." I respond with a half-smile. "But what I really want to know Sid, is how do I not screw this up?"

Sid gets a wide Cheshire cat smile. "Missy, you ain't gonna screw up nothin'. We didn't put yew in this job b'cause we like yew. We put yew there b'cause we see the fire, determination to be the best and the incredible energy yew bring to the role. We know we're gonna be better b'cause of yew."

"But where do I start?" I'm not getting answers but more

platitudes.

"Yew start by bein' yew."

The Professor

Sid gave me his usual bear hug and sent me on my way. I just love him as a human being and need to treasure every minute I get to spend with him.

About seven-thirty I get a call on my cell. Elijah. "How was your day?" I can tell by his tone of voice that his wasn't great.

"I learned a few things. Did you?"

"Same stuff I learned last year."

"Sorry, but what can you expect? Any chance you can get moved up into AP classes?"

"I'm taking graduate courses now. Would need permission to take doctoral level."

"Maybe I can intercede on your behalf." I don't know if I can, but I would think the school district would have to respond to someone who represents a significant community employer like I do. I'd be willing to go to bat for him.

"Let's talk about that if we're still here on Friday."

"How are things at home?"

"I found the paper I wrote that brought me to the attention of the government. I haven't sent it in yet. You were right."

"My advice? Burn that paper. You don't want anyone finding it."

I hear the silence at his end and realize there is more to the story. "There may be a problem."

"Who has a copy?" I know exactly what he's going to say, but let him tell me.

"My physics professor. I asked him to give me comments before I sent it in."

"How long has he had it?"

"Only a couple days. If I'm lucky he hasn't gotten to it yet. I know he has a lot of papers to read, but he also knows I have a deadline on submission."

"You need to get hold of him tomorrow and ask him to send it back to you. Tell him you've discovered some errors or something."

I can try." Doesn't sound particularly convinced it will make any difference.

"Do we need to come back two weeks ago? Before you submitted it?"

Elijah doesn't answer.

"What aren't you telling me?"

"Bubbles aren't that close together yet." He admits. "Has to be at least a year."

"So, we come back a year ago. We're only trying to find a future where you're not wanted by the government. There have to be more of them than where you're wanted."

"That's just it. All the new bubbles from here are after I sent in the paper."

"Hold on. I'm probably the last person you want trying to figure out this whole bubbles bisection theory."

"That's an interesting name, I'll have to remember it."

Something occurs to me. "You said I was assigned to your case, but you didn't think the version of me that existed in this time was up to winning."

"I went ahead and saw she was not."

"Was that your first trip?" I'm trying to get a time line here.

Elijah nods. "When I went back, I found you in court. You were larger than life. Prepared, succinct, direct, there was no arguing with you. I was just blown away by your courtroom performance and so was the judge."

"So, what's the issue?" I'm not getting the answer I'm looking for.

"You haven't gone home yet."

Home? "No, why?"

"You'll understand when you do."

Overloading

Elijah asked if I've been home yet. He obviously knew it might change my perspective about being in this bubble. I check my driver license to be sure and find I'm still living at Cirque.

As I approach the door, I have no idea what my demeanor should be when I see Noah, if he's here in this world. Of course, the door recognizes me and unlocks as I approach. I open the door and listen for his sounds, but I don't hear them. He's not at the table, in fact his computer isn't there either. The art is there. His art. The art I missed when Mia and I were living here, sometime in the future. In a different bubble, a different time and place. Not here.

Apparently, I've gotten home earlier than Noah. I wonder if that's usual or whether we had words and he's staying away as long as possible, so he doesn't have to continue that discussion, whatever it was.

The clock tells me it's approaching eight o'clock. Probably had something to eat out this late, although I didn't. Do I make up something light for both of us knowing he might just come in and not even sit down with me? I so much want to talk with him. The few days I had with him when I came through this, or a bubble very close to this one were special to me because I felt loved by someone, even though I couldn't figure out a way to bridge the disappointment he had in me. Maybe now I can change the direction of our relationship. I want to but have no idea where he is.

I check the 'frig. Salad greens. A few vegetables. I could have a green salad. That's about all I want to eat as I'm really not hungry. It's not like I'm eating a lot and can afford to skip more meals than I am already. I wonder if it's a side effect of being in one time for a few days and then moving to another for even fewer days. And I just got here today.

My cell rings. Noah's name comes up.

"Noah. Is everything all right?" I ask almost out of breath.

"Everything's fine. Why?"

"Where are you?" I don't want it to sound demanding or panicky, but I can't help revealing both.

"Nashville. I'm at the Pediatrics conference. HCA is the sponsor this year. Did you forget?"

I'm disappointed that he won't be home tonight. Elijah seems bent on moving on to another bubble soon. Will I even see him this time through? "I'm sorry. Yes, I forgot."

"I just got in from dinner with the Owners of HCA. They're doing some incredible things. It's amazing. With the scale they've achieved they can pull resources to work initiatives and create centers of excellence with just incredible equipment and the best staff."

Knowing he goes to work for them in a few years I assume this dinner was the beginning of either that courtship of him, or opening doors if he decided he wanted to leave Baylor because of me.

"Is that a model you can work with at Baylor?" I ask since he seems to want to talk about it.

"In a limited way. We don't have the resources they have. Their network is huge in comparison to ours. Yes, there are a few things we can do that would be similar, but I'll have to do it for a whole lot less money."

"Sounds like you're still mulling how to do it." I respond to what I hear and where his mind is at.

"Don't know how I would go about it yet, but there's definite possibilities that could improve patient care."

I let that sit for a moment before continuing. "Are you ready to change the subject?" I ask to make sure he's finished discussing his day.

"Sure, what's on your mind?" He sounds curious but guarded.

"Us. I want to talk about us. Where are we going? How are you feeling about our relationship, about me? That's why I was disappointed when I realized you won't be home tonight."

"Can this wait until I get back?" He almost sounds annoyed I want to talk now.

"We might continue it then, but I'd really like to talk about it now, if you're up to it."

"If you want to talk, I want to talk." I hear the hurt feelings from something I've said or done.

"Where are we?" I begin.

"That's the question we seem to dance around. Some days you seem to be fine with what we've created between us. Others… well, it's like you're a stranger who comes home to discover me there and you don't quite know what to do with me. That's hard for me because I need someone I can talk to about the good days and the bad days. Someone who can feel good with me when I have a success. When I've stopped the progression. When I've extended a life that appeared to be nearly over. Some days you're that rock I can come home to and unload what's troubling me. Let me get it out so I can regain some semblance of balance. And then there are the days when you're so caught up in your world. You don't have time for me. That's when I have trouble restoring the balance. That's when I need you the most and you're not there for me. That's hard."

"I'm sorry," is all I can say for a long moment. Then I try to respond, "I'm not a rock. I'm like you. I absorb things. When you come home and unload your day, I absorb your troubles, I end up mixing them up with my own and then I have to figure out what to do with both sets. I know that's not an excuse, but I wanted you to know I'm not ignoring you. It's just there are some days when your pain and mine become overwhelming. I don't know what to do."

"I didn't mean you're like a rock where what I say just bounces off, if that's what you're thinking." Noah is quieter. *I'm not sure if this is the first time we've had this conversation. I'm guessing how I would have reacted. I hope I'm not making this worse for all of us.* Noah continues, "What I was trying to say is you were there for me. Solid. Helping me deal with my day and helping me understand that tomorrow will be better, or not, but, in any case, we're together and we will solve any problems we have together. And then you change, or so it seems. You're not there. We're not working through our days together. I'm left to try to figure out how to reconcile things and you seem to be somewhere else. I have no idea how to help you because when you go off, you're in your head, somewhere. I don't know what's wrong because you won't talk about it. You're just gone. And then there are nights like tonight. You want to know how we get back on track. I can't tell you how many times we've had this conversation. I always say the same thing and you always say you're sorry. But nothing changes. We end up in the same place. Don't you understand that I want to help you be present in our relationship? But until you are, I don't know what to do for you. As a result, I have no idea where we are going as a couple."

"I don't know how to deal with the darkness I see in you." I try to explain but know it's inadequate.

"Do you need to see a professional?"

"I'm not crazy, Noah."

"I'm not implying you are. I'm suggesting a counselor. Someone who can help you sort things out. Help you understand how to deal with your pain. If you can get a handle on just that, then maybe my issues won't be so overwhelming for you. Maybe you will learn techniques to help you manage the turmoil in our lives. Learn how to deal with each other in a balanced way where we can be what the other needs."

"I'm not seeing a counselor," is my flat response. "If it got out, and it would, it would undermine me at work. I'd probably be out as Managing Partner in a matter of months."

Attention

I find Professor Amit Bedoya an interesting experiment in combining parenthood. His mother is Indian Hindu. His father is Peruvian Catholic. Between them they raised a mixed-up agnostic who took refuge in physics to explain a world that made absolutely no sense to him. I meet with him in his elaborate laboratory at Southern Methodist University in Dallas. Dr. Bedoya is short of stature, a dark mop of hair, dark expressive eyes that seem constantly wondering about something or other. Today he is dressed in jeans and a New York Giants hoodie. That tells me he is a deliberate provocateur as no one wears a Giants sweatshirt in the home of the Dallas Cowboys.

"Elijah? You wanted to talk to me about Elijah. But you are an attorney. I don't understand."

"Elijah Mason wrote a paper he gave to you and asked for comments. He was planning to submit it for publication. That was why he wanted your thoughts."

Dr. Bedoya has to consider my statement to see if it aligns with anything he remembers. "A paper. Hmmm."

"It would have been about a week ago, from what he said."

"What is the issue with this paper?" Dr. Bedoya is neither acknowledging nor denying knowing anything about it. That tells me he has probably read it and is still trying to decide what to think of it.

"He decided against submitting it and wishes to reconsider his theory in light of errors."

"I would like to know more about the errors." Dr. Bedoya has clearly read it.

"That's just the problem. There are other parts of the paper that may have merit. He wants to protect whatever value may reside there."

"Why would he send a lawyer to see me? I don't understand your role."

"I am here to retrieve the copy and any other copies you may have made and ensure you neither discuss, attempt to use or in any other respects attempt to replicate any aspect of the novel portions of the paper."

"That's impossible. He has built upon general physics theories which are in the public domain. I cannot tell you I will never attempt to use general theory in my work." *Defensive offense, hmmm.*

"Dr. Bedoya, you are talking with a trial attorney who has made her living litigating people just like you. The agreement I have for your signature has been vetted by dozens of courts and comports to the various intellectual property traps that exist around public domain and novel concepts. That's not a defense you can use."

"The agreement must be prospective." He looks like he is feeling trapped.

"What do you mean?"

"You cannot prohibit discussions I may have already had with colleagues and others."

"Others?" the cat is already out of the bag.

"I have a relationship with the Defense Advanced Research Projects Agency. I have discussed his theory with my Program Director."

"Have you provided a copy of the paper?"

Dr. Bedoya shakes his head just once, like other Hindus I have seen. "Elijah did not suggest I should not provide copies to other potential reviewers. He was looking for input. How to make it better. Dr. Patel is knee-deep in the most advanced theoretical project validation work in the world."

"For military applications." I point out.

"Is that a problem? We're talking theory here. We're talking whether there might be Federal funding to conduct research that could validate his theory. I am doing him a favor. DARPA might be willing to provide a scholarship for him where he can conduct laboratory experiments. It could put him on a fast track for his doctorate. Maybe even post-doctoral funding. Do you have any idea how hard it is to find post-doc funding in physics?"

"No, Dr. Bedoya. I have no idea about that as I'm a lawyer trying to give Elijah an opportunity to correct some theoretical mistakes he has made before they are put on display for the entire world's ridicule." I have to make this strong and appeal to Dr. Bedoya's self-interests as the person advocating for Elijah's ideas.

I see this comment strikes home. Dr. Bedoya seems to realize the potential impact of too wide a discussion of a flawed theory. "But few theories aren't improved by robust discussion. Getting his ideas into the mainstream forums will bring out the best minds considering his ideas. They are novel, I have to admit. Goes in a whole different direction than the mainstream theories and research. No, Miss… what was your name?"

"Wilcox."

"No, Miss Wilcox, I haven't damaged Elijah by bringing attention to his theory, as raw and potentially flawed as it may be. It's novel. The fact that it could lead to an entirely different conception of how our multi-verse operates is worthy of consideration."

"Dr. Bedoya. Is the subject of his theorization your specialty?"

Dr. Bedoya stiffens. "I am a nuclear physicist."

"Particle physics if your resume is correct."

"Yes, but I am probably as knowledgeable about this area as anyone, if only because no one is actively researching it."

"So, you admit this is not your specialty. You will acknowledge that as the author, Elijah has the right to withdraw his novel idea from consideration by the wider academic and non-academic interested communities, and that you have not advised him as to what parties have received his flawed work."

"This is not a court room, Miss Wilcox."

"No, but I'm giving you a preview of the questions you will have to answer if I have to take you there to withdraw Elijah's paper from wider discussion and consideration."

"You can't hold me liable for trying to help one of my brightest students." That answers my question about whether this paper is really Elijah's. I was wondering about that.

"Are you sure this paper is his work?"

Dr. Bedoya's wondering eyes now have something else to consider. He ponders my question for a long moment and then nods. "I would say this is his work. Elijah looks at physics from a unique perspective. He asks questions that affirm to me he has long ago gone past the content of the advanced course he is taking from me. He asks questions my doctoral students do not think to ask, trying to understand advanced relationships and asking what if questions I've never considered. So, I would definitely say this is his original work."

"I get the sense you like Elijah."

"Like him? Yes, I think he is a brilliant creative mind. And the fact he's still in high school taking graduate physics tells you he will go far with the proper guidance and opportunities."

"And you're trying to help him." I already know the answer but want him to see he may not be in what he is doing.

"I am."

"What can help him more than anything at this time is to pull back this paper. Help him establish a better first impression on the wider physics community. Allow him to decide if he wants to participate in Department of Defense related research. Permit him to develop his concept and theory as far as he can before others advance it in directions that may not be in alignment with his original intent."

"What are you saying? That Elijah is afraid to lose control of his theory?"

"He wants to get it right so it will stand on its own, rather than watch others distort or ridicule his concepts. As you said, he's still in high school. Not even Einstein was still in high school when he released his first theory. He had time to reflect on it. Do the math. Elijah needs that time too."

"Einstein lived in a very different time." Dr. Bedoya informs me. "The first paper out there is generally seen as the foundation. That's why I encouraged him to publish his ideas. But when I did that, I had no idea what that theory was. I had no idea how revolutionary a thinker he is. Is he an Einstein? Not today. Could he become one? I would say if his theory is correct, he may well have a similar impact on the scientific community."

"So, you are unwilling to respect his wishes."

Dr. Bedoya shakes his head just once again. I don't think he's reflexively saying no. I think the shake of his head is a realization of what he is saying. He looks at me with a pained expression. He is clearly conflicted. "I'm afraid I cannot."

Happy

"So, what did you do?" Elijah asks. We are having lunch at a café across the street from the SMU campus as most of his classes are here rather than his high school. I've just left Dr. Bedoya's lab and wanted to fill him in before he goes to class with the Doctor.

"I asked him to recall it. Got him to sign a prospective agreement, with a modification that the limitations are in place only so long as the paper remains unpublished, which is fair. If it's public domain then he should be able to use it in his work."

"So, Dr. Bedoya is the one who sent it to the Department of Defense." Elijah mulls.

"He is really excited for you. Thinks you could be on a fast track for a doctorate. Is that what you want? To be an academic researcher?"

Elijah takes a bite of his veggie wrap and chews while he considers my question. I wait.

"That is one possibility," Elijah finally responds.

"If you could do anything, what would it be?" I push since his response was less than enthusiastic.

"Explore different bubbles. Validate my theory, see how it all actually works." Elijah smiles at me, "I'm glad you made me come up with that horsey ducky explanation. Now I'm thinking of bubbles rather than space-time or time-place spheres when they really are bubbles, floating in the universe, bumping into each other from time-to-time. And that's where ghosts come from. At least, that's what I think. When the bubbles bump into each other you can see into the other bubble, you see shadows and your mind fills in the details from what you know in your bubble. But that's why you can't really interact with ghosts. They don't exist where you do. They exist in parallel to where and when you do."

"Let me see if I'm following you," he has my attention about the ghost.

"I'm sorry. Concepts come to me and I talk my way through them. That's how I develop the idea."

"No problem, but you're saying bubbles explain ghosts."

"They could." Elijah offers.

"But you're saying our mind fills in the blanks. What we think we see is not what we actually see."

"I think so." Elijah seems happy I'm following him.

"So, a bubble bumps into our bubble." An image pops into my mind. "Who was that woman I saw running back in my original bubble? She looked just like me and she was real."

"Are you sure? You said she disappeared on you multiple times."

"Is that something you did?" I'm beginning to wonder since that whole series of ghosts happened just before the first transit.

"No. I didn't create your ghost. But from what you said it may have been a side effect of my travels. I came back and visited your courtroom on one of those days. And I traveled to a different bubble on the other. I wonder if my travel has side effects like you've described. People see things related to my transit, but they dismiss them, or they think they've seen ghosts, as you did."

"But what about the runner?"

"I have no idea about that. You said she was right on the street with you. Passed by you on more than one occasion."

"You said there is an exchange at transit. That whoever comes in to a bubble sends whoever is the same person in that bubble to the other bubble."

Elijah is thinking this through with me and nods.

I continue. "Could it be there's a transition that occurs where both occupy the same bubble, separated by your magnetic field and that one of the pair moves in and out in an uncontrolled fashion? That would kind of describe what happened. She was me. She even said hello. So, she knew I was there. But instability or whatever caused her to come into and out of my bubble that morning. What do you think?"

"I think you're an excellent attorney, but scientific phenomenon is not your strength."

"Well, then." I respond hurt at his characterization of my attempt to explain what I saw. "I'll let you explain it all to me some time. When you've figured it out."

"You're making the assumption I will be able to figure it out. Maybe it was all just a recurring dream. That would explain it better than anything I can offer from my theory."

He's not going to say anything more about the ghost. "Which brings us back to what is it you really want to do." I follow his transition back to my question.

"What do you want to do?" Elijah turns my question around. "I know you're a lawyer and all. But what do you really want to do?"

I haven't given this any consideration. I've just been along for the ride to keep him out of trouble. And on this ride, I've already explored two different jobs in the matter of a couple of weeks. "Maybe we are both restless souls who will never be happy, but will forever learn, discover and move on to the next adventure." I'm not sure I buy this but put it out there to see how he reacts.

Elijah looks off towards the SMU campus across the street. "There are many different ways to, how did you put it? Forever learn, discover and move on to the next adventure? I can do that in a lab. You can do that in your law office. We can do that on a sailboat or by bubble jumping. We haven't done the sailboat yet, but that could be the next one."

"You're saying we have choices."

"That's what the different bubbles represent to me. Each bubble results from different choices the people living within have made. That's why there is so much variety out there. Eight billion people all making different choices. Sometimes they make one choice. That takes their life and those in their bubble in one direction. In another bubble they make the same choice but someone else makes a different one than they did before. That takes that bubble off in a different direction. There are so many permutations on what an individual's life could be like that there has to be at least one where we would both be happy."

"Even though you have no idea what it will take to make you happy and neither do I. All you know is making weapons related systems for the Department of Defense is not it."

Elijah frowns as he looks back across the street again.

"I take it you have a class at one." I guess.

"Dr. Bedoya's. I'm not looking forward to listening to his lecture because I'm sure it will have something to do with Intellectual freedom and intellectual property and how physics is the study of the laws of nature and nature is the property of all of us."

"You've heard the lecture before." I realize.

"Last year. But then it wasn't tinged by his encounter with you." Elijah notes.

"You ought to enjoy listening for the differences then. How did we change history in this bubble, which isn't the same bubble you were in a year ago."

"You're starting to understand. That's scary." Elijah grins at me.

"We have a choice to make, again."

"I know. I expect Dr. Bedoya has unleashed something here he can't stop. We will be in court next year fighting the custody hearing. It will all end up in the same place."

"And that's not what you want." I seek to confirm.

Elijah shakes his head. "1956 is starting to look more appealing."

"Can we think about a time maybe not quite that far back?"

"My age is an issue. If we go back ten years, I can't occupy my life because I am clearly not six."

Survive

I get the call from Mr. Mason at the office. "Miss Wilcox. This is Harold Mason. You've been recommended as someone we need to retain. It seems the US Government, for some reason, believes it needs to take our son from us."

"Did you…" *Back up.* "Did someone from the government call you, visit with you or send you a letter?"

"We received a letter."

"And what did this letter specifically say?"

"It's a subpoena, for us to appear in court in the matter of the US Department of Defense vs. Elijah Mohammed Mason."

"Is there a court date on the subpoena?"

"Next Friday."

"And does it say anything about custody of Elijah or how did you get to that conclusion?"

"Specifically states that the US Department of Defense has determined that Elijah Mohammed Mason should be transferred to the custody of the US Department of Defense immediately as a matter of National Security."

"Do you have any idea why the Department of Defense believes you son is a national security concern? By the way, how old is your son?"

"He's sixteen and no, I have no earthly idea what this is all about."

"I'll be happy to represent you and your son in this matter. Do you have access to a fax or could you scan the subpoena and send it to me? Next Friday isn't much time. Maybe it would be better for me to come to your home this evening. What would be a good time?"

"Is eight too late?"

Noah won't be home tonight since he's still in Nashville. "Eight is fine."

"Do you need an address?" Harold Mason asks, apparently surprised I haven't asked. "It's 71 Sunset near White Rock." *I remember being there after we got the stay, but they were packing then.*

"Uber will find it. Thank you for your call Mr. Mason. I will see you at eight. We can plot out an appropriate response then."

I grab a bite to eat at Café Momentum, after leaving the office. I don't recognize anyone this evening and call an Uber about seven-thirty. The ride up to White Rock Lake isn't long but the traffic can make it slow going. I arrive at their small-ish house right on time. Harold Mason answers the door and I introduce myself. He introduces me to his wife and then Elijah comes out and just nods to me.

Mr. Mason brings me in to the dining room. The subpoena is waiting for me. I quickly read it over, although I've seen it before, in a different bubble. "I'll file for a delay with the court in the morning."

We discuss the details of the subpoena and general strategy for an hour or more. Then I get up to leave, shake hands with each, including Elijah and work my way to the front door as I call for an Uber to take me home. A final good-bye and the car picks me up. Once in the car Elijah calls almost instantly.

"That was fun."

"Second time through for you. We have to start the process. I'll get that done in the morning."

"What if I want to leave in the morning?" Elijah has had it with this bubble already.

"We should probably wait until after I can get the request for postponement filed."

"Why? Neither of us will be here after we leave. No reason to postpone. They have the hearing and we simply don't appear. Maybe we're wanted as a result in every branch from this world, but so what?"

"The so what is if you decide you want to go forward again at some point. Then you can't be you in that future. First of all because you won't already exist, but also because people will be looking for you. Let me file a motion to dismiss and request a postponement which will be on record. If we are ever intercepted, we have a court proceeding on record.

"Sounds like you'd rather stay here and fight through now that you know the government's case."

"Is this my first-choice bubble?" I respond unsure. "Too many things are at play. I suppose there are parts of my life that would be good for me here, and other parts… well I just don't know yet."

"Meaning Noah." Elijah instantly jumps to the tone of my voice.

I don't answer his assumption. "Life is going to be hard no matter what bubble we jump to. As you've pointed out others make choices that affect us. We decide to choose something differently than we did previously and the bubble changes. All we can do is find a point in time where the world is friendlier than at other times. But the fact of the matter is that with all the choices being made at any given moment, the world we find perfect for us now will change. There is no perpetually perfect place."

"How do you know Dallas in 1956 isn't?"

"We've been able to step into the lives we would have." I point out. "Even our cell phones and apartment key fobs worked. We were able to pick up quickly because another version of ourselves paved the way for us. But going back to 1956? My parents weren't even born yet. I'm older than my grandparents would have been then. We're talking about a very different place. We have to establish new identities, find a place to live and I need to get a job. I'll have to get an office job, typing or answering phones. No one is going to hire me to do anything professional."

"But you could do most anything as a lawyer, you know all about business."

"But two things, I will have no degrees I can show anyone and I'm also a woman. In 1956 Dallas, being a woman means if I didn't inherit the family business I'm no one of consequence. I can starve to death as far as most people will be concerned. I'm not going to get a break, I'm not going to be given equal treatment. Old white men rule the universe."

"It can't be as bad as you're painting it" Elijah dismisses my alarmist reaction.

"It's going to be worse, and that's why I need a little time to collect things we are going to need if we are making that trip. Things to help us survive."

Half-wit

It's five am two days later. I couldn't make the necessary arrangements that night since everything had long ago closed. Here I am at the Winspear waiting for Elijah, dressed in blue jeans a plain top and light sweater that won't look really out of place in 1956. I carry a cloth bag I found to carry our important supplies. Elijah soon arrives dressed in cut-off jeans, a Led Zeppelin t-shirt and basketball shoes. He glances at me with a puzzled expression but seems to pass it off.

"I have a question."

Elijah shrugs like 'go ahead and ask'.

"If this device doesn't exist in that bubble, how do we get somewhere else when we decide we've had enough?"

Elijah opens the door to the cabinet and removes a cell-phone like device. "This is a controller that will activate this unit from any other bubble and bring us through here. Then we can hop to another bubble."

"Does it use batteries?" I wonder looking at it.

"Of course."

"How long will those batteries last if we can't recharge?"

Elijah frowns and reaches into the cabinet. "Good point, I'll bring the charger."

"What else will we be dependent on that won't exist there?"

"What do you mean?"

"Any medicines? Aspirins even? I don't know, but we need to

bring anything with us we will need this time."

"I'm good."

I'm real reluctant. I know it's going to be a shock to the system. Elijah opens the portal and the fog begins to engulf us. He takes my hand and leads me only a few steps before I feel the electric pulse on my skin. I'm now in a land before technology. The fog begins to clear. I see the stars still visible in the morning sky because the city lights are so much lower, and the downtown buildings all seem to have fewer floors. I turn to look around. The Winspear and all of the arts buildings are gone with old office buildings occupying what I know as the Arts District. The Woodall Rodgers Freeway isn't there and the downtown area simply extends northward.

"Okay. Does any of this look familiar?" I glance around.

Elijah seems to be lost. I don't blame him. None of the familiar landscapes can be seen. "Where's the Reunion Tower? I can always tell where I am from that."

"Hasn't been built yet," I inform him.

"What do you mean?"

"Reunion Tower was built in the mid-seventies." I recall. "Not even a thought in 1956."

"What about school? Can I just enroll in college?"

"We could do that, but first rule of school here, even if you know the teacher is wrong, don't tell them. And when you take a test? Tell them what they told you, even if it's wrong."

"Why would I do that?" Elijah is suspicious I have some agenda to make him look silly.

"Because otherwise you'll either get kicked out of class or fail the course."

I see Elijah resisting my advice. "First step is we need to go to a jewelry store to get some money. Then go find a furnished apartment. We need a place to get settled."

"Why can't we just use your credit cards?" Elijah seems puzzled.

"Haven't been invented yet, and we don't have a bank account anyway."

"What do you mean?" Elijah can't believe we have no money.

"Do you have any?"

"No, but my parents…" He starts to realize we have a problem.

"Who haven't been born yet…"

"Oh." Elijah looks at me like a deer staring into headlights.

"Don't worry, I exchanged money for gold and silver. I'm going to take a real beating but at least we can exchange it for dollars now."

"Why would you take a beating on it? Gold is gold."

"Yes, but on an inflation-based index, I'm only getting pennies on the dollar. Hopefully it will be enough until I can get a job and collect a paycheck."

"I have a question?" Elijah realizes his parents aren't with us. "Did you bring enough to pay my tuition at SMU?"

"No. You may have to drop out of school and get a job until we can make enough."

"You planned that, didn't you?" Elijah is clearly angry with me. "That I'd have to drop out of school and get a job. Make me want to leave because I'm bored here."

"No. You can go to public school, which will be free or get a job to raise tuition. I had to do that when I was in law school. Just remember, it was your idea to come here."

Elijah pulls his cell phone from his pocket. It doesn't register. "What's wrong with the cell coverage?"

"There is no cell coverage. I told you that before we came."

"How am I supposed to look up anything?" Elijah appears to be totally confused.

"There's nothing to look up. There's no internet, there's no Google, there's no Facebook, there's no Instagram, there's no Twitter, email or Snapchat either. So, basically, even if it worked there would be no content."

"What kind of a place is this?" Elijah puts the phone back in his pocket.

"This is the age before technology. We're still more than a year before Sputnik is launched into orbit."

"Sputnik?" *Oops. Have to back up.*

"That's right. You don't know history. First man-made satellite put into orbit by Russia."

Elijah just shakes it off as non-consequential. "Maybe I could go to work for the space program."

"You wouldn't be much help. None of the tools you're used to using exist. No computers, no spreadsheets, no databases or ability to crunch large data sets. You would be no more use to them than I would. You may know theory, but the tools to build things you take for granted don't exist."

"How can that be?" Elijah can't imagine a world without computers

"You're the time traveler. It's ironic that you're traveling all over the universe, but you don't know anything about time, or history or how technology progresses. You just expect what you've known to be there. So, the best place for you will always be in the future where even better tools than you're used to will exist because somewhere along the way someone built them. But you don't have to be patient, help someone build them. You just pull out your device and go further into the future where someone else has made the breakthrough you need to achieve your breakthrough."

"Are you mad at me?" Elijah asks exasperated at my venting at him.

"No, I'm mad at me, for feeding into this. There's no way we should be here. You can't do what you do best, and neither can I."

"You'd rather be back in your boring office, trying to talk your attorneys down off the ledge? That's no place for you."

I'm surprised at the judgment about me he's just voiced. "Maybe not but I am good at it. I'm not going to be good at being a secretary to some half-wit old man."

"You haven't even tried to get a job yet. How do you know that's what will happen? With what you know about business and what business did well over the years you should be able to make a killing in the stock market."

Psyche

I sell my gold and silver for pennies on the dollar only the dollar buys a whole lot more in 1956. We find a furnished two-bedroom apartment downtown as we both are looking for jobs in the downtown area. And the job search starts tomorrow.

We enter a neighborhood market. Elijah goes up and down the aisles and then comes back to whisper to me, "Where do I find bottled water?"

"In 1985." I respond having no idea when bottled water became readily available, but knowing it isn't this year.

"Let's get out of here. There's nothing I want."

I buy a few toiletries I know we will both need and meet him outside. He looks in my bag and nods to himself. "Yeah, I'll need to shower at some point." I take that as acceptance. When we get back to the apartment he asks, "Where would we find fast food?"

"San Bernardino, California. McDonalds opened there last year. Or you might find a Chic-fil-A if you want to go to Atlanta, they opened in 1949."

"Why are you a smartass all of a sudden?"

"You keep wanting to live in the world that won't be here for another thirty years or more." I remind him. "We can jump to a future bubble any time you want."

"No, I want to at least give this a chance." Elijah is dead serious. "See if we can make it here. Everyone fantasizes about what they'd do if they could go back in time. They all think they would become millionaires or president of something. Well, we're here. Let's see if we can take advantage of it."

"I take it you're hungry?" I respond.

"Aren't you?"

"Let's go over to the Woolworths. They have a lunch counter."

"What's a Woolworths?"

When we arrive at the Woolworths the lunch counter is busy. We have to wait. Elijah looks at the food people are eating. "What is that?"

"Fried Chicken, mashed potatoes, gravy and collards."

Elijah apparently has lost his appetite, "How can people eat that?"

"They would say the same thing about your veggie wrap."

"But this is all so unhealthy." Elijah shakes his head.

"Health food…"

"I know. No one ate health food until the late 1980s." Elijah is finally understanding.

"Actually, the Natural Food Association was formed in Atlanta, Texas three years ago, 1953. But Rachel Carson didn't publish Silent Spring about what pesticides were doing to us until 1963."

"Great, I'm going to be eating raw pesticides for the next seven years." Elijah is clearly unhappy.

"A lot longer than that because it was probably another decade before much really changed. You see people made decisions about what they want to eat or buy. If you like your veggie wrap, you'll eat it until someone comes out with a pesticide rating for what's in your wrap.

Then maybe you'll change. Just because a book came out on a subject doesn't mean anyone did anything different for quite some time."

"And I take it the next thing you're going to tell me is that just because I wrote a paper about the Multi-verse Bubble Theory that not much will change for a decade or more."

"Einstein published his General Theory of Relativity in 1923. The atom bomb didn't become a reality until 1945."

Two seats at the counter open up. We move to take them but a guy and his wife who came in behind us push past to take them.

"You going to just let him do that?" Elijah is incredulous at the couple.

I put my arm out to hold him back, "We don't know the lay of the land here. Confrontation is never a good thing when you don't know the rules."

Elijah grimaces. "I'm not hungry, let's get something later," his voice sounds angry and confused.

We leave the lunch counter and head over to the Dallas Public Library. Elijah follows me into the reading room. I pull a Dallas Morning News off the rack and go to the classified ads. I start going down. As I thought, laborers, clerks and secretaries. A few door-to-door or outside sales jobs. And then I find one for a local real estate company looking for experienced commercial real estate development professionals. They have a companion ad for experienced commercial real estate leasing agents. I point out the ads to Elijah. "Worth responding?"

"For you maybe, but I don't see anything here for me."

I point to an ad that was off by itself in a box. "Geophysical Services. Oil field technology, but they're getting into other areas. I'll bet you could get a job as a technician to start."

"Sure. Just long enough to make tuition."

I pull him aside, "You've said you want to explore the bubbles. Going to school isn't exploring the bubbles. If you want to know what life is like in your creations, you need to live the life here as everyone here lives it. Dropping in for a few days doesn't tell you enough to validate any theory you might want to come up with. As I remember, coming here was your idea. Now it's up to us to make this work."

"I don't know why I let you come along." Elijah responds upset with my lecture.

"And if you had you wouldn't have stayed a whole day because you would have had no place to live and would have headed home as soon as you got hungry." I'm being my usual tactful self.

"You must think I'm just a spoiled kid."

"No, I think you're a brilliant spoiled kid."

Elijah raises his eyebrows realizing the truth to what I'm thinking. Laughs. "You got me. Yeah, I don't know how long I would have held out here with nothing working."

"Again, let me ask do you want to jump on to the next place where technology works and you can either go to school or at least be able to work with the tools or stay on here?"

Elijah looks deep inside himself. "I've never had to do something that was hard. It's about time I find out what I'm made of. See if I can rough it in the age before technology."

"You might just find you're more resourceful than you think." I support his decision.

We leave the library and are wandering the streets, looking about. "Now that we're going to be here a while, there's something I want to do. It involves taking a bus north."

"You want to go to Alaska?"

"No, North Dallas. My maternal grandparents are living there now. My father's parents don't arrive until a few years from now. I'd like to meet my maternal grandparents."

"Why?"

"To understand what they were like when they were still full of hopes and dreams, before they had my mother, before the world started grinding on them. By the time I came along, they were tired of trying to make ends meet. Having to give up one thing after another in order to get their daughter through school, to pay for her wedding, to pay off their house so they wouldn't still have a mortgage when they retired from a weekly paycheck. I think it will be fascinating to meet them, to learn of their dreams and what dreams drove them."

"You're really negative about this time." Elijah observes the tone of my voice.

"Not so much. If you had spent any time studying history 1956 is just eleven years after the end of the war. Less than twenty past the Great Depression. The scars of both of those events are still in the psyches of the people of this era. They're conservative because they've seen people lose everything. They're close knit because nearly everyone either lost a relative or knows friends and neighbors who did during the war. This period in time is a study of the transition our country made in flexing its muscles as the leader of the free world. People in this era are proud of what they have accomplished. Companies are growing and with them jobs for people who finish school. People are beginning to think that the peace that came out of the last war can last. The countries who lost are reintegrating into the world economy. They have a sense of optimism for the future which is taking root for the first time in a long time."

"I have no idea what you're talking about." Elijah informs me.

The Big City

The bus leaves us on the corner of Garland Road and Gaston, about a block and half from my grandparent's house, located on Tucker near Casa Loma. This area is at the base of White Rock Lake which I used to come visit on summer weekends. The houses here were mostly built in the 1920s, so now they are nearing thirty years old. Many are starting to show the need for a fresh coat of paint. The yards are all tidy. For the most part the houses and yards are well kept.

"My grandparents bought their house in 1951, when my grandfather was promoted to department manager at the Neiman Marcus store in downtown." I tell Elijah what I know of them. "I remember he used to joke that he started out in jocks and socks for the boys who were playing sports and ended up in ladies' underwear. And through it all he never rose above department manager. He never went to college. By the time he was able to be promoted beyond department manager all the men who went to school on the GI bill were looking for jobs with their newly minted college degrees. He was his own worst enemy in that regard. My mother often told me I was going on to college and graduate school. No one was going to beat me out for a job because I didn't have the right degrees."

We find the house. A two-bedroom bungalow. "It seemed a lot bigger when I was coming here regularly. It was also a different shade of color, white now. I remember it being a beige or maybe that was just the weathering of the white paint I'm now seeing. The tree in the front yard seems almost to be a dwarf in regards to the giant I remember that shaded the front porch." I continue my memories.

"What are we going to say to them? Like who we are and why we're here?" Elijah whispers.

"My grandmother's mother died very young, like thirty-two or something. They were never close to that side of the family because her father re-married right after. Said he needed a wife to take care of my grandmother and her siblings while he worked the ranch. They had a place up near Denton, which back then was like on the other side of the moon. Now it's a far suburb. I'll tell them I'm a distant cousin's daughter of her mother and I'm trying to put together a family tree."

"That's about as lame an excuse as I've ever heard." Elijah dismisses me. "Who cares about relatives who died a long time ago?" Elijah doesn't offer a better suggestion.

I knock on the door. In a moment a woman in her late twenties, who bears a resemblance to my grandmother comes to the door. She's about my height, she has my blonde hair and my smile. I know where those features came from and hope she doesn't notice the resemblance. "May I help you?"

"Are you Mary Carter?" I ask.

"I am. And who might you be?" Friendly but cautious.

"I'm Jane Wilcox and this is my brother Elijah."

"Never would have put you together." She looks at us more closely. "How can I help you?"

"I think we're related through your mother?" I sort of half inform her and half ask. "She was Amelia Proctor?"

"Yes. But she died a long time ago." Grandma seems puzzled.

"I know. I'm trying to put together a family tree. So, I was hoping you could help me fill in some blanks about who was who."

"Well, I never really paid much attention to any of that. Father would talk about relatives once in a while, but I never really figured out who they were. After my father remarried, I don't know as I ever saw my grandparents on her side after that."

"You mind if we come in? See how much we might be able to reconstruct?"

My grandmother opens the door, but seems to be unsure if she's doing the right thing.

As we enter the tiny living area my grandfather enters from the bathroom. I would know those sparkling blue eyes anywhere. I always wanted them, but that was not to be as mine turned greenish before my second birthday. Grandpa always used to refer to them as his emeralds. Said I'd always be rich because of my jewel eyes.

Grandma introduces us and explains the purpose of our visit. My grandfather shakes our hands and welcomes us to his humble home, before seating himself next to his wife and listens to the discussion.

"Your mother's mother was Abigail Adams Proctor. Her husband was Harold Henry Proctor. Is that correct?"

"Gee, it's been so long since I even thought about any of this." My grandmother looks to her husband for help, but he just shrugs. "Abigail. That sounds right. Henry, I don't know about him."

"Abigail was born in 1871 in Kearny, Nebraska and Henry was born in 1867 in Topeka, Kansas. They met in Oklahoma City in 1888. Henry went back to work on the family farm in Topeka, but wrote letters back and forth to Abigail who became a school teacher in Denton. Henry moved to Denton when they married in 1893. The records aren't all that complete, but it appears they had at least ten children. The records would suggest that two or more were stillborn. Amelia was born in 1904 and was the youngest. And if the records are correct you were born in 1926."

"That's more detail than I have. Have you written this all down somewhere?"

"I have." I smile. "Unfortunately, since I didn't know I was going to have any time to connect with you this time through Dallas I didn't think to bring a copy. But I'd be happy to send it to you."

"That would be wonderful. I just never thought too much about any of that. Who they were or where they came from. The way you tell it, almost seems like they're neighbors or friends or something. Knowing where they moved here from. I always just thought I was a Texan and my family had been here forever. So, Kansas and Nebraska on my mother's side. Thank you for sharing that."

"Do you know anything about your father's side?" I want to keep her engaged.

"Oh, let me think about it. I don't have any facts or dates or anything like that. I might be able to come up with a name or two."

"Whatever you can remember will be helpful and I'll see what I can find."

"Heavens. It must have taken you years to find out all you did."

"We're not in a hurry." I try to put her at ease. "It's just something I'm interested in."

"My father is Richard Buchholtz." Mary looks shyly at her husband. "John here kids me about being a kraut. But I'm only half German. And I have to remind him I don't particularly like sauerkraut or even cooked cabbage. So, I keep trying to convince him to call me something else. Maybe someday." My grandmother touches her husband on his chest and smiles at him. He is non-committal. I can't tell you how many times I've seen that expression.

I wait and she continues. "So, my father married my mother. And they bought a few acres from her father. Later he would buy more from other neighbors and eventually he had over a hundred. But mom died when she was, gee, what was she? Twenty-four or twenty-five? I was only three or four years old, so I don't really remember her. My father remarried within a year. That's about all I know about that."

"You don't remember your father's father?" I look for something she might remember.

"Struck by lightning bringing in the hay before I was born. It was hard for my father. He kept up the family place and his for a lot of years."

"Why did he do that?"

"My father had three sisters who inherited the farm." Grandma informs me. "Father bought his piece, and grandfather gave the rest to father's sisters. That didn't go down well. The sisters lived together in the house they grew up in. None married. So, my father had to work their farm plus his own so they wouldn't starve."

"Why didn't he just convince them to sell it to him and live off the money they got for selling the land?" I ask having never heard this story before.

"Father couldn't have paid them much, so it worked out better for them to sell the crops and pay the taxes and living expenses from that."

"Sounds like your father wasn't happy about the arrangement." I try to understand.

"What else could he do?" Mary Buchholtz Carter shrugs her thin shoulders.

Do you remember any of his sister's names?" I ask to keep this like a genealogy discussion.

"Aunt Bertha, Aunt Simone, and Aunt what was her name? Oh, Aunt Marlene."

"Simone? Sounds French?" I ask.

"Yes. There was something about that. Give me a minute. Oh…"

She turns to her husband for inspiration, help, support... anything to jog her memory.

"You said something about that once." John Carter reminds her. "Something about your grandfather had brought his wife back from a trip to the big city. You never said what city."

Grandma smiles in remembrance. "She was French, Grandma Buchholtz always said she never intended to marry a kraut." My grandmother looks pleased in a way I've rarely seen.

Expensive

"What about your side Gr... uh John?"

"I never spent any time trying to think about any of this stuff. It doesn't help me sell garments at Neiman so no sense worrying about it."

"What do you worry about?" I try to sound interested and not combative or belittling his lack of interest in his ancestry.

"I worry about them Russians. They got the bomb and that means we aren't safe. I worry about the politicians down at city hall. They keep wanting to build new schools and raise my taxes when I can just barely afford the mortgage and taxes I got now. I worry about Mary here. You see we wanted to have children and we just don't know if it will ever happen."

"John. Why are you telling them that?" Mary seems upset with him, and I can understand why. This is also something I never heard about.

"What do the doctors say?" I inquire.

"Doctors? What about doctors?" John responds.

"Does her doctor have a theory? My boyfriend's a doctor is why I'm asking."

"Is he a good doctor? Maybe my Mary should see him." Grandpa responds.

"He's a very good doctor. But he's not a gynecologist."

"A what?" Grandpa responds confused.

"So, you think there's hope for us. To have a child?" Grandma asks almost afraid to.

"Depends on what you're experiencing." I try to respond neutrally so it doesn't sound prying.

"Miscarriages." John responds dejectedly. "Three miscarriages."

"You should go see your gyne… your doctor and let him or her do…"

"Are there female doctors in Dallas?" Mary asks surprised I would say that.

I realize the blunder I made, "I really don't know the doctors here."

"Where do you live?" Grandpa asks.

"Chicago", I offer hoping there are female doctors there in 1956.

Grandpa sits back, "Oh."

"I was born in Dallas, but moved there for school and stayed for work." I rush to fix the faux-pas.

"You went to school in Chicago? What do you do?" Grandpa asks.

"I'm a lawyer. I work for a large law firm there."

"You make good money as a lawyer?" Grandpa continues.

"I do all right." I respond.

"I'm just reflecting on your clothes. Don't look like you're well off." Grandpa looks at Elijah and points. "But I've been wondering, what's that airship on your shirt for? I've not seen that before. Must be something they only do in Chicago."

"They're really quite common." Elijah responds without thinking.

"So, that's something I have to look forward to?" John Carter, garment merchant asks.

Elijah nods and Grandpa gets that same look. The one that means he can't believe what someone is telling him. Whatever it is, it's crazy besides.

"You said you work in garments for Neiman?" I try to get him to talk more.

"That's right. Practically run the whole section." My grandfather is clearly proud of his work.

"How long have you been there?" I continue since he only gave a curt answer.

"Went there in 1948 right after I was discharged from the Army Quartermaster Corp. That's where I learned about buying things.

"So, you were still in after they started demobilizing the forces." I note. This is also new.

"Somebody had to keep the lights on after all the fighters left."

"So, you never fought?" I confirm, knowing this answer.

"I went in September 1943. On my seventeenth birthday. Went overseas, but only got as far as England. They kept me there the rest of the war. When they brought me home they needed someone who could figure out where all the equipment went we took over there. Didn't want it to fall into the hands of them Russians. Who knew what they would do with it if they got it. Probably come on in the rest of the way and run right over Europe since so much it had already been destroyed. So, they brought me back to Fort Benning. I sat there until they mustered me out. Went calling on Neiman the day I got back. Their only question was had I bought uniforms for the Army? I answered in the affirmative and that was all they wanted to know."

I had heard bits of this story. More now with it being still fresh in his mind. "So, how did you meet Mary?"

Grandpa looks at her lovingly and Grandma looks at me as if embarrassed. "That is an interesting story. Probably the most interesting story you'll get from this visit. As you may know Neiman's has a lunch counter up on four. I try to make it a habit of eating there once a week so I can see what my shoppers look like, what bags they're carrying things like that. Anything that might help me decide what to order. Anyway, Mary is working behind the counter one day when I go in. She'd just started working there about two weeks before I met her, but since I could only afford to eat there once a week, I'd not been in on her days before. Since she was serving the counter and I usually sat at one of the tables with a couple of the buyers in my department I had to make a decision. Do I stay with my buyers or do I go introduce myself to this cutie behind the counter. Well I'm sure you think I sat at the counter, but I didn't. I watched her instead. She just seemed to be too good to be true. I wanted to see if she really was. Anyway George, the younger of my two buyers dared me to go introduce myself, but I told him I wasn't ready. George told me that if I wait until I'm ready she'll be somebody's grandmother. Could you imagine this lovely creature being a grandmother?"

I smile but don't answer as clearly I can.

"So, George, he takes my fate into his hands. He goes to the lunch counter supervisor and tells her I have this huge crush on Mary. He wonders if she can come join us for a few minutes if he gives the supervisor a few bucks. Well, we're in there at the busiest time of the day. The supervisor says to come back after the rush. But George isn't about to take no for an answer. He tells the supervisor I'll come help serve for the next half hour to get ahead of the crowd if she can come sit with us for the next fifteen minutes before we have to go back to work."

Grandma shakes her head, "Not exactly how it happened."

"What? I came and served the lunch crowd for a half hour and you came and sat with us afterwards so I could meet you formally," my grandfather responds thinking she's wrong.

"Yes, that part happened, but John and George both had to come up and serve the lunch crowd. George told my supervisor he wanted to meet me, but his buddy would help if she would agree."

"I didn't know George did that?" Grandpa seems genuinely surprised. "I was the one who was crazy for you."

"But George was the one who made the play," Grandma points out.

"That son-of-a ..." Grandpa looks peeved. "Oh, pardon my French. I just..." Grandpa can't finish the though aloud.

"So, if George was the one who made the play, how did you end up with Gr.... John?" I ask.

"John was much cuter and a much better dancer. George was nice and all, but he was just a buyer. That's all he was ever going to be. John is in the management training program. He's going to be a store manager or vice president someday. You just watch. I knew if I stuck with John it would be a better life, no matter how it all turned out. John is just such a loving guy. And fun loving. Do you know what we do to have fun?"

I shake my head.

"We go down to the lake and watch the geese take off and land at sunset. It's just a magnificent sight. And it doesn't cost us anything except our time. That way we can save our money and pay off the mortgage. That's our plan. To pay off this house in less than thirty years. Take that money we put into a mortgage and we're going to travel to all the places in Europe that John never got to see when the war was on. That's going to be grand when we finally get to take that trip. See the world. See Europe when people aren't shooting at each other. That will be some trip."

"We've taken enough of your time. I really want to thank you for opening up your home to us. But if I might leave with just one thought. See a gyne… doctor about your miscarriages. There might be something that can be done."

"The docs haven't figured it out yet." Grandpa responds, but Grandma winks at me.

The Secret

On the way back to the bus I ask Elijah, "You okay?"

"They seem like real nice people." He dismisses my question.

"Do you want to find your grandparents?"

Elijah shakes his head.

"That because you don't know where to find them or because you really don't want to meet them?"

"I don't know how to find them," he finally answers.

"One set is in Fort Worth and the other in Oak Cliff. I looked them up when I was doing research on my grandparent's genealogy."

"So, you planned this little visit," Elijah accuses me apparently unhappy.

"When we decided to come to 1956, it was something I just knew I needed to do. Help me reconnect with my roots, something you apparently don't feel a need to do."

"When I was growing up my grandmother lived in Oak Cliff. My mother's mother. I never see her anymore. She's real old. Mom decided she has to take care of her mother. My father won't go, so she does during her lunch hour because she works over that way. I think mom took that job just so she could be close if her mother needed her."

"You don't remember your Grandfather?"

"He was never around. Don't know the story behind that. Don't remember ever having even seen him. That's why Grandma never had anything. She worked just to pay bills and that was that. Mom had to get a full scholarship to go to school. Grandma couldn't pay a nickel towards it."

"What did your father think about his mother-in-law?"

"He doesn't like her." Elijah apparently doesn't want to say what he really thinks. "Says she's a leech because my mother's always buying her groceries or paying a bill she can't. He wanted her to go into a home somewhere. Sell the old house and give the money to him and my mom. Pay them back for all the money my mom had given Grandma over the years. But my mother won't let her. Said Grandma paid off the mortgage so it's her house."

"Is that the source of the tension between your parents?"

"I'm just a kid, how am I supposed to know? All I can say is it's not been pleasant for as long as I can remember. I think my father would never leave because my mother would have taken half of everything he's saved over all their years together. He may be a horny bastard, but he's also cheap. He's not giving my mother one dime because he thinks she's been bleeding him dry to support her mother."

"Horny bastard?" I'm reacting to the description of his father.

"He's got friends," is all Elijah will say.

I remember the earlier comments, I nod, "What about his parents?"

"He doesn't have anything to do with them. I don't know why, but I've never even met them. Whatever happened was before I was born, from what I can tell."

"Why don't we go by your grandmother's house? You can see the house and decide."

Elijah gives in reluctantly. We board the bus and change

downtown for Oak Cliff. I'm able to find the house relatively easily, realizing it's not so far from the Texas Theater that will become infamous in a few years as part of the Kennedy assassination. The house is tiny. Maybe seven hundred square feet. The yard is just bone-dry dirt. No plants, flowers or grass like the other houses all up and down the street. The house could use a coat of paint.

"Want to meet them? We can pretend to be census takers for the city. How's that?"

"Sure. You're used to getting people to talk." Elijah steps back.

I go ahead of Elijah and knock on the door. A short woman answers it. She's a bit plump, with stringy blonde hair and a huge mole on her cheek with hair coming out of it. "What do you want?"

"Hi. Are you Matilda Songstrem?"

"Yes," she looks at us blankly.

"We're census takers from the City of Dallas. We gather information about the people living in the city so we can decide which streets need paving, where to replace or build new sewers, change out traffic or street lighting, that kind of thing. But in order to make those decisions about your tax dollars we'd like to ask you and your husband some questions."

"My husband's not here," she responds almost without thinking.

"That's all right. You can answer for both of you. Do you mind if we come in?" I ask.

Matilda's eyes get big at the idea of us coming inside. "I don't think so."

"Okay." I retreat to put her at ease. "Your husband's name is Willem Songstrem?"

"Yeah." Although she is slower to answer as if she is thinking either about his name or whether he is her husband.

"Does your husband live here with you?"

Again, her eyes get large as if she's not sure how she should answer. "This is his home."

"But is he currently living here with you?" I push. "This is important for us to allocate the city budget equitably. If he's not living here another part of the city may need the funds more."

Elijah shakes his head at me. I wonder what that's all about but can't stop to ask now.

"I haven't seen him… in a year… maybe. Could be a little longer. He comes and goes. I'll see him again when life brings him back this way."

I'm trying to put the pieces of the puzzle together in my mind. "So, this isn't the first time he's left you for an extended period of time?"

"He works around. Some times he's out on rigs in the gulf. Some times he's out in the Permian. I hear tell he's even done some work up Pennsylvania way. Times aren't great. So, you got to make a living where and when you can."

A piece comes into place. "So, he works in oil production?"

"Completion he calls it."

That fits. "Do you have any children living with you?"

"My daughter died a few days after she was born. Went to sleep in her crib and never woke up the next morning. Lord must have come and taken her in the night. Lord works in mysterious ways is all I can say about that."

Elijah seems puzzled about something. I keep going. "No children since?"

"Willem's not been here long enough since she died. I think he blames me for her passing, but there's nothing I could have done. She was fussy when I put her down and then nothing through the night. Not a peep. If there was something wrong, I would have heard it. I hardly sleep at all. And since, I won't even close my eyes at night. Not even to blink. He'll come back someday. He'll run out of work, or money or whores to satisfy his itch. He'll come back and when he does, I'll get pregnant and this next time she'll grow into a strong woman. You'll see."

I know she's going to have to wait ten years for her husband to return, but he will so she's right about that. I can't imagine waiting a decade for my man to come back to me. And then I realize Noah waited a decade for me to come back to him.

"Mrs. Songstrem," Elijah asks, "Why do you stay here? This place is a dump."

Matilda Songstrem looks at Elijah, really looks at him. "You have his eyes. Who are you?"

"Nobody. I just work for the city gathering census data so I can earn tuition money."

"Tuition money. Well good for you. Going to school to make something of yourself even though you could be making good money out in the oil fields."

"If your husband is making good money in the oil field why are you living in this dump?" Elijah asks the question differently.

"I'm going to have a grandson someday. And I have a secret bank account that all the money Willem sends me goes into it. Someday my grandson is going to want to go to college. I'm going to make sure he has the money to go even if I have to live like this for the rest of my life."

"Why do you think you'll have a grandson?" I ask.

Matilda Songstrem looks at me as if that's none of my business.

INTER-WHAT?

As I wait for my interview, I think about the bus ride with Elijah back from his Grandmother's house. At first, he was quiet, apparently thinking through the encounter, but he ultimately seemed to want to talk about it.

"How could she do that?" he finally asked. "Live there all these years when she had money coming in? She could have lived a normal life. Maybe if she had she wouldn't have ended up the way she did."

"How was that?"

"She's a mess. I mean she has so many health problems."

"But you said she's still living in that same house."

Elijah shakes his head, "I just don't understand."

"Do you remember me talking about people of her generation lived through the Great Depression, followed by the Second World War?"

"What does that have to do with her killing herself?" Elijah demands.

"It's a mindset. In the depression there wasn't enough to eat, money for clothes or winter coats, or heat in the winter. One out of four people was out of work. There were homeless camps under bridges and overpasses. So many people didn't have the basics they needed to live that the message was handed down from parent to child that you save every penny you can. You never knew when the world was going to fall apart again."

"But she was saving that money for me and didn't even know I would ever be born."

"People have faith in different things." I reflect more to myself than him. "Some have faith in themselves; that they can persevere in any situation. Some people have faith in the people around them; that they will always be there. Some people have faith in an unseen God. Whatever you put your faith in, it enables you to endure anything you're faced with. In this instance I think, and I could be wrong, that your grandmother had faith in your grandfather, that he would ultimately come back to her. She had faith that they would have a family. She was going to make sure you never had to endure what she chose to. I know that may sound crazy to a brilliant spoiled kid, but it's not. It's who she is."

"And I supposed the next thing you're going to tell me is I should respect her. Respect that she was crazy to deprive herself of basic things, things that would have made her healthier, helped her live a more productive life. How can I respect that?"

"What you need to respect is that it was her choice. She is apparently the kind of person who doesn't want things for herself. She wants to help and please others. A lot of people are like that. Few take those traits to the extreme your grandmother has. But you still need to respect her for being true to who she is."

"What does that mean? Being true to who she is?" Elijah doesn't like this conversation.

"It means she doesn't make excuses. She doesn't change her mind half way through and say, 'oh I was just kidding. She decided she's going to provide a better future for a child she is decades away from ever even meeting. But that hasn't stopped her. Hasn't deterred her. She's constant in her resolution to do this one thing."

"I would have spent the money." Elijah shakes his head again.

As I think about that conversation a tall thin man wearing a Texas summer suit and string tie comes out of the office behind me. He glances down and displays a curious look. "Why you must be Miss Wilcox. I'm so very pleased to meet you. Won't you come in and visit with me for a bit?" he gestures towards his office. Upon entering I get a very different impression of this man. His office walls are covered with pictures of buildings and acreage, maps, some aerial photos and a few newspaper articles. On the old wooden table he uses for a desk are blueprints and drawings and contract documents.

"Appears you're hands on in developing your projects", I remark as I sit down next to the table as there are no other chairs.

"I'm in every detail of every project right down to the moisture in the concrete we pour and the amount of money we pay for land. I'm in front of the city council looking for zoning changes, for the city to run sewer and water and build new streets so my tenants can get to the space they rent from me."

"Always lease. You don't do a build to suit." I test my understanding of his business model.

"Never have and never will. Why would I give up the remaining value of a building when I can lease it off to someone else, keep the cash flowing, and pour it all back into the next building and the next."

"A much smarter way of doing it."

"Miss Wilcox, why do I get the impression you know a thing or two about real estate development?"

"I've worked on site selection teams for companies looking for the optimal national location for distribution and support facilities."

"When did you do that? You hardly look old enough to drive."

"I appreciate the compliment sir, but I have nearly fifteen years of experience doing deals for companies all over the country. I have a good understanding of who will need warehousing and logistical support in the Dallas and Fort Worth region in the next few years." I hesitate and then plunge on. "But what could really just cause this area to explode is a single airport serving both cities. An airport where Dallas could build world class airline and freight hauling services."

I have his full attention. "Now why would you ever come up with a notion like that? The railroads haul the goods Americans buy. We warehouse it here and deliver it all over the south."

"If you were to look at the numbers on tons of freight moved, you would see the interstate highway system the federal government is building is already eating into the dominance of the rail system." I inform him. "And when it's complete, it will accelerate. As people get used to getting what they order quicker, they will want it quicker still. That's where an international airport in Dallas will open us up to serve the world. Why bring your freight into New York or LA when you have to wait weeks or months and then pay huge longshore haulage costs? If you can fly it into Dallas and just pay an airport landing fee, it's so much faster and will be cheaper to deliver anywhere in middle America."

"Have you looked at air freight costs? I mean they're ungodly," he responds.

"Today when only a small amount of freight goes that way. But it's going to take twenty years or more to get a new airport built. By then we could be landing men on the moon."

"That's not going to happen Miss Wilcox." He shakes his head. "You almost had me with your knowledge of trucking and the interstate highways, but an airport?"

"Sir, only those who see what it will take to forge a new industry or serve one that is growing become truly wealthy. Talk to the people over at American Airlines. They're small right now, but as people earn more, flying to see relatives at the holidays will become normal.

Businessmen will fly to meetings in New York, Los Angeles or Chicago. In a few years businesses that can react quicker than their competition will win the customers. And that's where you come in."

"Me?"

"With your business model, you can build in advance of signed leases. You could have space that a company setting up operations in Dallas and Fort Worth can move into the day they first come to town if they want. No more waiting a year to get in business while someone builds a building for them. You could build larger buildings you can divide up and have multiple tenants in the single envelope. You could build closer to the interstate highways, airports and in some instances the rail yards when heavy freight will still come in by rail. Steel, pumps for the oil fields, pipe to get the oil out of the fields and to the markets. All of that could come through your warehouses, modular buildings and intermodal hubs."

"Inter-what?"

The Future

Elijah meets me back at the apartment about six. He looks beat. I'm cooking hamburgers for us to eat. I'd never had to go buy ground beef, mix in eggs and spices and breadcrumbs and hand press it into a hamburger, but I wasn't ready to go find a restaurant again after the Woolworth's experience.

"How did your interviews go?" I ask to get him to engage with me.

"If you're expecting me to be the breadwinner here, we might as well go look for another bubble to jump to," he sounds defeated.

"Why is that?" I press.

"These people! They just seem to think they're the only one with half a brain. I mean they're talking about such simple concepts. You know? An integrated circuit? That's like the foundation of every circuit board in the world. And they talk about it like it's this nirvana. They seem to think if they can only figure out how to make it work, they can end world hunger or something."

"It hasn't been invented yet," I inform him.

"I knew you were going to say that." Elijah shoots back. "But the people I'm talking to aren't chip makers. I mean they make instruments for drilling oil. How low tech can you get?"

"If they haven't invented the integrated circuit yet, who's going to make a chip without a circuit?"

"What are you talking about?" Elijah isn't following me.

"You just said, they aren't chip makers. And they aren't, but they will be."

"Nobody's going to take an oil field instruments company and turn it into a chip maker."

"The company you interviewed at?" I set him up. "In a few years the integrated circuit will be invented there. A few years from now they'll change their name to Texas Instruments."

"You're telling me I interviewed at Texas Instruments before they were Texas Instruments, when they only had a few hundred employees? At the beginning."

"That's exactly what you did." I confirm.

"This is getting surreal. I mean why would I want to work there before they become the company they will become? Before they start working on interesting application chips? It just doesn't make sense to me."

"You listening or have you shut down?"

"I'm listening." Elijah acts like he did something wrong. "What do you want?"

"I want you to do the one thing you say you do better than anyone. I want you to think."

"Okay." Elijah knows he's not going to like this discussion. "You got my attention."

"In the time we came from what was the big scientific challenge?"

"Pushing Moore's law." Elijah doesn't hesitate. "We are starting to see we can't double computing power on a single chip every year and a half to two years forever. So, we need to find a way to approach density from a different direction."

"I don't know what you just said, but in this time, an integrated circuit is much the same problem." I inform him. "The best minds are all working that problem. Companies are investing a lot of money to make it a reality. Don't you see, every age has a different set of challenges, none more daunting than the other when viewed in the context of what is known and the tools available to work with?"

"Where do you get all this from?" Elijah isn't sure he believes me.

"You forget, I was managing partner of a major law firm."

"Only for a few days." He tries to temper my self-assurance.

"Only because you kept getting into trouble and had to get out of town. No listen, I was a corporate litigator for more than a decade. My clients were the major companies in Dallas and around the country. I learned a lot just by listening and asking a few questions."

"Are you feeding me the line that every age has its challenges and what may seem rudimentary really is hard because the tools and foundational knowledge needed to solve it are lacking?"

"Relative to any other age, yes." I confirm his analysis.

"So, you're trying to convince me that helping to create the first integrated circuit here is as important an accomplishment as inventing Space-time transit will be in seventy-years?"

"When they give out Nobel prizes, they don't say the one they gave out last year isn't important anymore." I point out. "They give out an award for the most important scientific achievement of that year. So, if it's a Nobel you're looking for, one awarded in 1956 is as important as one awarded in 2026."

"Fair point." Elijah seems to muse over my point.

"But you're not buying it," I react to the tone of his response.

"Never thought about a Nobel." Elijah muses. "But now that you mention it, did the guy at TI get one?"

"It seems to me he did, but not until many years later."

"What are we doing here?" Elijah finally sits down as I serve him the overcooked hamburger.

"Eating."

"No, I mean what are we doing here?" Elijah isn't sure what I just put in front of him. "I've never eaten anything that looked or smelled like this. And where are the fries and a shake?"

"Redondo Beach, my friend. Have a nice walk."

"Elijah takes a bite. He holds it in his mouth for a moment, assessing it. I'm not sure if it's about to come back out or not, but then he turns up the corner of his mouth and tries to talk with his mouth full, "This is a lot juicer than McDonalds."

"Better you just chew."

Elijah does, watching my face as I take a much smaller bite. It's not McDonalds, but I'm afraid to admit it tastes a lot like the hamburgers my mother used to make when we were saving for a new car or something expensive. Our diets got a lot leaner. There was less on the table. Desert became a once in a while instead of a couple times a week. Nice to know I cook nearly as bad as my mother even though I almost never cook at home other than in a microwave.

"What are you thinking about?" Elijah wants to know.

"How my mother used to cook."

"You didn't learn from her? I thought that was one of those things a mother's supposed to do for her daughter. Teach her how to cook. Just like a father's supposed to teach his kid how to fix things."

"That's absolutely the way it is in 1956, but not so much in the future."

"What changed?" Elijah seems to be trying to understand history, something new for him.

"Fast food, packaged foods in groceries, women didn't need to cook from scratch anymore. They buy a frozen burrito and microwave it."

"Which still hasn't been invented," he notes with some self-assurance.

"Right. And fathers teaching their sons to fix things? How many things have you fixed in your house? Everything is disposable and the new product does more for less money than what you throw out."

"That's what the engineers of 1956 started?"

"It started before now, really. Pretty much after the war. But it just took a while for it to become prevalent in a lot of different products. That comes back to tools like cheaper and cheaper computers, then cell phones and all the new technology we take for granted."

"I don't know. They offered me a job, but it's like slave wages," Elijah admits, embarrassed.

"How much?"

"A hundred a week. That's like five grand a year. Who would work for that?"

"The cost of living has gone up 850% since now, so that's nearly $48,000 in the future."

Cost

Over the next several days we continue to interview for positions. In an age without email it takes a while to hear from the companies we are interviewing with. I meet with people from oil and gas companies, companies that make oil field structural steel for wells, pumps for oil extraction, and even Braniff International Airways, which I know will go out of business in a few years. But since the money from selling the gold and silver won't last, I need a job.

Elijah has more difficulty getting interviews as he is perceived as being very young. But those who take the chance on him seem to be impressed. Once he understood what kind of salary makes sense based on the cost of living now, he relaxed. He seems to be more willing to consider jobs that he isn't really looking at as a career, but in Dallas there aren't many companies that need his particular skills. At least not yet.

Saturday can't come quickly enough as far as Elijah is concerned. And every day seems to weigh down on him more. The fact that everything just seems to take so long isn't making it any easier. I'm not sure how long he will stick this out as he spends long periods just sitting at the apartment table thinking through something he won't discuss. I finally ask him, "Have you solved it yet?"

Elijah slowly disengages from his thoughts. Shakes his head before looking up. "What?"

"Have you solved it yet?" I'm less timid this time.

"Solved what?"

"The problem you've been working on almost since we arrived."

"I want to see them." Elijah responds almost in a whisper.

Now I'm the one who isn't sure what we're talking about.

"My grandparents. The one's I've never met."

"Your father's parents." I seek confirmation.

Elijah nods and finally engages my eyes. I can see he's been wrestling with this question since we visited with his mother's mother. He learned a lot about her in that short meeting. Things he never knew but had never had an interest in before.

I look at the clock on the wall and suggest, "We could go see them now. It will be evening by the time we get there so they should be home."

"What did you find out about them when you were looking this all up?

"I'd rather you find that out from your visit." I won't prep him at the cost of possibly biasing him one way or the other.

"Let's do this." Elijah rises.

We take the Greyhound bus from the downtown station in Dallas to the downtown station in Fort Worth. I look at open fields. But I see in my head buildings I've seen in the future, in a different bubble maybe, but they will come. I don't know what most of them will be, but it reminds me of the ghosts on the other side of the dimensional portal. Not so much as a fog hiding things in the shadows, but the image of future buildings that will someday sit in these wide-open fields.

Elijah is quiet most of the way. He's looking about but not talking about what's there versus what's not there yet. I think he's very nervous about being rejected by his father's parents, even though I impressed on him that his father hasn't even been born yet. He needs to relax as just like in our other visits, our ancestors aren't thinking about us as family.

I finally ask as we approach the Fort Worth Greyhound bus station, "What do you think you're going to find?"

"That they're just hard people."

"What do you mean, hard?" I'm confused by the term he chose.

"That they just don't care about others. Into their own stuff, maybe. I don't know. I just haven't been able to understand why they never wanted to even meet me."

I hear the deep-seated hurt that has apparently haunted him his whole life. A crazy grandmother and a set of grandparents who don't care about him at all. He must be wondering what that says about him. Will he end up being unstable like Howard Hughes and so many other geniuses? I can see where he would wonder that. If all we do is set his mind to rest maybe he will feel better about himself. And if he does how will that change his attitude about validating his bubble transit theory? Will he finally settle down and try to live a normal, or what can be as close as possible to normal for someone as brilliant as he is?

We take the bus across town as his grandparents live on the south-side near Texas Christian University's campus. I lead him to the house. Probably eighteen hundred square feet, which is huge in comparison to Elijah's Grandmother's cottage. A stone pillared porch with a porch swing and four chairs greets us. A well-tanned woman sits in the swing, knitting what looks like a blanket. She is very short and I'm not tall. If she is five feet I would be surprised. Maybe ninety pounds. She has a healthy glow to her dark hair bordered face. She concentrates on her project and hasn't looked up even though we've stopped in front of her home. I step up on the porch. "Ma'am?"

She glances up with a curious look, but she needs to concentrate on what she's doing so I give her a moment to finish. Soon she puts the needles down. A broad smile. I glance at Elijah who seems surprised as I ask, "Maybe you can help us?"

"If I can," the bright smile continues.

"We're looking for Walter and Carolyn Mason. Do they live somewhere nearby?"

She seems curious, "I'm Carolyn. What can I do for you?"

"We're from Life Magazine."

"In New York?" She seems positively surprised. "Why would Life Magazine be interested in Walter and me?"

"One of your neighbors, who asked to remain anonymous, sent us a note about the film you and your husband have been making." I begin. "We'd like to talk with you about the project."

"Really?" Carolyn puts the knitting into a cloth bag then comes to shake our hands. "It's very nice to meet you. Did you really come all the way from New York City just to interview us?"

I nod. "Is Walter at home?"

"He's teaching a class at the university. It's a seminar on Film making. Some of the students in the class have been helping with the project. They're looking at dailies tonight. Trying to figure out if they have to reshoot parts."

Elijah and I take seats next to each other.

"What's wrong with me, I'm sure you'd like a lemonade. It's warm and I'm sure you're parched."

"Thank you," I say before Elijah can refuse as I'm sure he has no idea what lemonade is.

When Carolyn is inside, he asks me, "What's going on here?"

"Just go along with me."

Carolyn is back in a moment with a tray and four glasses. I accept the glass and take a sip, nodding and smiling. Elijah apparently sees what I'm doing and does the same.

"You and your husband are making a documentary film tracing the history of the Klu Klux Klan in Texas. That must not make you very popular with friends and neighbors." I begin.

"We are committed to bringing history to life for people. The fact that history has some ugly sides is a part of history. Who was it that said he who ignores history is condemned to repeat it?"

"George Santayana. A philosopher and writer." I respond without thinking.

I see Carolyn nod, apparently, we passed some test. "Well, that's what we're about, making sure we as a country don't go backwards. That we don't revisit the past. That we become cognizant of the people all around us who are with us nearly every day, but aren't seen or treated as people."

"And I take it your husband is the passionate one amongst you." I'm being facetious.

She nods and seems even more excited, "He is. This whole project was his idea. But once he explained what he wanted to do I was all in."

"Regardless of what it costs you." I seek confirmation

Causing Trouble

Carolyn Mason isn't happy with my question. She turns a little more guarded. "What are you planning to say about us and our project?"

"We don't know yet since we've just gotten started, but generally Life wants to inform the American public of topics that are worthy of their consideration. So, we would hope people who read about your project will want to see the film when it makes it into theaters."

Carolyn relaxes a bit, still trying to understand my question about cost. "That's what we hope will happen. That people all over the country will go to the theater and watch our film."

"You said your husband has been using students at the University to help with the project. What kind of reaction have you gotten from them?" Elijah asks.

"Reaction? They're all thrilled to be working on a real project rather than just making another student short."

"How is it you and your husband came to make this film in Fort Worth?" I ask.

"TCU is a great school. Even has Christian in its name. So we thought it might be more open minded about letting us do the original research and actual production here. We hoped it would support academic and intellectual freedom."

I notice Elijah perk up at that comment. "And you found it at TCU?" he asks.

"Absolutely. Everyone is so supportive. They've provided nearly everything we've asked for."

Elijah frowns for a moment, but lets it pass. I pick up the thread. "So, you're still filming? How long do you think it will take to complete it?"

If we can stick to the shooting schedule, we will finish principle photography by the end of the year and should be finished in September or so next year." Carolyn perks up and peeks over us, "Here comes Walter."

Carolyn waits for a solidly built blonde man of about six foot. He has the same build as Elijah only more muscular and a bit thinner. His longish hair hangs in his face. As he climbs the porch stairs, he pushes it back. "Walter, these nice people are from Life Magazine. They heard about our project."

"Walter seems hesitant to believe his wife. "Life Magazine you say?"

"Nice to meet you," I rise and extend my hand. Walter considers what his wife has said but finally shakes mine and then Elijah's.

"How did you come to hear of our little project?" Walter picks up the glass of lemonade his wife brought out for him, although the ice cubes have now partially melted. He takes a sip and then sits down beside his wife.

"One of your neighbors sent it in." I respond. "Our editor asked us to stop by and learn more. There's no guaranty we will publish this or any story we go out on. But from what Carolyn has been telling us I think this could be a compelling story."

"Life Magazine." Walter tries that on for size. He makes a decision after only a brief consideration. "Did Carolyn tell you we're probably a year from completion?"

"She did."

"I think a story at this point might be a bit premature." He slowly responds apparently searching for words to ensure we don't just write him off. "A lot happens in a year. And if I told you today that I'm going to release a book, or walk across the Grand Canyon on a tightrope, by the time a year comes around you've completely forgotten about it."

"I agree, but when we were sent out we didn't know your release schedule."

Walter Mason is preoccupied. I think I know what he's thinking, and it isn't about audiences. It's about people who will try to stop his film's release if word gets out too soon. Walter nods. "What can I tell you about the film that Carolyn hasn't?"

"Your wife gave us her perspective as to why you chose to take on a difficult subject like this. Would you share your thoughts on why this film is essential for everyone to see?"

"Do you think most people are happy with their lives?" Walter asks.

"I take it the key word for you is most." I respond carefully.

Walter seems pleased, as if I passed a test as I did earlier with Carolyn. "It is. But what's your answer?"

"Given the billions of people who live in abject poverty the world over I would have to say no."

Walter considers my comment, but it wasn't what he was looking for. "What about in this country?"

"Same answer, we still have more than half our population living at or below the poverty level. Middle class means you make a dollar an hour more than your poverty level neighbor."

"A dollar an hour is a lot." Walter responds, and I realize my mistake. *It was too much in 1956.*

"You're focused on the abusive relationship that white people have with the colored and Asians."

"We locked up the Japanese in the war, did you know that?" Walter tests me again.

I nod.

"We enslaved people." He begins to rant. "Treated them as property. And we abandoned them when we freed them. Made them make their way in our land of freedom without any help from those who enslaved them and brought them here. That's not right. If we're Christians, we extend a hand to our brothers. Help them up. Give them a chance. Treat them as the equals they are."

Elijah listens closely. Then asks, "But not everyone agrees with you."

"No, they don't." Walter admits. "And that's why this film will be so powerful. Everyone who has gone to work every day and ignored what is going on around us will see what we all have permitted to happen in our midst. Once you see it, you can't just ignore it. You can't tolerate those who treat your brother as an animal or worse. Don't you understand? That's what this project is all about. No one else will make this film. Look at the mainstream films. If we see a colored person, they are a domestic, or entertainer, or doing menial work. Colored are never shown as heaven forbid, doctors or lawyers. We just got our first colored professional baseball players, even though they've had their own leagues for decades. That wasn't right. At least that gives me hope. Rosa Parks refusing to move to the back of the bus last year in Montgomery. The door has opened a crack. We start seeing the colored as equals in the things we do, maybe we will begin to accept them as the same as you and me."

"Why do you refer to them as colored?" I ask.

"Them?" Walter reacts. "They aren't them. They're us. We're all men and women period. That's the message of the film. And with it we're trying to change everyone's mind-set including yours."

I let the silence gather, then ask, "How would you like us to proceed?"

"I prefer to maintain a low profile on this for now." Walter lowers his voice out of caution.

"We'll come back next year." I offer, knowing we won't.

Another Choice

Elijah is quiet on the bus back, apparently trying to understand what he just experienced. I'm sure it must have caught him totally by surprise. The film they are making may explain why he'd never met them, why his father never spoke of them, although I suspect there may be one more reason. I give him space. Respect his need to put what he learned into perspective.

Once we are on the intercity bus back to Dallas, he finally asks me, "You knew."

"When I did my homework on my own grandparents in 1956, I thought you might want to meet yours. So, yes. I located them and then read a little about them. Why did you never Google them? Weren't you curious?"

Elijah shrugs. "They never existed. Never a word about them. Neither Mom nor my father. I didn't know if they had died when my father was small, or if they had just banished him for something he did. Those were the two possibilities that occurred to me."

"Why do you always refer to him as your father and never Dad? While your mother is Mom." I ask picking up on something I hadn't thought about earlier.

Elijah frowns, "I do that?"

"You do." I confirm my observation for him to see if he will analyze his own behavior, whether he can look objectively at his feelings.

He struggles with the thought for a moment before continuing. "My father always has a different agenda than Mom. I don't know if that makes sense. When he is home, he is usually grumpy about one thing or another. Takes it out on Mom a lot. But he just leaves me alone. Maybe that's why I got so into science. I have to learn everything on my own because Mom is too busy with Grandma and her own work and he is just never there."

"What do you think happens when your grandparents release their film next year?" I ask to see if he has any idea of what lies before them.

"Some people probably aren't going to be happy." Elijah offers, but I can tell he understands more than he's saying.

"And what happens to them?" I push.

"He loses his job?" Elijah is trying to put the pieces together.

"And their home we just visited? It will be fire-bombed and burn to the ground."

Elijah's eyes open wide. "Do they die?"

"No, but they will be run out of town. They'll end up in the liberal bastion of Denton, which is just thirty miles north, but a whole different world. The North Texas State College is there. Walter will get a job as an English professor on the condition he not make any more films. But he still has to hide the fact your grandmother is black. They can't be legally married in Texas until 1967 after the Supreme Court ruling. Your father will be born in Denton before that. He will grow up labeled by others, but I think he will label himself because of who his parents are and the film they made."

"My grandmother…" Elijah starts to ask me, but draws his own conclusion.

The bus arrives at the Greyhound station in Dallas.

"I'd like to go over to the Lake. Watch the geese come in for a landing at sunset as my grandparents do. You can go back to the apartment if you want, but I want to understand the simple pleasure it gives them."

Elijah shrugs, apparently doesn't want to be alone. I wasn't sure.

We arrive at White Rock Lake just before sunset. The southern edge beckons, which is the closest to my grandparent's house. We find a bench near the lake and sit down, just looking out over the shimmering water. A slight breeze in my face allows me to clear my lungs. I feel the cooling presence of the moving air. The long rays of the setting sun stretch out over the darkening blue of the lake water.

"Is this why you came back with me?" Elijah asks. "To meet your grandparents? To understand their lives and how the choices they made affect you?"

"When you suggested this time, I thought there was no way I would want to live here. Even when we got here, I tried to convince you to go elsewhere. It was evident to me you would struggle here without all the toys you depend on and with who you really are.

"I never thought about my grandparents. I was just trying to find a time when the government wouldn't be after me. And the fact I'm still just a teenager? I don't want to give up these years I have to learn what I can be. What I can do. What I can contribute to the knowledge we have. I want to be free to explore not only the world, but the multi-verse. To see what's really out there. To understand it first hand, not just conceptually."

"And now that you're here, what do you think?" I still hear the wanderlust in his voice.

"I guess I wasn't ready to come here." Elijah admits. "I have to create a whole new life, not step into another me's. You know in some ways that's really exciting and liberating. I get to write the book on me.

I become what I chose to become. Not the extension of the me that was here."

"How has what you've learned about yourself affected your thinking?"

"About what?" Elijah isn't following me.

"Do you see anything of the type of people your grandparents are in this time in yourself?"

Elijah nods once understanding my question. "I see the conviction of my father's parents in me. I see the singular focus of my mother's mother. I wasn't going to give up on my ideas no matter how many times I went down blind alleys in trying to build the portal device. I knew what the device had to do. I knew the basic technology that would be needed to enable the transit. But there were parts that just didn't exist. I had to figure out how to make them myself."

"What do you think about it now that you know where those traits came from and what they led your grandparents to do? What consequences they suffered, endured, managed as a result of those choices?"

"The bubbles are different from each other, not only because they're offset by time, but because of the choices the people living in those bubbles have made. So, I'm not sure what I'm seeing here is the last word on the traits I have."

I shake my head, "I don't agree with you. I think the traits you have are genetic. The choices you make are a result of your traits, but not solely determined by them. I think, as you said, your and my grandparents could have made different choices and we would be different people, but we would have the same traits because they're biologic."

"You're saying that if Walter never made that film, but some stop action horror flick that made millions, I would be the same person, traitwise, but my father may have embraced his parents and they would have helped shape my values growing up. We would have been better off. Maybe my father would have gone into films like his father and we would have lived in LA or someplace. The choices would have made my life different, but I would have still been the same person."

"I think that's what I'm seeing. If my grandfather had gone back to school to get his degree, he might have become the store manager rather than ladies undergarments department manager. Would that have changed my life? Maybe. Hard for me to know. If they didn't go see a fertility doc would I even be here? It all comes down to the choices we make. And that's why the multi-verse becomes so hard to navigate."

As the sun finally sets and the sky is all aglow the geese come in to land on the variegated color shimmering water. "Spectacular. Clearly worth the price." I note, probably more to myself than Elijah.

"Where do we go from here?" Elijah asks me, even though I've been wondering the same thing.

I can't take my eyes off the geese that have now landed and are swimming towards us. "You're the tour guide." I respond.

"Is there more here for us or is it time to move on?"

"I don't know if there is a perfect world, bubble, time-dimension, whatever you want to call it out there for both of us." I begin. "I was comfortable being managing partner at VV&U. I was comfortable being a Texas State Supreme Court Justice. Here, I'm not comfortable, don't know what I will become. That's a little scary. It would also be a lot more work for me to make something of myself here. But you alluded to it. We have a chance to make ourselves into what we want to be by the choices we make here. We're not foreordained to be anything because of who we were growing up. We don't have to live up to anyone else's expectations, or limit ourselves because of them. We also have the luxury of having insights into what's going to happen in the next sixty years. This might be my one chance to make a fortune."

"Sounds like you want to stay on," Elijah gives voice to what he thinks he's hearing.

I nod, tentatively. "For a while. I don't know if I might change my mind next week or next year. And it's all right if you want to go on to your next time of interest. As long as you promise to check back in with me periodically. That way you can validate your theory about the multiverse and I can validate myself." *I'm really not sure of anything I just said. Can I face this time alone? It would be so easy to go back to either of the other time-dimensions we visited, but those belong to another version of me… I don't know.*

Elijah looks out over the lake which has now turned black as the night settles in. "I brought you here so I'll stay on with you. At least for a while. See if we can get jobs. How's that?"

THE END

About the Author

dhtreichler toured the global garden spots as a defense contractor executive for fifteen years. His assignments covered intelligence, training and battlefield systems integrating state of the art technology to keep Americans safe. During this time he authored seven novels exploring the role of increasingly sophisticated technology in transforming our lives and how men and women establish relationships in a mediated world.

Keep up with all of dhtreichler's latest work and essays at www.dhtreichler.com.

Also by dhtreichler

HOPE

Emergence

Barely Human

The Ghost in the Machine: a novel

World Without Work

The Great American Cat Novel

My Life as a Frog

Life After

The Tragic Flaw

Succession

The End Game

I Believe in You

Rik's

The Illustrated Bearmas Reader – Ralph's Ordeals

The First Bearmas

Made in the USA
Lexington, KY
02 December 2019

57940994R00168